Advance Praise For Brutal Disclosure

"Polin delivers an incredibly authentic view of America's gritty underbelly from an expat's perspective."

-US Review of Books

"Compelling...This is a terrific novel...from beginning to end."

-Readers' Favorite Book Reviews

"Brutal Disclosure is a winner."

-Midwest Book Reviews

"...reminded me of early Irvine Welsh or Roddy Doyle."

Literary Titan

BRUTAL DISCLOSURE

A DECLAN O'NEILL NOVEL

KEVIN POLIN

Published by Atlantic Press
Durham, North Carolina

Brutal Disclosure
A Declan O'Neill Thriller

ISBN (ebook): 979-8-9935023-0-4
ISBN (paperback): 979-8-9935023-1-1
ISBN (hardcover): 979-8-9935023-2-8
ISBN (audiobook): 979-8-9935023-3-5

Library of Congress Control Number (LCCN): 2025923361

Cover design by ebooklaunch.com
Cover photograph by Kevin Polin
Author photograph by Chi-Duen Poon
Edited by Atlantic Publishing
Copy editing by Lini Ge

Tarot card illustration from the 1909 Rider–Waite deck, public domain.

Printed in the United States of America

First Edition 2025

For my Dad, and for Lini

Knight of Swords Tarot Card

BRUTAL DISCLOSURE

Chapter One

Declan O'Neill's brother, Sean, lay dead on the pavement eight stories below the living room window of the council flat he shared with his mother. Lying on his bed, staring at the nicotine-stained ceiling, Declan's body was stiff as he gripped the blanket with both hands at his sides. He felt like vomiting, but it seemed as if his stomach just didn't have the energy. His mind churned: over and over again with thoughts of his brother—his beautiful brother. Blue and orange lights cut through the night air outside and swirled lightly around the room from the emergency vehicles in the street below.

Through the door, he could hear the familiar clink of a vodka bottle tapping against a glass as his mother poured herself another drink in the living room. Declan also heard the police detective talking to his mother.

"Mrs. O'Neill, was anyone else in the flat when your son jumped from the roof?"

"J-just me and my other son Declan," stuttered Rose O'Neill.

"Does anyone else live here with you?"

"No, just Declan."

"And, do all the tenants have access to the rooftop?"

"Tenants aren't allowed up there, but Sean and Declan knew how to fiddle the door lock. They go up there together all the time to smoke. They call it their 'Thinking Place.'"

"I see."

Suddenly, there was a smash as, apparently, the glass of vodka fell to the floor. Mrs. O'Neill screamed and then cried, "My boy, my gorgeous boy." Dimly, Declan could hear a woman police officer try to console his mother.

A few moments later, several light taps on the door echoed through Declan's bedroom. Declan turned over on his side and faced the wall. A few moments passed, and the taps came again.

"Fuck off," Declan said.

"Declan, I just want a word or two, then we can be out of your way," said the detective.

The police officer turned the handle and stepped into the room. Declan sat up on his bed, looked out the grimy window, and watched below as two ambulance men placed a stretcher next to his brother's body as a forensics officer in white overalls and a police photographer stood by. He saw people he knew watching the spectacle from behind the police tape. Neighbors, friends from school, shop owners, and a tall, Eastern European man, all watched Sean's body being scooped off the concrete and flopped onto the stretcher.

Declan looked up over the rows of tenement houses that stretched over a mile to the Brighton coast. His mother's eighth-floor council flat afforded him a high vantage point to survey the now sedate seaside town. Declan could not understand how most people seemed to be going about their business as usual while his brother's body was taken into the ambulance. People ducked into the corner shop for cigarettes or milk, a group of older men staggered home from The Railway pub, and drivers walked in and out of the bus depot at the end of his street as a shift change transpired—all as if just another evening.

The detective cleared his throat, and Declan looked over at him. Declan watched as the detective surveyed the room, taking in the remnants of a wardrobe scattered about the floor: splintered wood like broken limbs, clothes piled in dirty heaps, and shards of broken mirror reflecting dark shadows. Declan had smashed up the wardrobe just moments before the detective had arrived at the flat.

"Any idea why your brother did this to himself?" asked the detective.

Declan blinked several times before replying, "Aren't you the detective? Why don't you tell me?"

"You were here at the time?"

"Yes, asleep until I heard the police sirens."

The detective paused. Observed a book on the floor, *L'Étranger*, then looked back at Declan.

"Look, son. I'm sorry you have to deal with this. You must know something about what's going on? Why would he do this?"

"You mean with the Russians?"

"Maybe. What do you know about them?"

"All I know is one or two of them seem to run the whole drug operation over this estate, but the local lads do the actual dealing."

"Do you think your brother was mixed up with them?"

Declan turned and looked out of the window again.

"He didn't sell drugs."

"Did you ever see him speaking with these Russian types?"

Declan didn't answer.

"Look, son. We think he was a launderer for them. We've been watching the bastards for months."

"A what?"

"A money launderer. Since he was English, he could go in most of the bookies unnoticed and funnel all the drug money through the electronic betting machines. He rotated in and out of every betting shop south of London. Betting the drug money and turning it into legit money—all for a ten percent loss set by the bookmaker by law."

"He didn't tell me what he did. I knew he was mixed up in it, but why would he do this? He had a lot of dreams. We both did...do."

"From what we know, Sean got too greedy for his own good."

"You mean that trip he made to China?"

"Yes. We looked up his passport and ran some checks. We believe he was in Macau for two weeks, gambling about a hundred thousand pounds of the Russians' money."

"Jesus. He told us he was going on some sort of sightseeing trip. We thought he had stopped gambling."

"He got himself in a terrible mess with the worst kind of people."

"Well, he's paid for it now, hasn't he?" stated Declan.

"Declan, I shouldn't be telling you this. But I will, for your own safety. These guys have taken over all the estates and nightclubs and are making a fortune pushing drugs to all the locals and the tourists that come into Brighton. There are no other gangs like 'em in England. These are mostly ex-military blokes, who'll stop at nothing to make sure a debt is paid. These men are animals. I'm just warning you that you and your mother need to be very careful, 'cause these guys will likely come after you for your brother's debt, since they may think he gave you at least some of it. If I were you, I would keep a low profile for a while."

"Why don't you arrest them? Can't you do something about this? My brother is dead, and he wouldn't be if those bastards were locked up."

"We don't have enough to put them away for serious charges. They are cunning—they let younger kids like your brother take the real risks. We are on to them. But need more time to have a solid case." The officer cleared his throat and continued, "Anyway, I have told you much more than I should have."

Declan turned, reached for his cigarettes and lighter on the bedside cabinet, and said, "Well, don't worry about me, I'm getting out of this place."

"Getting out? Where?"

"Anywhere. Probably America."

The detective took a deep breath and looked down at the wooden fragments of the wardrobe and then said, "Be careful over there, son. Those yanks sort out their problems with guns. They may talk English there, but America's still the bloody wild west."

Chapter Two

Seven days after his brother's death, Declan approached his mother in the living room of their flat. She had just finished her morning vodka. Declan poured her another drink. "You've never poured me a drink in your life. What's going on?"

"Mum, I have to tell you something."

"What now?"

"I'm leaving for New York City. You know the Russians aren't going to forget about Sean's debt. So, I'm going to fly over to America, make as much money as I can, then come back and pack us up and take us back to Ireland. The Russians won't find us over there, and even if they do, Dad's old Sinn Fein mates will help us."

His mother instantly lunged at Declan and grabbed his arm and chest.

"Jesus God! You'll leave me here to those animals. You're just like your father, leaving me on me own! Don't go Declan. For God's sake!"

"Come on, mum, it's not like that. It's me they want."

"But what am I going to do?" replied his mother with tears streaming down her cheeks.

"Just be careful with yourself. Chris will look in on you, too. It's the only way—I can stay away until things settle down here and then return with enough money to move us back to Ireland. I want to have enough money to set you up in a nice place. If we go over there now, you'll be in welfare housing with not much chance of moving out. This seems the best option. I am going to make something of myself.

There's good money to be made there and made quickly. I can make some kind of future so we can both benefit. I'm going to do it. I *will* make it over there."

"Oh Jesus have mercy on me," cried Mrs. O'Neill before falling to the floor, sobbing.

Declan helped her to the couch but she was inconsolable. Declan quietly went back to his room, picked up his backpack, and crept out of the flat, ignoring his mother's wailing.

He knew his mother was right. He knew there might be a good chance he might never return. He knew too much had happened in the past and felt he had no option but to escape and try to make a life for himself. He had never been that close to his mother. He missed his father immensely, but could never relate to his mother.

Perhaps the years of neglect he and his brother suffered at the hands of their mother had had an adverse effect on him. Perhaps his mother's frequent disappearances where Sean would have to look after his little brother for days and sometimes weeks. Perhaps it was the strange men knocking at their door late at night, looking for their mum. Perhaps the occasional visit from the police and social workers were also partly to blame. And worst of all, perhaps the frequent teasing at school with jibes such as, "Your mom's just an old prostitute," or "Hey Declan, can I shag your mom for two quid?" And the one that got him the most, "Go back to Ireland you Fenian bastard. You don't belong here." The ensuing fights and expulsions from school took their toll on Declan.

This all left him with no love of England.

***

AT ONE P.M. THE same day, Declan O'Neill left the Windsor Castle Pub in Heathrow Airport's Terminal Three. He had drunk three pints of Stella Artois lager while watching a news show that reported exclusively on President Bush's initial phase of Operation Enduring Freedom in Afghanistan and the search for Osama Bin Laden. Within twenty minutes, he had boarded a Virgin Atlantic 747 jet bound for New York City. His first plane trip, ignorant of assigned seating and almost drunk, Declan randomly chose a window seat towards the back of the half-full aircraft. After putting his only luggage in the overhead bin—a small hiker's backpack—he sat down and fumbled in his jacket pocket for a cigarette and lighter. He placed the comforting Benson and Hedges cigarette between his lips. A stewardess in a bright red skirt suit with matching lipstick appeared. "Sorry, sir, there is no smoking allowed on this aircraft."

"Sorry."

Declan carefully placed the cigarette in the seatback in front of him, half protruding from the magazine pouch as if to remind him a small comfort was waiting when he arrived in America. He ran his fingers through his thick mop of wild black hair, looked out the window, and watched baggage handlers load suitcases, bags, and boxes onto a conveyor that dragged them on into the plane's underbelly. He wondered why everyone packed so many items. He expected to be gone for an extended amount of time—maybe a lifetime—and yet after days of preparation, he calculated he would only need what he could carry in his small backpack. There was a pair of jeans, a short and long sleeved shirt, several pairs of underpants and socks, a motorcycle magazine, a paperback copy of George Orwell's *Down and Out in Paris and London*, a map of New York City, a notebook and pen, a small bottle of Jamaican Rum he'd bought from the Duty Free shop, two packets of salt and vinegar crisps, toothbrush and toothpaste, stick of deodorant, a small towel, and a four-by-six-inch school photograph of himself with his brother taken several years ago.

As he continued to wonder what was in some of the enormous suitcases, he sensed someone standing in the aisle looking at him. He turned to see a dark-haired, somewhat frumpy girl, wearing black-rimmed rectangular glasses, who looked to be about the same age as himself—nineteen. She held up her ticket and said in a high-pitched American accent, "I think you are in my seat."

"Oh," was all Declan could muster in his embarrassed state.

"Don't worry; I can sit in the aisle seat."

"Thanks. Sorry about that."

"No big deal. I'm Isabella."

"Hello, I'm Declan."

Isabella wedged her small backpack under the seat in front of her, plopped herself down, and released a sigh. She threw her dark, shoulder-length hair behind her ears and continued, "You going to New York City or travelling on somewhere else?"

"New York. Yes, staying there for a while."

Isabella bent forward and rummaged in the side of her backpack until she pulled out a paperback book. Sitting back up, she turned to Declan and asked, "Family there?"

"No, I'm gonna check out New York for a bit then travel on somewhere else."

"A backpacker? I've been in England studying British Lit. for a semester. But, I didn't backpack."

"That's nice."

"Where are you from?"

"I'm Irish but grew up in Brighton. It's on the south coast."

"Yes, I've been there. All those beautiful Victorian buildings. And that old iron pier. I loved it."

Declan thought about how little he knew about the Victorian buildings in his hometown, but he knew the pier very well. He recalled the summer days he and his brother had spent wandering about the pier and the surrounding beach area. He remembered the salty air, the sunburn on his back, the candy-floss vendors, and then he remembered his brother was now dead. It occurred to him, too, that as much as he missed his brother, he must not cry.

"Did you go on a tour?" asked Declan.

"No. Just myself. I did most of my sightseeing in England on my own."

Isabella was the first American Declan had ever been able to get to know, and she was everything he'd imagined: loud, gregarious, unpretentious, friendly, and didn't seem to have a care in the world. He felt at ease with her and was happy to be spared the silence and awkwardness that would have undoubtedly occurred if she had been English.

The plane took off. It was a cloudy, grey, damp day, but Declan was able to see the lush green English countryside quite clearly as the aircraft lifted higher into the sky. He wondered how long he would be gone from his home; he wondered if it were possible he would never return. He felt sad, but quickly dismissed the feeling by reminding himself that he had no future in England. His brother was gone, job prospects were poor, and he didn't want to find out what the Russian drug gang was going to do with him. But more than that, he wanted to make some money so he could help his mother move back to Ireland. Declan didn't understand why, but he felt embarrassed by his predicament and couldn't bring himself to tell Isabella of the real reasons for his departure. For now, he felt his backpacking story would work well as a cover.

As the plane rose higher into the English sky, the TV monitors overhead played a news report of more anti-government protests in London. The protesters didn't seem to have a unified message—some gathered against high taxation, some against supporting the war on terrorism, some against global warming, and many came to protest against excessive police powers. Declan felt everyone seemed to be unhappy in the world—or at least in England. He turned to Isabella and noted she wasn't interested in the news reports. She was absorbed in a book: Jane Austen's *Sense and Sensibility*. He took a deep breath and tried to relax. He remembered the novel's main characters, sisters Elinor and Marianne, and began to recall the book's plot. He looked over to Isabella again and wondered who she might like most. Probably the more sensible Elinor, he thought, given Isabella's practical manner. But then again, perhaps she was romantic, like Marianne. *Perhaps that was why she came to England?*

On reaching cruising altitude, the "Fasten Seatbelt" light chimed off. Isabella bent down, rummaged in her backpack, pulled out a plastic-wrapped chicken sandwich, and placed it on her knees. She carefully unwrapped it and nibbled at the crusts. Her eyes darted towards Declan as she became conscious of him looking over.

Declan quickly masked his grin with a cough and asked, "So, what will you do when you return home?"

Isabella carefully placed the sandwich back on her knees and replied, "Not much. I have a few months off before I return to NYU. I've got two more years to go, then I'm done."

"What then?"

"I'm graduating in Finance, so hope to get a job with a good investment company. If that doesn't pan out, I'll probably work for my dad's investment firm."

Declan felt confirmation on his initial impression that Isabella was most like the sensible Elinor.

"You live in New York City?" asked Declan.

"Long Island. Great Neck—it's a town east of the city."

"Oh, that sounds nice."

"Yeah, it is. What about you? After travelling, will you return to England and go back to college?"

"Yes, that's right."

Declan chuckled grimly to himself. Having dropped out of college nearly a year ago, he was unlikely to get back in. Moreover, England was awash with unemployed youths—Declan's chances of a job with no experience were slim. In any case, he had made a plan, of sorts, and was going through with it.

***

WITH THE PLANE NOW well over the Atlantic Ocean, the stewardess came by serving drinks. Declan ordered a beer, and Isabella ordered a Coke. Declan took a mouthful of the beer, then relaxed back into the comfort of his seat.

"What's it like living in Brighton? It's so different there. Do you go to the beach a lot?"

"Not really. I did when I was little. But now I hardly go down there. Except in the winter for walks."

"Oh."

"In my spare time I play guitar. I was in a band but cropped out."

"What happened?"

"It's a long story."

"I don't mind—we have a long time to go on this flight."

Declan took another swig of beer and recalled the last time their band played. It was autumn and Declan was with his brother Sean, who played bass guitar; Chris, his best friend, who played rhythm guitar, sang lead, and wrote their few original songs; and their friend Tony, who played drums. Declan played lead guitar. The gig was at the small, dimly-lit British Legion Club. However, after playing a few cover numbers from the band Green Day, they went into two of their own punk compositions: "Hitler Was a Mate of Mine" and "The Second World War—What a Waste of Time."

The first song had a section where Chris went into a tirade of almost a stream of consciousness with rants that talked of the benefits of a "Hitler-led Europe", where people could prosper "under the banner of *egalitarian* society led by the Nazi party." He would also, usually, denigrate Churchill as a "fat bumbling idiot" who had led England in the wrong direction with his alliance with the "Yanks."

The group was promptly ejected from the club amid angry patrons and had most of their equipment confiscated by the Legion's management.

Declan looked over at Isabella and saw her Star of David necklace. He felt incredibly foolish. Foolish to have been part of a band that insulted military personnel, and foolish for not realizing how much of an insult his band's songs would cause Jewish people. He suddenly was struck that they were singing songs that supported the deaths of beautiful beings such as Isabella. Before meeting Isabella, he knew no Jewish people. But now, sitting next to her, he seemed to understand the power of words when repeated, even jokingly, to ignorant people. *These words have the power to change nations and millions of lives*, he thought.

He turned to Isabella and said, "Honestly, we weren't that good. Just a group of friends playing some dumb punk songs. Did it for a laugh, really. I'm not really into punk either. More on the Radiohead and Depeche Mode side of things. I even listen to classical music quite a bit."

"OK," replied Isabella.

She then asked, "So, is Declan an Irish name?"

"Yes, it's my Dad's name. He and me mum are from a town called Lurgan. It's close to Belfast."

Declan decided not to tell Isabella about his father's death—killed in a Belfast security checkpoint "shooting accident"—as he thought it best not to seem *too* eager for sympathy.

"You don't sound Irish."

"We moved to England when I was a baby to get away from the troubles in the north."

"Well, this trip could work well for you since it's sort of cool to be Irish."

"Is it? Well then. I'll try and use that angle when I get there."

"Yeah, you should," said Isabella.

Declan looked out of the window of the plane and thought again about his band's lyrics. He wondered why he never thought deeply about what effect his band's lyrics would have had on the ex-servicemen at the Legion. He decided that he would try his best to examine how he conducted himself and make changes if necessary in America. He decided that in America, he would create a new, better Declan O'Neill—a person who would not be intimidated by anyone and who would follow his own righteous path and not make excuses.

The Captain announced the flight was approaching the mid-point of the Atlantic Ocean. He said the plane should land on time at New Jersey's Newark Airport.

Declan finished his beer and decided to try and talk with Isabella about something much different than his rock band. He remembered Isabella had been studying literature, so he thought this an easy topic: "So, what sort of books do you like to read?"

"Right now, I really like Joseph Addison."

Isabella looked at Declan, who nodded, and so she continued, "The period around the *Tatler* and *Spectator*."

"Yes, I've read some of his essays. I remember one where he walks about Westminster Abbey and talks with a friend. Nothing really happened, but it was interesting just hearing them talk. He seemed so concerned and well-mannered."

"That would be the *Sir Roger de Coverley Papers*. Those are my favorite essays from Addison—when he talks about Sir Roger," replied Isabella.

"Yes, a real insight into another time and place."

"You are right, a real insight."

"I remember them being really a kind and gentle sort of people. Always saying and doing the right thing. Always seemed to have the right answer for everything. It was like they could calmly handle anything that happened to them. Sort of blokes I'd like to be friends with. I don't know anyone remotely like 'em though."

"That's too bad. It's always good to have role models," responded Isabella, looking over at Declan.

"Yeah, 'spose so. But, we have his writings so it's like he's still here," replied Declan, tilting his head back into the seat and thinking deeply.

Isabella stared at Declan, "How does someone play in a punk rock band and enjoy reading Joseph Addison?" she asked.

"Don't know. Seems normal to me," replied Declan, who then took another swig of beer. "I 'spose I've always been a bit different than most people I know. I love literature, and, like I said, classical music. I sometimes feel I've been caught up in the wrong type of life. Do you ever feel that way, Isabella?"

Isabella turned away and looked at the seat back in front of her and replied slowly, "No, I don't really know."

Declan was drowsy after having drunk three beers and felt himself drifting into sleep. Then it occurred to him that, by the time he woke up, he may be in America. He felt scared—it was as if things were moving too fast. His heart beat rapidly. He sat up and drank some water. He wanted to sit on the plane as long as possible; he wanted to talk with Isabella longer. More than anything, he wanted to delay the uncertainty of where he was going to go when he arrived in New York City. He wished his friend Chris were with him. With Chris, they would be drinking and Chris would surely be telling him: "Don't worry, Dec, it's going to be a right laugh when we get to New York. So what if we don't know where we are going, we'll just have a few drinks and take the piss out of the Yanks. Sleep on benches, and if anyone gives us any lip, we'll tell 'em to 'Fuck Off!'"

At that moment, he missed his friend Chris almost as much as he missed his brother. He then recalled the times he and his brother lay on top of the roof of their block of flats. On cold, crisp winter nights, when the sky was particularly clear, Declan was sometimes able to point out several interesting objects, beyond the usual constellations, in the night sky: The Andromeda Galaxy, the Pleiades Star Cluster, and the edge of the Milky Way Galaxy. Sean was always complimentary of Declan's knowledge of astronomy and happy to lie back, smoke, and listen to his brother talk about the universe's composition. "You always were the smart one, Declan," his brother would say.

"That doesn't matter, Sean. I'm just glad I can share it with you."

"I don't know how you learned all this stuff. We went to the same schools, did the same classes and everything."

"The library. While you were off with your mates, I'd go to the library. Better than coming home to watch mum finish off another bottle of voddy."

"Yeah, right."

An emptiness grew inside Declan's stomach as he realized his closest companion would not return.

Declan looked out the window and all he could see was the vast blue Atlantic. He looked over at Isabella—her mouth slightly open, eyes closed and arms flopped by her side. He noticed Isabella had a faint whisper of a mustache. Her skin seemed so clear and delicate, and he wondered what it would be like to kiss her soft pink lips. He decided that as much as he liked Isabella, for some reason, he would not want to kiss her. Then he felt as if he was taking advantage of her by looking at her sleeping. He looked forward at the seat back in front of him.

The stewardess with the bright-red lipstick passed by and Declan asked for another beer. He noticed the woman's *Virgin Atlantic* lapel pin. He wondered if Isabella was a virgin. He felt sure she was. Technically, Declan realized he was a virgin too. "A drunken fumble with the local tart and shooting your wad early don't count," Chris had told him. Chris was a self-professed "Sexpert." He seemed to know all manner of things to do with sexual intercourse. Declan believed Chris obtained all of his sex information from the porno magazines he stole from his dad's workshop at the bus depot where his dad worked. "I unlock the bog window when I drop by to see my dad on Friday, then I sneak back in through the window on Sunday afternoon. If I nick just a magazine or two from one of the lockers, they won't notice. They've got 'undreds of magazines stacked up in those lockers. I've compiled quite a nice collection for myself. I want to index them into categories. Not sure what the categories will be right now, though."

Declan took the beer from the Stewardess's hands and said, "Thanks."

Isabella gently stirred awake. "I didn't mean to wake you," said Declan.

"That's OK, I feel like drinking a beer now."

"Have mine. I'll wait for the Stewardess to come back."

"Thanks."

Isabella carefully opened the can and drank a couple of sips before asking, "So what exactly are you going to do when you get to New Jersey?"

"Well, I'm going to get myself to New York City on a bus."

"Where are you going to stay? Do you have friends there?"

"No, don't know anyone in America. Not sure where I'm going to stay in New York either."

"What?" asked Isabella, sounding incredulous. "So *exactly* what are you going to do when you get into the City?"

"Well, I'll look around for a budget-type hotel."

Isabella laughed, "Are you kidding? There are no budget-type hotels in the City."

"Well, I'll find something, I suppose," said Declan, turning glumly to the window.

"God, I hope it works out for you," replied Isabella. Declan continued to look out the window but sensed Isabella staring at him. He rubbed the dark stubble on his distinct jawline and exhaled a deep sigh.

Isabella gulped two mouthfuls of the beer and said, "Listen. Let me give you my home number so you can give us a call if you ever get into trouble. Hopefully I'll have my cell phone back soon—I let the

last one expire when I went on this trip—and I can get that to you
later."

Declan turned toward her and could only muster, "OK."

"But, if I ever invite you out to Great Neck, please try to be on
your best behavior!"

"OK. It's a deal."

Isabella took a pen from her small bag under the seat, wrote her
name, Isabella Ber, and her phone number, 516-487-0900, on the back
of the airline magazine, then tore the piece off and handed it to Declan.

"Thanks," said Declan, wiping some wetness from his eye. He
couldn't quite understand this kindness. A sort of kindness he hadn't
experienced. He looked again at Isabella's face and was struck by how
soft and babyish it seemed to be. He wondered if maybe there could
be a chance for them to be together. But quickly dismissed it with the
realization that it would take almost a miracle for anything to work out
between them once they left the plane.

"You're welcome."

"You know, I'm not really in college and travelling like you. There
was a family tragedy, and I wanted to just get away."

"Oh, I see. I'm sorry about that. Well, I hope this trip helps you
out," replied Isabella who didn't seem too surprised by what Declan
said.

"Thanks."

***

AT FOUR P.M., THE plane landed uneventfully in New Jersey—just
another plane among three hundred landing that day in Newark. But
to Declan, the pang of twisting nervousness in his stomach reminded
him of how critical to the rest of his life this day would be. The thought
crossed his mind that he didn't have to do this—didn't have to walk
into the unknown. *I could always stay in the airport a few days and*

then just fly back—tell everyone it didn't work out, tell them the Yanks are arseholes and America is a dump. But, he reminded himself, there was nothing for him in England except sorrow. *I'm going to do this. I don't care what happens.*

After gathering their items, Declan and Isabella slowly and silently made their way from the plane along with their fellow passengers. Knowing they may never see each other again, it was as if they didn't want to add to the difficulty of saying goodbye, and so agreed to silence. Declan sensed a sort of sadness in Isabella—a hint of some kind of longing—that surprised him. It then crossed his mind that she had spent four months in England and may not have met anyone she cared for. Probably never met a new best friend, let alone a boyfriend. He wished he had met her in his home country. Wished he could have shown her around London and Brighton and stopped in parks, coffee shops to talk about Joseph Addison, Keats, Wilde, Shakespeare, others. It occurred to him that if he had met her in England, he would not be in this situation. *Christ, what am I doing?*

He watched her walk with her small backpack—a backpack carrying her pads, pens, snacks, and books. He then remembered her asleep on the plane seat. He remembered her small breasts, her Star of David necklace, her perfect skin. He suddenly wanted to help *her*. For some reason, he felt he could help *her* in some way. He imagined kissing her as she slept on the plane and her waking with a smile and embracing him. He imagined them walking off together through the airport to an apartment or a restaurant or a bar to talk about Sir Roger de Coverley. But then he dismissed the idea—he had no idea what would become of himself and was suddenly aware again that it was really *he* who needed some help.

After several minutes of winding through multiple hallways, they approached a fork in the hall where a large Black woman in a tight, dark blue uniform shouted: "U.S. citizens to the left, all others to the right." They stopped and turned to face each other. Declan politely held out his hand and said, "It was nice to meet you, Isabella."

"And it was nice to meet you, too, Declan. Please be careful here."

They shook hands, and Declan looked into Isabella's solemn gaze. She stood there as if expecting something else. Declan felt nervous, unsure what to do, gave a half wave, and said, "Bye now," then turned and walked towards the right and the non-citizens' queue. He knew Isabella was watching him, but he kept his gaze forward

Chapter Three

DECLAN PASSED THROUGH IMMIGRATION and Customs, entered the main airport area and looked at the throngs of people waiting to meet friends and family, many holding cell phones to their ears and following the progress of their loved ones. He wished he'd hear someone shout his name. He wished someone would tell him they have been expecting him and had all his arrangements ready. But he knew that wouldn't happen. He knew he was on his own.

He looked for a toilet and found the Men's Bathroom. Inside, he went to a cubicle, locked the door and carefully removed the money belt wrapped around his stomach under his shirt. He counted the money: five hundred and twenty-five pounds. This was the sum of his last unemployment check, the sale of his guitar and entire CD collection, and a small donation from his friend, Chris. He pulled out two of the fifty-pound notes and slid them into the front pocket of his jeans, then re-fixed the money belt tightly to his stomach. He found the nearest currency exchange booth and exchanged the one hundred pounds for one hundred and fifty-six dollars. "Have a nice day, Sir," said the vendor unconvincingly.

Declan frowned—he had expected at least one hundred and seventy-five dollars. He planned to use two fifty-pound notes per week. Living on cheap food and staying in the most affordable hotels, Declan believed he had five weeks' worth of money to find a job and become self-reliant in New York City. He felt sure this would be enough time and money. Besides, Chris had told him, "They'll be begging you to stay there–they love the English. They'll probably pay *you* to stay at their hotel."

Declan followed the signs to the "Transportation" area and found a booth where he could purchase a bus ticket to downtown New York City. The sign read "$16 one-way, $28 round-trip." Declan gave the man a $20 bill and asked for a one-way ticket. The vendor gave him a ticket and change without saying a word or even looking at him.

Outside, the May air chilled Declan as he boarded the bus; he passed only three people as he made his way to the back. The driver announced they would be leaving in ten minutes. Declan then realized that by the time the one-hour trip was over, it would be close to seven p.m. and starting to get dark. Another pang of nervousness spiked through his stomach as he realized he had nowhere to go. His only plan was to start walking the streets and seek a cheap hotel.

No sooner had the nervousness receded than it returned in full force as the bus turned east out of the airport, exposing the Manhattan skyline in the distance with the glistening beacon of The Empire State Building to the south. It also occurred to him that just one year ago, he would have seen the silhouettes of the twin towers, but now they had been destroyed. Declan took the small bottle of rum from his backpack and took a large swig, coughing as the alcohol scorched his throat—he was unused to drinking spirits of any kind. He took another swig and thought of his brother, Sean. Since Sean's death, Declan thought of him all the time. In fact, he believed he thought of his brother at least once every hour of each day. He mostly thought of the times they would talk to each other before sleeping—both lying in bed and sharing how their day had gone. The talks had given Declan a sense of bonding that he knew had helped shield him during difficult times when his mother was absent. It made him sad that Sean never got to live his dreams: "I want to live as an artist, even if I'm dead broke the whole time. All I want to do is paint. Paint and draw."

Sean always had a tough façade—he had to in order to protect Declan when his mum would disappear and bill collectors would knock at the door. But he was artistic at his core and always dreamed of playing the piano as well as pursuing his painting. But that was all gone now.

The talks with Sean had tapered in the last year, and Declan wondered if he would ever stop thinking of ways he could have prevented his brother's death. He was glad the subject never came up with Isabella. He didn't want this business being discussed with other people—especially Isabella. She had struck Declan as free—free from worries and cares and any unpleasantness. He was glad for her and wanted more than anything to have a life like hers. Life without his brother was almost unbearable. The image of the tangled mass of his brother's body in a bloodied heap at the foot of his block of flats seemed to be with him at every moment. He wanted to forget, and maybe here, in New York City, he could be free from it.

***

As CALCULATED, THE BUS entered the Port Authority transportation complex just minutes before seven o'clock. Port Authority spanned several blocks and three stories, with steel girders wrapping the façade. It looked like a prison complex to Declan. New York City had fallen under a blanket of grayness as the sun hurriedly set. The bus snaked its way through multiple turns within the bus terminal complex before coming to a stop. Declan hesitated as he disembarked the bus and entered the terminal. It was a dank, stifling, and rushed place, with people whisking by in a race for the exit, their hands clutching bags and phones. Declan noticed a darkened area of the perimeter of the complex had two homeless people huddled up on pieces of cardboard. One sleeping man had two pigeons perched nonchalantly on his cardboard blanket. Declan stood for a moment—taking in the whole scene—and thought it could pass for a makeshift British government shelter. Within seconds, two different homeless people approached him, and one asked, "Hey man, I'm really hungry. Can you spare a couple bucks?"

"No, sorry mate, I'm skint," replied Declan.

"Hey, where you from, man?" the man asked as he followed Declan, who had decided to make his own rush for the exit.

The second man said, "Hey, man, what about me? How 'bout a few bucks for me too?" The first man then said, "It's fucked up man. Get out while you can. Get back on the bus. Don't get sucked into this rat hole."

Both men followed Declan down the first escalator but gave up the chase as Declan turned and walked towards the second escalator that took him to the ground floor. The first hobo shouted down from the floor above, "You gonna regret it, man. This place is gonna fuck you up!"

Declan fleetingly wondered if he should just head back to the airport and go home. But he told himself he was tired, hungover, but had to keep going. At least for a few days to see how he can manage the situation.

Needing to pee, Declan looked for signs in the building, but finding any signage lacking, he approached a suited, pudgy, middle-aged man smoking a cigarette.

"Excuse me, mate. Could you tell me where the toilets are, please?"

For a few moments, it seemed the man would not respond. But then he replied, "Seriously? Well, you seem like a nice guy, so I'll give you some advice: This place is a shit show. And us worker drones will ignore you and not offer to help because we secretly hate the fact you are invading our miserable commuting lives after you just frolicked around the city all day, enjoying yourself. No one knows what the fuck is going on here—not even the customer service agents. There are five security cameras in the entire place, and not a single cop is in sight. Don't ever use the ticket machines else you'll be harassed by a bum looking for money. And you want the bathrooms? Well, the bathrooms haven't been cleaned since the Reagan administration—I know for a fact prison toilets are cleaner."

Declan stopped the man from continuing by saying, "OK, thanks," then turned and walked towards the escalator. The man shouted from behind, "Kid, go down to the first floor and spend four bucks in the Starbucks for a coffee. Use their bathroom."

Declan turned and said, "Thanks, mate."

As he made his way towards the Starbucks, a pregnant woman, smoking a cigarette, walked by and shouted, to no one in particular, "Who the fuck stole my bananas, you assholes?"

After visiting the Starbucks, Declan exited the building and walked out along 42nd Street in no particular direction. He passed an ice cream store, Madame Tussauds, Ripley's Believe it or Not, The Gap, and Red Lobster. It felt as if he were in an outdoor shopping mall. Everyone on the street appeared to be a tourist, and there were several police officers on foot patrol, who seemed to be there to give directions rather than prevent crime. The whole area was brightly lit and seemed a happy place. Pedestrians rushed about excitedly, a group of giggling girls walked by swinging large paper shopping bags, and a street performance band leader shouted, "Next performance in five minutes." It was in complete contrast to Port Authority, but it put Declan more at ease compared to the Port Authority scene.

After passing through Times Square—a place he often thought must be the center of the world—he noticed someone lurking in the shadows of a storefront. "Wha you need man?" the tall, skinny Black man wearing a Fila hat who slithered up to Declan asked in a low tone, and walked by his side.

"Nothing mate, ta," replied Declan.

The man followed him across the street, "Come on, man, you need a woman? A man? ID card? How about a Nokia cell phone?"

"No, thanks."

"Hey, you like boys? Yeah, is that it? No problem man. Hey, wait up, stop walking so fast, let's talk bizniss. Everyone need something."

Declan kept walking east and increased his pace a little faster, while grabbing the strap of his backpack tighter. "Well, fuck you, mother-fucker," said the man under his breath before quickly turning on his heels and heading back to his post.

There did not seem to be any hotels in sight, and within a few blocks the glare of 42nd Street's neon lights had faded, and a gloomy darkness engulfed the road ahead as Declan approached Madison Avenue. He decided to turn back and see if there were hotels on the west side of Port Authority and so made his way across the street, to hopefully avoid the hustler, and back toward Times Square. About ten minutes later, he cringed as he saw the hustler waving at him from within the shadowy shop entrance.

Declan hurried his way past the tourist establishments and wondered why the man had picked him out. A bar called Blarney Stone caught his eye, and the sight of the shamrock was a welcome symbol that tempted him inside. But he pressed on, wanting more than anything to get off the street to a place where he could lock his door and rest. He approached Port Authority and turned south on Eighth Avenue. Within a block, he came upon a Howard Johnson's hotel and made his way through the parking lot towards the front entrance.

Parked directly in front of the lobby was a large red Buick, with a Black man at the wheel, eating an ice cream cone and two teenage girls in the back seat, also eating ice cream cones.

Inside the hotel, the clerk at the desk was encased in a fort-like structure with just a tiny plastic sliding window exposing him to hotel guests. "How much for a room, please?" asked Declan.

"How long you staying?" asked the grimy clerk.

"One night."

"Are you a Social Security case?"

"No. I'm from England."

"Two hundred bucks. Cash only."

"OK. No thanks," replied Declan, looking down.

As he left the lobby, the black man leaned out of the Buick window and said, "Yo. Check out the back seat. Fifty for a half and half. Any one of them, customer's choice."

"No thanks."

"Hey! I'll throw in an ice cream too!" said the man, apparently serious, as Declan made his way through the parking lot towards Eighth Avenue.

A police cruiser brashly entered the parking lot, causing the man in the Buick to put his vehicle in gear and drive away quickly.

Declan thought again of Chris and imagined his friend would have instantly taken up the offer from the pimp. Probably would have wanted to try out some of the scenes from his porno magazines.

Further down Eighth Avenue, Declan passed several more hotels, all of which proved too expensive for his budget. By now, it was almost ten p.m. and Declan was becoming increasingly nervous. He felt stupid; stupid, he had put himself in this situation. He had no idea what to do. He could always call Isabella and tell her he was unable to find suitable accommodation. But he couldn't bring himself to do that. Instead, he did the only thing he knew—went back to the Irish pub he had earlier seen on 42nd Street.

He made his way as fast as he could to the relative security of the brightly lit and tourist-ridden 42nd Street area and onto The Blarney Stone Pub. Inside, he realized it was not the sort of pub he was familiar with, but more a place where people simply came in and got drunk at the bar. There was no socializing at the bar, no mingling—just serious drinkers staring at the small television whose purpose seemed to be to avert the need to talk.

He sat at the bar, and a fat, greasy-looking bartender, who sighed as he noticed Declan, said, "What you need?"

"I'll take a Guinness."

"We don't have Guinness."

"I thought you were an Irish pub?"

"We are."

"Well, I suppose I'll take a Budweiser then."

The barman slammed down the bottle of beer with an air of contempt and said, "Seven bucks."

The beer helped soothe Declan's nerves. He quickly drank the small bottle of beer and ordered another—choosing to ignore the fact he could ill afford such an expense.

Declan finished the second bottle and left.

***

Declan, tired and inebriated, walked south on Sixth Avenue with no real plan. Within thirty minutes, he came across the Waverly Theater that was about to screen a midnight showing of *The Rocky Horror Picture Show*. He walked up to the box office and purchased one ticket, thinking it would be a good way to sleep for at least a couple of hours.

Inside, Declan saw there were probably two hundred seats on the main level, more on the second floor balconies, and was surprised to see that probably a third of all the seats were taken. It appeared others had the same idea as him, as many were sleeping. The place smelled of piss and semen. Looking around, Declan saw there were three types of customers: those that came to sleep, those who were curious tourists (there were a crowd of Japanese off to the side), and those who were actually interested in the movie—many of whom were dressed in various items from the movie's characters: fishnet stockings, capes, wigs, and French maid outfits, among others.

Declan found a seat towards the back and side, but still found himself surrounded by people. There seemed to be all manner of conversations going on, with money, drugs, and information passing hands. Oddly, the first two rows, which were full, seemed to be off-limits and reserved strictly for genuine vagrants who were there simply to sleep.

A few minutes after he sat down, a man tapped Declan's shoulder, leaned over and said, "How ya doing. Name's Josh Rubenstein. Looks like we're the misfits here. Wondering if you wanna hook up and check out some of the other late-night entertainment around here?"

Declan turned and saw a youthful, pimply, dark-haired man wearing wire-rimmed glasses. "Well, no thanks, I'm OK where I am."

"Come on, man. I know all the best peep shows and strip clubs. They aren't easy to find these days unless you know where to go."

"No, mate, not interested."

"Well, we can even pick up a couple 'a hookers on Eighth Avenue. I know which ones to look for. You don't want no junkie or some bitch with a psycho pimp, and you definitely don't want to be robbed when they take you to their room. That's why it's best to go in pairs on these operations. Come on, man, it'll be a blast!"

"Sorry, mate, I've been travelling all day. Just want to rest here a while and catch the movie if you don't mind."

"Shit. Well, I'll be right back here if you change your mind.

"Yeah, cheers."

The movie started, and Declan wrapped his backpack strap around his arm and quickly slipped in and out of sleep. It was not an ideal situation, but he told himself it was better than walking the streets and, at any rate, only cost nine dollars. Every now and then, Declan would be woken by patrons throwing items around the theater—apparently, this was part of the show. Declan was hit by a toilet roll, some rice, and at one point was woken by water thrown over his head. As the movie progressed, patrons would shout comments in unison with the dialogue or as a sort of response to the on-screen action.

The cinema had a shadow cast, of sorts, who performed many of the scenes from the movie in front of the screen. However, the cast at the Waverly Theatre mainly consisted of middle-aged, perverted-looking men who, to Declan, seemed bordering on insane. One fat old man in makeup, garter belt, stockings, and basque, kept stomping up and down the aisles, shouting all sorts of indecipherable comments to no one in particular. At one point, he sat next to two teenage girls two rows in front of Declan, and said to them, "I'm a cuddler, and to me it's all about your orgasm." The girls quickly turned their heads from him, apparently due to the stench of his breath.

Declan nervously drifted in and out of sleep, finding it strange to open his eyes in a dreamlike state and see a big screen of tits, transvestites, and odd behavior in front of him. He felt anxious, almost afraid, but too tired to fight the fatigue.

In what seemed like just a few minutes, but was actually nearly two hours, the movie came to an end, and the lights went on. As people began to leave, several men placed themselves in areas of high foot traffic and looked brazenly at each person passing by. Occasionally, one would get a nod from someone, and they would turn and walk out together. Declan decided to stay put in his seat. A man to his left, dressed in stockings and a corset, walked down the aisle to leave and as he passed Declan, turned to squeeze by his legs, and thus exposed his penis hanging limply from over the top of his slightly pulled down black women's underwear. Declan looked away and took a deep breath. The man kept walking, and Declan noticed Josh Rubenstein approach the man and walk towards the exit with him.

Declan closed his eyes and tried to sleep some more. He thought to himself that if he could walk outside and know the sun would rise in just a couple of hours, he would be OK. Until then, he would cocoon himself in his own protective shield, a pretend shield that allowed him to ignore what was going on around him. He would focus on his goal: to make a new life in America and be able to return home and help his mother. That was why he had come, and that's what he would do. These incidents would be deflected by his shield, and he would not allow anyone or anything to penetrate his defenses. He had seen things of this nature before in England—the perverts in Brighton park, the prostitutes outside the corner pub at closing time, and, of course, the Russian mob dealing drugs—but he had never seen so much of it in just one evening. He knew he looked innocent; he knew he looked too young. *I will survive this*, he kept telling himself. Returning to England was not an option—not until he had achieved success in America. He would sleep on the streets or in the parks—if necessary. The most important thing he needed to do, he thought, was avoid any type of attack—knife, gun, or beating. But what he had learned more than anything as he sat in his cocoon in the Waverly was that this was going to be much, much more difficult than he'd imagined.

Chapter Four

Declan felt a jabbing sensation on his arm. He woke to find a bald, Hispanic-looking man with small eyes that seemed to be embedded in his face, prodding him with the end of a broom handle. "You gotta get out, we closing."

"Oh, right," replied Declan.

In a panic, he felt for his backpack and quickly calmed on finding the shoulder straps still wrapped around his arm. He got up, walked along the aisle of chairs, and felt his shoes pull on the sticky carpet. By now, there were no other patrons in the theatre, and as he approached the main door, a burly man, who was emptying a rubbish bin into a plastic bag, stopped what he was doing and, without saying a word, unlocked the main door to let Declan out.

The entrance area to the theatre was dimly lit by one flickering strip light. A lady in skin-tight elasticated pants, high heels, and a gray sweatshirt with its hood pulled over her head, arms folded, was crouching, back against the wall, by the front of the cinema. Several middle-aged men lurked in its darkened corners, one talking on his cell phone and the other writing a text message. One stepped out in Declan's path and asked, in a low tone, "Hey buddy, need a dime bag, crank, X?"

"No," replied Declan as he moved past the man firmly and quickly.

A police car slowly pulled up to the curb. The windows wound down, and both officers stared at the people in front of the cinema, who instantly scattered.

Declan felt overwhelmingly tired, but grateful to have slept for a couple of hours or so in the theatre. He wanted more than anything to find a bed and sleep the rest of the day.

After an hour or so of aimless walking, Declan found himself back on 42nd Street and saw it was transformed from the previous night—several industrious-looking individuals scurried around the stores, cleaning and preparing the areas in front. There were coffee shops, newspaper stands, and electronics stores all opening their shutters and clearing the night's deposit of garbage. Declan wanted to get as far from 42nd Street as he could—and decided to walk to Central Park, where he hoped to rest. He took a quick look at his map, then made his way to Times Square, where he turned north on Seventh Avenue and then onto Broadway.

***

AFTER ABOUT THIRTY MINUTES of walking, Declan came upon a delicatessen called, Artie's Deli, dressed in a large, colorful façade with a warm glow flowing onto the cold pavement. He looked at the menu outside—the prices seemed fairly reasonable. Inside, he sat at a small window table. Within a minute, a waitress in her fifties asked, "What'll it be, kid?"

"I'll have a cup of tea and some toast, please," replied Declan.

"You mean iced tea or hot tea?" the woman asked.

"Well, hot tea of course."

"I see, tea and toast, huh?"

"Yes, please."

"Kid, for nine-ninety-nine you can get our eggs, pancakes, and coffee special. Only available before eight a.m."

"What about tea? Can I have the tea with it?"

"Yeah, I'll let you substitute the coffee for tea. But don't tell anyone," replied the lady with a smirk.

"Is bacon available?"

"That's an extra four-seventy-five."

"OK. I'll just go with the special with tea, please."

"OK, I'll be right back with your *tea*," she said as the smirk turned to a wrinkly smile.

Sinking back into the relative comfort of the plastic chair, Declan took a deep breath. He looked down to see some dried white substance down the side of his jacket's arm. "That bastard!" he said. He pounced from his seat and rushed to the toilet, where he scrubbed off what he could only imagine was semen fired at him from Josh Rubenstein, who had sat behind him in the Waverly Theater. He washed his hands and face several times, went for a pee, and then washed his hands and face several more times. He then took off his jacket to check for anything else, and he also ran his hands through his hair—just in case. His hair was clear.

Returning to his table, his mood elevated as he found a glorious plate of eggs and pancakes, alongside a large cup of hot water with a "Lipton" teabag hanging from a piece of string. The tea bag was weak and didn't yield much flavor. Declan didn't worry. This would be a pleasant experience, given last night. He wolfed down the food.

To kill time, Declan ordered another cup of tea. "No free refills on the tea, kid. Only on the coffee."

"That's OK," replied Declan. "Also, could I have change for the newspaper machine?"

Declan spent an hour reading the *New York Mail* jobs section before realizing the coffee shop was getting busy and he should leave to make room for other patrons. He noticed customers had taken their checks to the front to pay, and so did the same. The waitress who served him was manning the till and asked, "Was everything OK?"

"Oh, yes, very nice," replied Declan.

Declan received his change and noticed a large glass container that said "Tips" on it. He saw it mostly contained dollar bills, so he took two dollar bills and placed them in the jar. He looked up at the waitress for guidance, who gave him a slight nod.

***

Declan left the coffee shop and continued walking north toward Central Park. By now, the sun had risen above the skyscrapers. With a full belly and the sun in his face, Declan finally felt as if he had arrived in New York City. He decided to completely forget about the previous night and pretend that breakfast at Artie's Deli was his real entrance into America. He started to feel optimistic for the first time and thought to himself that all he needed was a cheap, clean place to live and a half-decent job, and that would get him started on his new life. He looked up with widened eyes at the vast array of buildings and then around him at the streets spilling with people on their way to work. He felt sure there was a place for him in this city. *Surely there's space enough for one more person—room to squeeze in a poor kid from England.* He found the nearest pay phone and called two of the jobs he saw in the *New York Mail*. The first, a position for a Hotel Front Desk Clerk, had a friendly lady explain the general job details to Declan before asking, "Now, you are legal to work in the U.S., correct?"

Declan was unable to answer the lady's question and so hung up the phone. He immediately called the second job, a position for a Security Officer. The man who answered was gruff and to the point: "First, let's get this out of the way, you are a citizen or have a green card, right?"

Declan again hung up the phone.

Around nine a.m., Declan arrived at Columbus Circle and crossed the busy street to the park. He passed several large rock faces, a carousel, and then came upon a large open field. He walked to the far side where the sun was shining by the base of two massive flat rocks, laid down his backpack as a pillow, and immediately fell asleep on the grass.

It was well past one p.m. before Declan woke. The field area was now active with dozens of people eating lunch, playing with their dogs, or just lying in the springtime sun. He rose, gathered his backpack, and continued his walk through the park. After only a few minutes he came upon The Boathouse Café next to a lake. He walked inside and from the counter purchased their cheapest option: a hot dog and Coke "special" for five dollars. While receiving his change, he noticed a small sign in front of the cash register: "Dishwasher Wanted. Talk Manager."

Declan sat at a plastic table, ate his lunch, and thought about the dishwashing job. It wasn't what he had envisioned as his first American job. He recalled the advice Chris had given him just before he left: "You just gotta go over there and suss it all out. The Yanks don't know nothing. There's money over there for the taking. They'll believe anything you say, mate. They don't know you're from a council estate—all they care about is that you are English and you ain't Black. If you were Black I wouldn't even bother going. They still lynch 'em in some states. Anyway, if you keep moving and keep looking for opportunities, the right one will come your way eventually. It's the law of nature: keep moving and you'll succeed; stop and you'll get fucked up the ass."

Chris was always giving advice—it was as if he had done everything and had an answer for every situation, yet, in truth, Chris had never left the country and had hardly ever left Brighton. But, for some reason, his advice always seemed sound to Declan. And now it served as a source of comfort as he navigated New York City on his own.

Declan finished his lunch and approached one of the staff members behind the counter, a Black man in his late teens, "Can I speak to the manager, please, regarding the dishwashing job?"

"You want the dishwashing job. Are you serious?"

"Well, yes. I'd like to apply for it."

"OK, I'll get the manager."

Within a couple of minutes, a tall, muscular man in his late forties burst through a side door and thrust his hand at Declan. "Rooster Fisher. How are ya?"

"I'm well, thanks."

"You want the dishwashing job?"

"Yes."

"Sit down."

Rooster went on to explain, "Now this is a busy café. We get hundreds of customers each day. There's a lot of work and no time for standing around. It's go, go, go all the time. You are going to be tired each day. We need someone for the night shift: five p.m. till midnight. The café closes at ten p.m., but the dishwasher cleans up the kitchen and does some prep for the morning shift. Eight dollars an hour. Is this something you wanna do?"

"Yes, it sounds fine with me."

"Where are you from? What are you doing here?"

"I'm from England and taking a year off from college to travel. We call it a 'gap year.'"

"You legal to work?"

"Yeah, I have one of those student visas."

"So, you have a Social Security number?"

"Erm...yes."

"How long are you going to be living in New York City? We really need someone who's gonna stay a while."

"Well, I'll be here at least six months."

"That'll work."

Rooster then showed Declan around the kitchen area and seemed particularly proud of his dishwashing machine: "It's a state-of-the-art Hobart model. Heats the water to 180 degrees and can cycle a rack of dishes in one minute using less than a gallon of water. Or you can set it on the 'Pots and Pans' cycle, and it will do most of the pan scrubbing for you! I even bought the taller model so it can fit a two-foot baking sheet right inside. It has a de-lime cycle—you'll need to run that last thing at night. This machine is a dishwasher's dream—you hardly have to lift a damn finger."

"Nice," said Declan.

"OK, so that's your main job. Dishes should be a piece of cake with the Hobart, but you will need to scrub the tough pans before running 'em through. Also, glassware will need to be hand-dried. At the end of your shift, you will need to take out the rubber mats, hose them down, and mop your area. Each person in my restaurant is responsible for their own mats at their station."

"OK."

"One final thing: you'll also have some janitorial duties."

"Oh. I see."

"To keep our operating permit with the city, we had to agree to keep open a public bathroom at the side of the restaurant. So, anyone can use that bathroom, and with the scumbags in this park, it can get messy. Anyway, you would rotate cleaning it with our regular cleaner."

"Right."

"Anyway, that's the deal. Still want the job?"

"Yeah, sounds good to me."

Rooster thrust his hand out, looked Declan in the eye, and then seemed to try to crush his hand in the handshake.

He gave Declan an application form to fill out and told him to bring it in with him the next day before his first shift. Declan knew he was an illegal worker, but recalled what Chris had told him, "No one gives a toss over there about illegal workers. My uncle was over there once, and all you do is make up a Social Security number. Takes them over a year before they kick it out of the system and by then you are in a different job. Everyone's at it. It's a bloody free-for-all over there. You can't go wrong—it's all handed to you on a plate. There's so much money there, the government couldn't care less. Plus, they respect the English—it used to be our country."

On leaving the restaurant, Declan looked at the application form and saw that it did indeed ask for the Social Security number, but there was no sort of formatting, so he had no idea how many numbers to write down in the space provided. He decided to go to the main city library and research what a Social Security number looked like. He took out his map and saw the library was back down on 42nd Street at Fifth Avenue. He made his way there immediately.

***

THE LIBRARY WAS AN imposing structure and looked more like a courthouse. Declan found the public computer terminals and did an internet search on "US Social Security Number Format."

He quickly found what he needed:

> The Social Security number is a nine-digit number in the format "AAA-GG-SSSS." The number is divided into three parts. The Area Number, the first three digits, is assigned by the geographical region. The middle two digits are the Group Number. The group numbers range from 01 to 99. The last four digits are . They represent a straight numerical sequence of digits from 0001-9999 within the group.

The website entry went into much more detail on how the numbers were actually assigned, but Declan found what he wanted when he came across this passage:

> Numbers from 987-65-4320 to 987-65-4329 are reserved for use in advertisements.

Declan wrote each of the ten numbers in his notebook and decided to use them in all matters relating to employment. He was now able to complete his application form for the dishwashing job.

He then remembered talking with Isabella on the flight over and their discussion of Sir Roger de Coverley, so he went to the literature section and quickly found the author Joseph Addison. He found Addison's *The Sir Roger de Coverley Papers*, and came upon a passage that appealed to him:

> Our real blessings often appear to us in the shape of pains, losses and disappointments; but let us have patience and we soon shall see them in their proper figures.

***

ON LEAVING THE LIBRARY, Declan remembered he still needed to find a cheap hotel. He walked north on Fifth Avenue to the park and checked the prices on all the hotels he passed. Starting from the library, he found: The Mansfield at $275 per night, The Holiday Inn at $250 per night, Hotel Omni at $420 per night, The Pennsylvania at $380 per night, and The Crown Hotel at $255 per night. The last hotel he found before reaching the park was Trump Tower, and he considered it a waste of time even to check its prices. He was astonished to realize he would run out of money in a couple of days if he stayed at any of those hotels.

The sun began to set, and Declan came up with a new plan: he would sleep in Central Park for the next two days. He would buy a cheap, warm coat and two large rubbish bags to slip over his feet and upper body—he had seen this technique put to good use on a survival documentary on the BBC. In the meantime, he would eat a large dinner to keep him warm through the night, then go to a normal cinema and watch a late-night movie that would kill some time before he headed back to the park for some sleep. He hoped that once he started working at The Boathouse Café, he could ask around and find suggestions for cheap places to live, knowing that most of his fellow workers would not be able to afford expensive accommodations either.

The thought of sleeping outside in Central Park did not concern Declan—he remembered his brother had spent many nights sleeping under the Pier in Brighton. He recalled his brother telling him of the cold nights where the wind would howl off the sea and seem to blow right through his body. Declan knew he would not have this problem. He would have the plastic bags and would be surrounded by bushes or trees. He then felt sad. Sad that his brother sometimes chose to sleep on the freezing beach rather than sleep in his own bed. He didn't understand his brother's motives, didn't understand what it meant when the social worker told his mother that her son had "Severe Depression." He thought of his brother being dead. He had jumped to his death from the roof of their block of flats. Most people probably thought the Russians drove his brother to his death, but Declan knew there was more to it than that. Declan guessed his brother probably would have harmed himself later, given different circumstances. It was Declan who, several times, had to rescue his brother from situations that could have resulted in an unfortunate ending: like the time Sean said he was going to "fire bomb the Benefits Office" because they were often late with his unemployment check, or the time Sean sat in the middle of a pedestrian crossing on a busy Brighton road, holding up traffic for thirty minutes, because he was "pissed off with just about everything," or the time, just before his death, when Declan talked Sean out of jumping off the end of the pier because, "he wanted to see if the tide would pull him back on the beach or drag him off to France."

As the memories cut through him, Declan reached Pulitzer Fountain, a block before the park. He walked as close as he could to the streaming water and began to cry. Cried for the first time since his brother's funeral. It was as if the water from the gushing fountain was pulling the tears from his eyes, and it was as if the noise of the splashing water gave him the privacy he needed to cry for his brother. But, despite the tears, he became even more determined to be successful in New York City. Nothing could hurt him more than the death of his beautiful brother. With him gone, the world could no longer hurt him, no longer get to him. To Declan, there was nothing left on earth that could be taken from him. So, now that he was in New York City, he would not only save money to help his mother (and keep himself away from trouble), but he would also do his best to transform himself into a new, more productive and effective person, as well as an honorable one.

He walked west along Central Park South toward the setting sun. On reaching Broadway, he turned south. Within a couple of blocks, he strolled into a pharmacy and bought a small box of large garbage bags. "Thirty-nine gallon is the largest we have," said the assistant. He also bought a cheap plastic raincoat with a button-on hood. Putting the items in his backpack, he continued down Broadway and made his way to the AMC theatre. The movie that appealed to him most was *The Immigrant*. He bought a ticket and entered the clean, brightly-lit theatre with its bucket-type seating and plush carpeting. Declan had never seen a theater like it, and it made a stark contrast to the Waverly. He felt safe here, knowing that no one in the AMC Broadway Theater would likely masturbate over his arm.

The movie was entertaining, and Declan watched it twice. He found it to be bleak and almost hopeless for the main female character, who is forced into prostitution. But at the same time, Declan realized his situation would never get as bad as hers, and this in some way comforted him.

The theatre announced it was closing for the night. Declan did not want to move from his seat. He was tempted to simply stay there all night, but an usher came in and began sweeping all the aisles. On the way out, he went to the bathroom, which he found clean and sparkly. He decided he would try to sleep in one of the stalls and took his time washing his hands—waiting for everyone to leave. Within a few minutes, he was the only person in the bathroom, so went to the last stall in the row of five and locked the door. He put down the toilet seat, sat down, hung his backpack on a convenient door hook, then folded his arms and attempted to sleep. Within a few minutes, the clattering of a cleaning cart stirred him. Quickly, he raised his feet onto the toilet seat and wrapped his arms around his legs. He could hear a man whistling and singing in what sounded like Chinese. The man started to brush the floor with a broom, and one by one, kicked open the toilet stall doors. Declan began to panic. Within seconds, the man attempted to push open Declan's stall door. "Hey, somebody in there?"

Declan paused for a second and reluctantly replied, "Yes, just about to leave. Hold on."

Declan got to his feet, put on his backpack, flushed the toilet, then unlocked and left the stall. An Asian-looking man stood by holding a broom and looked at Declan suspiciously. Declan quickly made his way out of the cinema building.

By now it was past midnight. Walking north on Broadway, Declan decided to eat at the McDonald's to fill his belly in preparation for his night sleeping in the Park. Declan took as much time as he could to eat his Big Mac meal before leaving the restaurant. Continuing on Broadway, he came upon a luggage store that also, for some odd reason, sold an extensive collection of knives. Declan decided it would be wise to have some form of protection while sleeping outside. He went inside and asked the clerk if he could recommend a knife.

"What do you want it for, son?"

"General protection."

"KA-BAR. Seven-Inch blade, 1095 Carbon Steel. Best fighting knife in the world—only knife used by the US Marines."

"Yes, that sounds like exactly what I need."

Declan bought a KA-BAR and immediately stashed it in the front pocket of his backpack.

He slowly walked north back up Broadway and onto Central Park West. A certain amount of fear had overcome him by now, and he wondered if he should just keep walking all night and sleep in the morning. However, he knew he had to try and get at least some sleep to be ready for his new job, and he thought it would be more dangerous to be out on the open streets at night. Just then, he happened upon a sign for "Strawberry Fields." He turned into the park and realized it was some type of memorial for John Lennon—a beautiful mosaic carved out of stone lay in the ground, surrounded by a wonderful array of plants and flowers. Being there so late at night in that place of beauty felt surreal to Declan. He stood in the middle of the mosaic and thought for a minute about John Lennon and then, for some odd reason, his fear of the coming night faded. He wished that John were still alive, wished John were still living in his home just across this street in the Dakota Apartments.

Declan walked on into the park, crossed a road, and came to a lake. It was just feet from the roadway but flanked with dense bushes. Since there was no path around that part of the lake, Declan thought it a good place to sleep. He found a small area under a tree, took off his backpack, put on the plastic raincoat and hood. He cut a small hole in one of the garbage bags and slipped it over his head. Then, he sat on the ground and pulled the second bag up over his legs, put his small towel by the base of the tree for a pillow, pulled his backpack inside his garbage bag, and lay down.

He could hear the gentle lapping of the lake as he lay there, and every few minutes in the background the sound of police and fire engine sirens. Occasional cars passed and lit his whole area; however, the bushes protected him from any possible sighting. It took a few minutes to adjust, but Declan felt it wasn't too bad at all and soon he fell asleep.

Within an hour, Declan jumped up in a panic. Illuminated under the constant city glow were two large furry rats, nibbling through the garbage bag around his legs. He kicked them and watched as they nonchalantly plopped their way along the water's edge—dragging their long, slimy tails through the mud. Declan looked at his watch: still only two-thirty. He had three hours before he could get up. He consoled himself that in three hours, he would pack up and make his way down Broadway to Artie's Deli and order the breakfast special with tea in place of coffee. He sat up against the tree and counted at least seven rats scuttling within his view. In his semi-conscious state, he felt almost as if his skin was crawling with a disgusting slime, and he would be infected with it forever. For the next three hours, he drifted in and out of a nervous sleep, and each time he became aware of his surroundings, he told himself: "I have to do this. I have to keep going. Don't give up. Never give up."

CHAPTER FIVE

AT PRECISELY SIX A.M., Declan stood up, removed himself from the garbage bags, put on his backpack, and made his way along Central Park Driveway. Then he walked through Strawberry Fields and over the "Imagine" mosaic, south on Central Park West, tossing the plastic bags into a garbage can. Then it was onto Seventh Avenue, where he arrived at Artie's Deli just as they were opening at six-thirty a.m.

He was the first and only customer at the café, and the same waitress tended to him at the same window table. "Tea and Toast?" she asked, smiling.

"No, I'll take the pre-seven a.m. special with *hot* tea in place of coffee, please," replied Declan as he mustered a strained smile.

"Sure."

Declan went outside, bought a newspaper, and tried to forget the night. The waitress came back with his tea and said, "What's with the plastic thing you are wearing?"

Declan forgot he was wearing the transparent plastic raincoat, and, slightly embarrassed, replied, "Oh, it's just my travel raincoat. Keeps me dry."

"You expecting rain this morning?"

"No, not really."

The waitress, staring at him with a look of skepticism, replied, "You know, we have hotels around here."

Declan paused for a few seconds and replied, "Yeah, but they're bloody expensive, you know."

"What's your mother think of you coming over here like this?"

"Not sure."

The waitress, sensing Declan's unease, told him she'd be back as soon as his order was ready.

But Declan *did* know how his mother was most likely doing. She would be drinking vodka or cheap wine and watching reruns of her favorite old shows on TV.

Declan read the *New York Mail* headline: "Attack Points to the Work of Central Park Rapist." He went on to read:

> After a one-year silence, the Central Park Rapist may have brazenly struck again, investigators fear.
>
> The yet-unnamed sex fiend may be responsible for the assault of a twenty-six-year-old woman who was dragged behind some bushes on the 72nd Street Traverse Road and choked into unconsciousness at 1 a.m. yesterday, police sources said.
>
> The woman was also severely beaten in the attack and was working with investigators last night. Since she was beaten into unconsciousness, it is not yet known if she was raped.
>
> Police have retrieved DNA from four of the now sixteen victims.

The waitress then took a deep breath and continued, "Anyway, look, I gave you some extra eggs and pancakes. You look like you need it."

"Thanks so much."

She then pulled a chair next to Declan's and sat down.

"You know, I've been like you in the past. Been down on my luck and on my own. I know what it's like. So, anyway, why don't you go and clean yourself up in the bathroom? If you get here before seven, there's never anyone eating, so you can do that as long as you're in your predicament." She patted Declan's hand when she finished speaking.

"Thank you, I will," replied Declan, somewhat taken aback by the woman's kindness. It wasn't money, it wasn't a place to stay, but it was a gesture that gave Declan some hope in his situation. In just two days, he had come to understand how vital such small gestures were. He again recommitted himself to finding a new life in America—his time again in this country was reset to this morning in this coffee shop.

"And my name's Nancy, by the way."

"Mine's Declan, Declan O'Neill."

By seven-thirty, the coffee shop was more than half-full—and Declan took his cue to leave. He wrapped his plastic raincoat in his backpack, paid for his breakfast, and left several dollars in the tip jar. Nancy gave him another nod before he turned to leave. This time, he felt it more of a gesture of "good luck."

***

DECLAN WALKED TO THE library and read for most of the morning. He returned again to his trusted book, *The Sir Roger de Coverley Papers, from the Spectator* and read as much as he could until lunchtime. Reading the book reminded Declan of the times in the past he had read the works, mostly rainy afternoons in secondary school when there was nothing to do at lunchtime. Declan would always find an excuse to leave his friend, Chris, and wander off to the library. It was at that secondary school that the library had been a place of retreat for him and a place to extend his learning beyond what was offered in the school. It was as if he wanted to absorb as much as he could about life;

and the library, to him, held as much knowledge as he was willing to bear. A Sir Roger quote came to his mind:

> I would retire into the Town and get into the Crowd again as fast as I could, in order to be alone to observe others without being observed myself.

***

FROM THE LIBRARY, DECLAN walked north to Central Park and, since it was now sunny and warm, slept in a large grassy area close to the carousel. As he drifted in and out of sleep, he wondered how his mother was faring back home in Brighton. He had asked his friend Chris to keep an eye on her—to check on her every couple of days. He knew Chris would do his best to make sure she was well, but what could he really do if the Russians decided to seek some sort of vengeance on her?

He sat up on the grass and looked around. Just off to the side was a path where he watched as hurried Americans pressed forward with their day. Many looked fat to him, some glum-faced, all were self-contained units not wanting any contact with outsiders. He could tell from the taut, aggressive manner in which they walked that these people were probably not open to new friends. Declan wondered if he would make any friends in this new city. Such a thing hadn't occurred to him before. He wondered if it were possible he could live for years in this place and not have any meaningful contact with others. He dismissed this thought with the acknowledgement that it was part of the sacrifice for starting a new life.

***

DECLAN ARRIVED AT THE back entrance of The Boathouse Café just before four p.m. and asked a young Chinese man for Rooster Fisher. Within a minute, Rooster came charging towards Declan, thrust out his arm, and proceeded to almost crush Declan's hand in another display of dominance. In Declan's mind, it was a sort of ritual Rooster had in order to establish that he was in charge. But, what purpose this served, Declan wasn't sure.

"Come this way. I'll hand you over to our kitchen manager, Louie. What are you doing with that backpack?"

"Oh, it's just some things I didn't want to leave in my hotel room."

"Fine, you can just leave it in the storage room in the back."

Declan was led through a hallway lined with tins of soup, gravy, cooking oil, and all manner of preserved foods. Writing on a clipboard was a short, stubby man, half bald with a dark complexion. His face was intense as he turned to Declan.

"Louie, this is the Irish guy, Declan, I told you about. He's the new dishwasher. I'll leave him with you. Good luck Declan," said Rooster as he quickly disappeared into a nearby office and slammed the door.

Louie looked back at his clipboard and continued writing what appeared to be some kind of log of the restaurant's supplies. It felt like a minute or so, while Declan stood there not knowing what to say or do. He felt as if he were part of some test to see how he would react. Was this man going to let him stand there until he finished his work and not say anything? He couldn't completely ignore Declan, since he needed to show him his duties. Declan adjusted the backpack over his shoulder and cleared his throat. "I'll be right with yer, buddy," said Louie.

Louie then hung up the clipboard, turned his back on Declan, and said, "This way."

He led Declan to the small kitchen area, where already one sink was full of pans and baking sheets. "This will be where you'll spend most of your time. The pans are always dropped in this first sink.

You can run them through the washer one time but they'll probably still need to be scrubbed. Those can wait until you have a break with the regular items that come through over here on this table. Now the servers are going to be bringing in plates, cups, cutlery, and glasses. You'll scrape off the food into this food bin. When the food bin is full, take it out and empty it into the large container at the back. I'll show you that in a minute. You have to scrape as much of the food off as possible—the washers are good, but it'll save you time later in any rewash runs. And believe me, the servers will return any dirty plates. I do random checks too of all the cleaned items and will kick back anything that is not spotless. Another thing is you have to get the glassware back fast. They go in a separate cycle so you may have only half a rack full of them. But the servers are always running out of glasses, so deal with those first."

"Right," said Declan, focusing as much as he could.

"Once a rack is clean, place all the dishes on the storage shelves back here. The glasses will have to be hand-dried to get the spots off. Pots and pans will go back in the kitchen area. I'll show you where in a minute. If you are not busy, keep busy. Tidy the place up, sweep the floors, clean the mats. I don't like to see anyone standing around. If you disappear for more than a few minutes, I'll be screaming for yer. Always wear an apron—they are right here by the door. Keep one on at all times here—it's an inspection item and we have to keep our standards up. The last franchise was kicked out for low sanitary scores on the City inspection. To keep our license, we need to cover our ass at all times. That goes for the shitter too. Did Rooster tell you about the public shitter?"

"Yes."

"Good. You'll have to clean it once a day. You and a couple of the other guys take turns. We have to clean it four times a day. If anyone fucks up cleaning it—they get fired immediately. Got it?"

"Yes."

"I'll get Sanat to show you how to clean it tonight, then you'll be on your own. You get one break around six p.m. when we have a slow period. Just ask one of the chefs for a sandwich and go eat it in the storage area."

"Sure."

"Got it?"

"Yes."

"OK, I'll be around all evening if you have any questions."

"Thanks."

Louie then walked to the office in a hunched-over style as if he were a football player, ready to slam his shoulder into the next person that was unlucky enough to walk in his path.

Declan put on an apron and began scrubbing the pans in the sink. As people passed by his work area, most would say an obligatory "hi" but not much else. Most didn't seem to want to be there, and if they had a few spare minutes, they would talk on their cell phones or send text messages. It felt like an unhappy, depressing place to him.

After finishing the pans, Declan could not figure out how to work the dishwashing machine, so he reluctantly knocked on the office door. Louie opened it and said, "What's up?"

Declan noticed Rooster with his feet crossed on the table, nonchalantly reading *Sports Illustrated*.

"Could you show me how to run the machine? Also, I need to know where to put the pots and where to empty the food bin."

"OK, follow me," said Louie, with an air of irritation in his voice, and proceeded to show Declan how to operate the dishwashing machine.

Throughout the night, the pots, pans, dishes, cups, cutlery and glasses kept coming. It seemed a never-ending stream. Declan had no time to eat since he didn't want to take a chance that Louie would come out of the office and see a mountain of dishes lined up. He soon learned to empty the food bin before it got half full—he could hardly lift it when it was full—and was laughed at by one of the servers the first time he struggled to lift the overflowing food container.

Declan quickly observed two types of waiters: those who scraped the food from their plates into the food bin and those who simply threw plates of half-finished meals on the table. To him, scraping the plates marked a line between a person of decency and one of selfishness. *What made the non-scrapers think they were above this sort of work?* To Declan, they were not far from dishwashers themselves.

Later, as the stream of dishes dwindled to a trickle, Louie approached Declan, holding a black garbage bag and said, "Yo. I need you to empty the garbage can in the restaurant by the front door. Take the full bag to the dumpster out back."

Declan took the garbage bag, dried his hands, and proceeded through the kitchen doors into the restaurant. As he approached the garbage bin container, he noticed three teenagers sitting at a nearby table who were laughing. Declan suddenly felt self-conscious as he pulled the garbage bin out from the wooden container. He overheard one of the kids say, "Check out garbage boy," and then more laughter. After tying up the full garbage bag, Declan lifted it over his shoulder and heard one of the teens say, "I'm gonna take a picture of garbage boy and send it to the group." They laughed as one of them took a picture, with his Nokia phone, of Declan holding the garbage bag. The teen then continued, "I'm titling it, 'loser garbage boy doing a trash pick-up at The Boathouse.'"

Declan said nothing and quickly left the area. He felt sad as he threw the garbage bag into the dumpster. He sat on a milk crate next to the dumpster and smoked a cigarette before returning to work in the kitchen. He again wondered if he had done the right thing in leaving England. He realized in a way the teenagers were correct: he was completely in the wrong place right now. He felt he had much more to offer the United States, but here he was emptying trash cans. He took a deep breath. He was tired, nervous, and embarrassed. He wondered if he should just throw off his overalls and take the subway to the airport and return home. "No," was his answer. He would encapsulate himself in an invisible mental protective membrane and go about his business until he had found success in America. There was no alternative. This was it. No turning back.

***

AT TEN P.M., ALL of the servers had left, and Louie introduced Declan to a skinny Indian-looking man. "Sanat, this is the new guy. He'll help you close up."

"OK, very nice. What is your name?" asked Sanat.

"Declan," he said, turning to Louie to remind him of his name—he had not called him by his name since meeting him.

Louie turned and walked off and, as an afterthought, said, "See you guys tomorrow."

"Nice to meet you, Declan," said Sanat.

"You too."

"Well, once you've had a chance to clean up your station, I'll show you how we close up."

"OK, right."

Declan took out all the heavy rubber mats, scrubbed them with a broom and soap, and returned them to his kitchen area. He then scrubbed down the dishwashing machine and the dish tables in his area.

"You'll also have to dump out the food bin and clean it, then clean out the food chute. Also, all the garbage cans need to be emptied and tossed in the dumpster out back. After that, it's just the bathrooms outside, and then we lock up."

Declan noticed how quickly Sanat skipped over the bathroom cleaning part.

"So, what do you do once we've done the lockup?" asked Declan.

"I'm the sandwich chef. I prepare several hundred sandwiches for tomorrow's day crew. I also do salads and stock the hamburger bins with frozen burgers and hot dogs so they are thawed out for tomorrow. Plus, I'm basically the night watchman. If no one was here, this place would be broken into every night. Alarms are no good here—no one listens to them. So, they made this position for me—I double as the night watchman and call the cops if someone breaks in."

"Have you been broken into then?"

"Oh, yes, at least once a month. I just lock myself in this storage room—it has metal walls and the door is safe. They put a telephone in here for me."

"Wow."

Declan finished his cleaning chores and Sanat led him to the public bathrooms with their mopping and cleaning equipment.

"Declan, this is a bad job. All scumbags in the city use this place. What I do is not even look at it too much. Just do the job really quickly, but well. Then get out and lock it up. I then wash my hands several times and take a thirty-minute break as my reward. It's not too bad today, but it can be in a terrible state sometimes."

"Sure, I understand."

"OK, first, take this Comet powder and throw it all over the toilets, seats, urinals, wash basins, mirrors, everything. Then take a few of these cloths, damp them down, and then just wash each of the toilets and everything hard and fast. Next, go back with a couple more dry cloths and lightly polish all the basins, then throw all the cloths in the garbage and empty the garbage can. Next, sprinkle a whole can of this Comet all over the floor, then mop it. Do you know how to sweep mop?"

"No."

"Easy. Just swing the mop side to side and slightly forward and you sort of mop and brush at the same time. Do it from that far corner to the door and move the cleaning cart back with you. When you get to the door, put the cart outside and brush all the floor crap out and into the bushes. And that's it. Ten-minutes. Now, you do the Ladies—it's usually easier."

Declan quickly found, as Sanat had said, using the Comet liberally was the key. "Rooster don't like the way we eat through boxes of Comet, but it's the only way to do this job and not puke sometimes. Be prepared for anything in this job. You never know what you'll find in these bathrooms. I even found a guy sleeping in one of the stalls the other day."

"Wow. Fancy that," replied Declan, smiling.

After they finished cleaning, Sanat offered Declan one of the enormous sandwiches he was making. "Take as much as you want: Corned Beef, Pastrami, or Roast Beef. All good stuff—half a pound of meat in each of them."

"Nice."

Declan hurriedly ate a Roast Beef Sandwich. "That was the best sandwich I have ever eaten. I am not joking. Fantastic!"

"Have another, my friend, no problem."

Declan did and was full after eating it. "Take a drink from the fridge. Don't worry. No one here. Only us."

Declan sat down and felt thankful for Sanat's kindness. "Why are you in New York, Declan?" asked Sanat as he ate one of his corned beef sandwiches.

Declan thought he could tell this man the truth. Unlike Isabella, he felt Sanat would understand his situation, "I'm trying to start a new life here. Things were not so good for me in England, so I decided to come here for a fresh start. At first it was just to get away and make some money to help my mother, but now it's even more than that. Now I want to really make a start for myself here."

"Well, you are young. A fresh start will be easy for you. You are strong, handsome, and white. You should do fine. But why this dish-washing job? They usually hire ex-cons and mental cases for that job."

"First thing that came my way. Like I said, only been here a couple of days. I don't expect it will last. Probably why Louie ignores me."

"Yes, you will find something better."

"And what about you? Why are you here?"

"I am from Sri Lanka. My wife and children were killed by the government. They accused us of being terrorists. I was lucky to escape and have been here for one year now. I do this job and stay safe. I have nothing else to live for anymore."

"I'm so sorry, Sanat. Really, I am. You make my situation seem quite petty."

"No, no, it is not petty. I can tell this is an important time for you. This may be the most important thing you ever do with your life—coming here to America at this early age."

"Yes, you may be right."

Sanat handed Declan a piece of paper. "Here, before you go. Take this AT&T number. You can use it to call your family. Just go to a public phone and dial the whole fourteen digits, wait for the dial tone again and then dial your number for England. The call is free."

"How d'you get this?"

"It's a scam the Africans run. They hang about the telephone booths and watch the tourists and businessmen use their calling cards, then memorize the number and write it down. They sell the number for ten dollars a pop. They usually last about two to four weeks, but are well worth the money. Best place to use them is in hotels like the Hilton or Trump Tower; they have nice carpets and chairs in the lounge area, where you can sit and talk for hours. Just buy a drink from the bar and security won't question you."

"Wow, thanks Sanat. This is really kind of you."

"If you need another, just look for the African guys hanging about at the entrance of the subway at Columbus Circle; they have the numbers there. Don't pay more than ten bucks."

Sanat finished his sandwich and drink, then stood and said, "Well, I have to continue with tomorrow's prep. Where are you staying?"

"Ermmm...close by. Not too far."

"Oh, well OK. Be careful going home. They don't have any cops in this park at night."

"OK, thanks."

"Bye Declan."

***

DECLAN'S PLAN FOR THAT night was to sleep in the vicinity of The Metropolitan Museum of Art on Fifth Avenue. The part of Central Park surrounding the building was nicely kept, and it seemed it would be a pleasant area to sleep, being close to such a world-renowned museum.

Declan walked twice around the museum until he found what he thought was a good place—directly behind the back of the building, close to a conservatory-like structure, there was a strong growth of bushes surrounding a tree. Declan climbed into the bushy cave, of sorts, removed his backpack, put on his transparent plastic raincoat, and placed his small towel down for a pillow. He rested his head against the tree and felt nearly comfortable in his position. After a while, Declan thought it wouldn't be so bad to actually live in the bushes. He could put together a "camping kit" of sorts and stash it in a locker somewhere and pick it up each night for his overnight stay in the bushes. Declan thought about what this kit might contain. A flashlight, small tarp, sleeping bag, first aid kit, snacks, and water, among other things. It didn't take long before he fell asleep.

About four a.m., Declan woke to hear a woman's scream in the distance. Declan was unsure how far away the scream was. He stood up and listened, but heard nothing more. Now feeling uneasy, Declan grabbed his backpack and towel, surged through the rear of the bushes and walked towards the side of the museum, and what he hoped was safety, since he knew the building would have security guards in the lobby area.

Declan hurried to the front of the museum, where he climbed the steps and sat at the top as close to the front entryway as possible. Inside, a security guard took notice of him but quickly returned his focus to a small television. By five a.m., Declan started his slow walk to Artie's Deli.

Chapter Six

The night in the park left Declan's nerves frayed and his body and mind further exhausted. To make matters worse, he felt he had to keep walking with purpose to help prevent himself from being picked up by the police, who seemed to be everywhere, or from being mugged. He felt as if the city was now preying on him. It was hard, harder than he had ever imagined, but, curiously, at the same time he felt alive. More alive than he had ever been. Alive because he was doing something. Alive because more than anything, he wanted his life to be something—anything. Alive because it was better to be in battle rather than like his brother, dead.

He tilted his head back and took in the sheer vertical stretch of glass and steel all around him as the skyscrapers pressed into the low clouds. The City was coming to life as taxi horns mingled with the din of hundreds of conversations. Everything seemed excessive, almost unbelievable. His excitement grew. He absolutely knew that if he could just survive these first few weeks, he could thrive in this place. Not only thrive, but do something great, even spectacular.

He arrived at Artie's Deli. Having breakfast and talking to Nancy had become his respite in just three short days. "So, what's on the agenda today?" asked Nancy.

"Yesterday was the first day of my new job, so I'm going to take it easy and be ready for my shift tonight."

"That's great. Where are you working?"

"Boathouse Café, in the park."

"What do you do?"

"I'm a waiter," replied Declan, too embarrassed to tell her he was a dishwasher.

"Well done. Maybe I'll drop by and see how you are doing sometime."

"Sure," replied Declan, warily.

After eating breakfast and reading the newspaper, things approached normality for Declan. He felt he had made progress—but still, he needed to find a cheap place to stay.

***

AFTER SAYING GOODBYE TO Nancy, Declan walked the few blocks to Trump Tower on Fifth Avenue. Inside, he did as Sanat suggested and walked directly past the front desk as if he were a hotel guest. In the alcove by the bathrooms were phone booths. Declan sat down in one of the plush chairs and used the AT&T card number for the first time. As if by magic, he heard the familiar British dial tone, and then his friend Chris' voice.

"Hello mate, 'ow are you? Dec here."

"Blimey, Dec, where are you? What are you doing? What the 'ell is going on?" replied Chris.

"Doing OK. Bit of a struggle, to be honest. Not as easy as I thought it would be. But I'm pushing on."

"Did you find a place to stay yet?

"No, not exactly."

"Where are you staying then?"

"Well, just crashing in the park at the moment. It's not so bad. I get up early and have a nice breakfast, so that's something to look forward to."

"Fucking hell mate, have you looked in the paper for a pad?"

"Yeah, the problem is it's just so expensive here. I'm down to about three hundred dollars so I can't afford rent, and hotels are at least two hundred dollars a night. My only option right now is to sleep rough until I can find a roommate or something."

"Yeah, right. So you are working then?"

"Yeah."

"Doing what?"

"Dishwasher in Central Park."

Chris laughed and said, "So, you went all the way to America to become a dishwasher!"

"It's just a start until I get on my feet."

"Sorry mate, didn't mean to laugh. I hope you get fixed up soon. 'Ave you met any birds yet?"

"No, not really. I'm busy trying to find a place to stay and a better job."

"Yeah right."

"How's my mum?"

"Oh, just saw her yesterday. She seemed pretty cheerful. Said she was going to try and get her mobile switched back on so you can phone her direct."

Declan knew that was unlikely to happen.

"Any news on the band?"

"No. You've only been gone a few days. It's gonna take time to replace you and your brother." Chris paused. Declan knew the pause was for mentioning his brother—Chris realized he had made a mistake in bringing up the subject. Chris changed topics. "I'm still working on getting my bloody amplifiers back from the Legion. I think I might have a few pints and go down there and apologize. But, Tony's not interested in doing the public apology bit."

"Surprising. He lost most of his drum kit," replied Declan.

"Yeah, right."

"Anyway, I hope you get the gear back and get the band back together."

There was an awkward pause. As if suddenly a chasm had opened between them both. Declan realized he really didn't care about the band or its equipment. He had far too many things to address with his situation right now. And, he thought Chris knew this. He thought Chris must know that this was probably the start of a very different Declan, and that their friendship would be forever changed as their lives took very different courses.

Then Chris said, "There was something I need to tell yer."

"Yeah?"

"I bumped into one of the Russian pushers outside the pub last night."

"Oh, yeah?"

"Yeah. And well, looks like they know you are in Manhattan. He told me to give you a message that they have an operation there and will be looking for you so you can return the hundred thousand pounds you owe them."

"Christ, how did they know where I am?"

"Well, probably a slip of the tongue in the pub before you left might have been picked up by one of their local associates."

"Shit."

Another awkward silence followed.

"Well, look, mate, make sure you phone every few days. We want to be sure you are doing OK. I wish I was there with you," said Chris.

"I wish you were here too, mate."

"If it weren't for the fact I have a few things in the pipeline here, I'd be there with you right now. We'd show those Yankee bastards a thing or two! Anyway, take care of yourself and phone soon."

"Will, do. Bye, mate."

Declan sat back, exhaled and felt the familiar queasiness in his stomach as he thought about the Russians having an operation in

Manhattan. He also pondered what Chris meant by "things in the pipeline." He knew there was no pipeline, knew there was no real reason for Chris not to be with him in New York. Declan couldn't quite grasp what the difference in them was, but knew there was some *thing* powerful inside him that drove him to New York City, some *thing* strong that made it fine to sleep in a park with rats, put up with terrible conditions and continue on. He didn't know what that *thing* was, but knew it made some sort of difference between himself and Chris. Whatever it was, Declan was glad he had it as he exited through the heavy gold-colored doors of the Trump Tower with an air of confidence about him.

***

DECLAN MADE HIS WAY to Fifth Avenue then south to the library. Inside, he again read, *The Sir Roger de Coverley Papers* and came across a couple of quotations that appealed to him:

> I came to my estate in my twenty-second year, and resolved to follow the steps of the most worthy of my ancestors who have inhabited this spot of earth before me, in all the methods of hospitality and good neighborhood, for the sake of my fame; and in country sports and recreations, for the sake of my health.

> When I reflect upon this woman, I do not know whether in the main I am the worse for having loved her: whenever she is recalled to my imagination my youth returns, and I feel a forgotten warmth in my veins. This affliction in my life has streaked all my conduct with a softness, of which I should otherwise have been in-

capable. It is, perhaps, to this dear image in my heart
owing that I am apt to relent, that I easily forgive, and
that many desirable things are grown into my temper,
which I should not have arrived at by better motives
than the thought of being one day hers.

Why the Sir Coverley writings appealed to Declan so much, he did
not know. However, he felt there was so much decency in the man,
so much righteousness, so much humanity, it made him feel better
knowing that such people could exist. In Declan's world, people were
harsh, combative, manipulative and ready to take advantage of anyone
in their path. That a man like Sir Roger was imagined in the mind of
a writer made him feel it was possible that such a man could exist. It
gave Declan much comfort in knowing that one day he might know
someone like Sir Roger, might even have someone like Sir Roger as a
friend, might even, perhaps, be able to emulate Sir Roger in some way
or manner.

At the very least, reading Sir Roger would become Declan's an-
tidote to the harsh realities he faced in New York City. He decided
at that point that whatever bad experiences happened to him in this
place, he would combat them with visits to the library and read some
of his favorite writers and absorb their wisdom: Shakespeare, Addison,
Socrates, Dickens, Orwell, Milton, among others. He stayed in the
library for most of the day, venturing outside only to buy a hot dog
from one of the street vendors.

***

IT STARTED TO RAIN as Declan walked north on Fifth Avenue toward
Central Park. He put on his cheap plastic raincoat and made his way to
The Boathouse Café. Once inside, Louie somehow saw him without

looking and said, "Hey Darren, we're usually slow when it rains, so any downtime you have, I need you to take out each of the garbage cans from the restaurant and scrub them down out the back."

"Yes, sure. And my name is Declan," replied Declan.

"Also, it's your day off tomorrow, right?"

"Yes, I believe so. The schedule just worked out that way."

With that, Louie walked away.

The shift went relatively fast and soon Sanat arrived which brought a smile to Declan and a hearty handshake between both men.

"Hey assholes, get back to work!" shouted Louie, who seemed to have been lurking in the shadows of the kitchen area.

Declan did not know what to make of Louie. He knew New Yorkers were supposed to be rough around the edges, but this man appeared to have no manners or respect for anyone. Declan wondered how this man could actually meet and talk with other people outside of work.

Later, when everyone else had left and Declan and Sanat were doing the closing routine, Declan asked Sanat about Louie. "He's very typical of some of the people here in New York City. They have no time for anyone. It's a harsh place. People will ignore you since everyone is afraid of everyone else—they all think everyone is going to mug, kill, or rape them. Or, at the least, rip them off. I've been here over a year, and my only friends are from my own country or other foreigners. I don't have any American friends. It's a shame."

"Yeah, it is a shame. Hopefully, people aren't like this in other places in America."

"I'm not so sure. It could be the same all over this country."

Both men sat on milk crates in the back area of the restaurant by the dumpsters. Declan lit a cigarette. "Declan, you look very tired my friend."

"I am. I'm very tired."

With that, Sanat leaned over and raised his index finger towards Declan's face. Declan did not know what to make of his actions and froze. Gently, Sanat wiped away some of the sleep from the inside corner of Declan's left eye.

"Yes, you are exhausted. You need to sleep properly. You know, you are a very very attractive young man."

Declan looked away. He felt saddened all of a sudden. It seemed that this man might actually be showing kindness with sexual motives. He felt let down again. He wondered if he would have to quit the job since it would be easy for Sanat to cause problems for him.

"Look, I know you have no place to stay right now."

"You do?" asked Declan.

"Yes, it's pretty obvious by your face. Plus, not many people come to work with a backpack stuffed with clothes."

"Oh," replied Declan before taking a large inhale off his cigarette and looking down at the ground.

"So, if you like, you can sleep in the storage room. It's quiet back there, and I hardly have to go inside once I have my supplies taken out for the night. You could lay down some potato sacks and make a sort of bed. It's better than being outside."

"Yes. Yes, you are right. But I have to ask you something: are you gay?"

"Yes. But it's no problem, I will not touch you if that is what you are wondering. You are very handsome and I am happy to just spend this time with you."

"I see. I didn't mean to sound harsh."

"It's not a problem."

"But I'm curious, you had a wife and children, and you are gay?"

"Yes. It was something I had to do for my family. But I've always known I was gay. And being gay in Sri Lanka is illegal."

"Illegal?"

"Yes. Engaging in any homosexual act is considered 'gross indecency' and is against the law."

"So, you could go to prison?"

"Not really prison. But, you can be fined or whipped. Most of the time people are made to go to government psychological re-education programs."

"Bloody hell."

Declan lit another cigarette as Sanat finished drinking a cup of tea.

"I won't get you in trouble, will I, sleeping here?" asked Declan. "That Louie is a right bastard."

"No. No one ever comes here after midnight—unless there's a break-in. And in that case you could leave before the police get here. That would be rare anyway. No one ever gets here before six a.m. So as long as you are gone by then it will be fine," replied Sanat.

"That would be brilliant. Thanks so much. I can help you do your work too, if you like."

"That's OK."

After their break, both men rearranged some vegetable boxes and placed about six potato sacks on the floor in the back of the storage room. Declan laid his head down.

"Thanks Sanat," said Declan.

"It's OK. I'll wake you about half-past five."

Within a few minutes, Declan was deeply asleep.

Chapter Seven

As he had promised, Sanat woke Declan at five-thirty: "Good morning. Did you sleep well?"

"Yes. Thanks."

"Well, if you are quick you can have a cup of tea before you leave."

"Thanks Sanat. Sounds good."

Declan realized it was the first morning he had awakened in America without a pang of fear in his stomach. He valued this man's kindness and he was also happy he kept his promise of not making any untoward advances to him.

He drank the tea quickly, picked up his backpack, and made his way out of the back entrance of the restaurant—not wanting to chance seeing Louie or Rooster coming through the front door. He turned briefly to wave to Sanat before making his way through the darkened park towards Sixth Avenue.

As he exited the park and entered a safer zone, Declan slowed his pace and ambled the several remaining blocks to Artie's Deli. He did not want to get there before they opened—he did not want to seem too desperate.

***

After finishing breakfast at the Deli he went to the library and spent the morning there. Around lunchtime, he left the library, deciding to look into the prices of MP3 players. Chris had told him electronics were cheap in New York City, "They're almost giving the shit away." Declan was interested in buying one once he had saved some money, but for now, he would just look at the various models and their prices. He made his way west on 42nd Street, passing Bryant Park and then north on Sixth Avenue, where he had seen many electronics stores on his first night in the city.

After looking in two stores, he crossed the street to another shop hidden under some scaffolding that stretched from the front of the store and over to the street's edge. As Declan walked under the darkened canopy, he noticed two Black youths sitting on one of the scaffolding cross-struts. One was rapping along to 50 Cent while listening on his MP3 player, which made Declan look over. Declan made his way to the shop window and saw another Black youth leaning against the far side of the window, looking directly at him. Declan locked eyes with the youth and was taken aback by his piercing stare. Declan looked away and felt shaken by the youth's aggressive posture. The youth then made some sort of signal to his friends sitting on the scaffolding by the street edge. They slunk down, and one of the teens approached Declan. Dressed in denim overalls, and a New York Yankees wool hat, he stood by Declan and looked up at him, saying nothing. Declan turned and noticed his upper torso was large and muscular.

"What you wan, man?"

"Just looking for MP3 players," replied Declan, trying not to show his nervousness.

"We got doze. Don't pay these prices—these goddam Arabs will rip you off. Come over here. We got some stuff in the bag."

"Well..." before he could say anything more, the boy grabbed his elbow and pushed him to the side of the store. His two friends looked around the street for any observers and then surrounded Declan and bundled him down a rubbish-littered side alley, then behind a dumpster. Two of them grabbed Declan by the collar of his jacket and held him against the wall. After a pause, the apparent ringleader who had been standing by the window said, "Motherfucker, we need fifty bucks urgently. My boys and me got to get fifty bucks today else we gonna fuck someone up. Now you can give me the fifty bucks and you walk outta here. But if you don't; well, you gonna get more fucked up than you ever been fucked up."

"I haven't got fifty bucks."

"Then what the fuck you looking in all these stores? We been watching your white ass looking in all these stores up here."

"I'm gonna buy one when I get my first paycheck next week. I'm just looking right now."

"You ain't no tourist?"

"No."

One of the two youths then said, "Dwayne, let's just fuck him up, man. Drop his ass and take what he got."

"Yeah, strip his ass for the cash. He loaded, man," said the other youth.

"Now hold on boys, let's give him a chance here. So, white boy, you got those fifty bucks?"

"No. Fuck off," and with that Declan threw the two men away from him and ran to the back of the alley, grabbed inside the front pocket of his backpack, and pulled out the seven-inch KA-BAR knife.

"Now, any you come near me and I'm gonna slice ya," said Declan.

The three men stood with jaws dropped. Dwayne, hands on hips and with a smirk on his face, said, "Hey man, it's only fifty bucks we want. Just throw down some cash an we outta here."

"Fuck off. You'll have to come through this knife to get at me. I ain't taking any more shit."

"Hey where you from man?" said one of the other youths.

"Shit City."

"OK, man, look, we ain't gonna hurt yer. We'll just back up outta here. OK?"

"Get on with it then," said Declan.

The three men looked at each other, smiled and nonchalantly walked to the street with a swagger in their stride. Declan put his backpack on, hid the knife up his sleeve, and then walked to the street. He noted the three men had taken their same earlier positions. In an act of defiance, Declan walked directly under the scaffolding in full view of them, rather than walking in the opposite direction away from the men.

Dwayne, at the far end of the scaffolding, had a wide grin on his face and said, as Declan passed him, "Hey, white boy. I like your style, man. Why don't you hang out with us for a while?"

"What?" blurted one of his sidekicks.

Declan stood in the open street away from the shadows of the scaffolding and said, "What's your angle now? Gonna jump me down the street?"

"No, way. We could have jumped you back there and killed you. But it's not worth it. We only take easy pickings; if it's not easy, it causes too much trouble. Got you figured out wrong. You not like the normal tourist white boys we get here so I'm thinking we could give you a special tour of our hood in Brooklyn."

"You crazy, Dwayne?" shouted the other sidekick.

"No, man. We going back home so let's take this guy from 'Shit City' with us and show him how we live. What about it, white boy? No strings attached, leave when you want. Plus, it'll be good for business having a white boy hanging with us."

Declan thought about this proposition and was worried but intrigued. Their world was one he knew nothing of. The only risk he felt he faced was that they would eventually steal his money belt. But, with everything that had happened to him, so far, he thought this was a way to connect with some new people. He realized that he and they were probably from the same social strata, and he knew the young Black men did not know that about him. And Declan wanted to see what that social strata was like for Black people in New York City.

"OK, I'll come. But the British Embassy knows exactly where I am, and if I don't contact them tonight, there'll be a major fucking international incident," replied Declan in an ineffective attempt to add some importance to himself.

"Shit, there won't be no problem. You never gonna get our tour from anywhere else, so let's go."

As if an order, the two other boys slipped off the scaffolding, and then all three of them walked in formation south on Sixth Avenue—taking up most of the pavement and forcing other pedestrians to move—with Declan following behind. The youths walked with a swagger and style that Declan had never seen before; it was as if they owned the entire sidewalk. They seemed unconcerned about anyone's opinion of them. The response from people as they saw the three of them walking was the same: eyes widened, and then a quick step to the side and an accelerated walk away. No one dared to break the gang's formation—they looked, and were, a formidable group. Even two policemen, standing across the street watching the group, did nothing. Declan knew this would not happen in England; the police would almost certainly approach them. However, in England, it would have been rare to see a group of young men walking in this fashion down a busy street. Declan felt guiltily exhilarated by the group: exhilarated and impressed. He had only seen this sort of thing in soccer matches when London and Northern teams came south to Brighton and wrecked the town.

Turning onto 42nd Street, they stopped at the first small vending store. Inside, Dwayne said, "Hey, what's your name?"

"Declan."

"I'm Dwayne and this is Axe and Roller. What forty you want?"

"Forty?" asked Declan.

"Forty—beer. Malt liquor. Old English, Colt 45, or King Cobra?"

"I'll take the Old English."

Each man took one large bottle of forty-ounce malt liquor to the front counter, which were then each placed in individual paper bags by the Chinese store worker who said, "Twelve Ninety Six."

Dwayne paid for the beers, and the men walked out of the store. Declan took a swig of the beer and coughed.

"Hey white boy, can't handle the forties?" Dwayne asked.

"Oh, yeah. Just a bit different. Good deal for three dollars each."

"Yeah, this is all we drink."

Walking through 42nd Street with this group of men was as exciting as anything Declan had ever done. Drinking beer on the street while walking and defiantly taking up all the pavement space was thrilling. The three men had a complete disregard for the over-commercialized establishments and the heavily spending tourists the area attracted.

"Welcome to New York, motherfuckers," said Roller as the group passed a group of Japanese tourists.

***

THE MEN WALKED TO the Port Authority subway entrance, down the steps and swiftly jumped the turnstiles, ignoring the ticket clerk nearby. Roller, in front of Declan, smoothly hopped on top of the turnstile and skipped lightly to the other side in a well-practiced manner—with MP3 player in one hand and beer bottle in the other. Declan nervously followed as quickly as he could, fumbling to get his backpack and beer over the turnstiles and looking over at the ticket clerk who folded his arms and frowned as he observed Declan's amateurish performance.

As the men walked along the platform, the dozen or so people gathered hastily made an opening for them—the men seemed to create a wake of people wherever they walked. They found an empty bench and sat on the seat backs; Declan leaned against the wall.

Several minutes later, the "A" train pulled to a screeching stop at the station, and Declan followed the three young men as they boarded and spread themselves out over two benches facing each other. No one else entered the same car as the men, and there were only five other people in the car—all of them white. Roller turned to his colleagues and said, "So, we ain't coming back wit noting," said Roller.

"Yeah, noting. 'Cept this white motherfucker," replied Axe, turning to Declan with a piercing stare.

"Well, we can try tomorrow—more people will be in town then," said Dwayne.

"So, that's what you guys do, just head downtown to rip people off?" said Declan.

"What!" said Dwyane. "We don't rip nobody off. We hustlers, we pick up money wherever we can. To SUR-VIVE, that's all. We can't get no jobs so we does whatever else we can."

"Why can't you find jobs?"

"Well, for one, there ain't none, and for second, we Black," replied Dwayne.

The others nodded in agreement and Roller started to rap along to another 50 Cent song on his MP3 player, "Psycho," that all three young men sang in unison and went along the lines of:

> *I'm a psycho, crazy, mad as hell*
> *I will kill you with my blade if you push me*

The train turned east as it passed the Canal Street station and proceeded under the East River and into Brooklyn. Within a few stops, Declan noticed that only Black faces were standing at each station. The view outside gave way from busy commercial areas to block upon block of blackened, littered, almost-abandoned residential streets. The train eventually arrived at Euclid Avenue Station.

***

THE MEN EXITED THE train station south onto Euclid Avenue. The four men, with Declan tagging at the back, owned the street once again. Within a few blocks, they came to a small corner store with boarded-up windows and doors. Strangely, to Declan, the sign on the door read "Open." Dwayne shouted back to Declan, "Declan—another forty?"

"Sure," replied Declan who followed him in, while Axe and Roller stayed outside and talked to someone standing by a pay phone.

Inside the store, Dwayne placed one Old English 800 and three Colt 45s on the counter. "I'll pay for these. My turn, I think," said Declan.

"Thanks," said Dwayne.

Outside, Axe was arguing with the man standing at the phone. "Hey, back off motherfucker!" said Dwayne.

The man at the pay phone looked to be in his forties, with eyes sunken, patchy afro hair, partly hunched back, and wearing dirt-ridden clothing.

As Declan watched from inside, it occurred to him that, if he was unlucky, he could quite possibly end up like this man in the future: scrounging and hustling for anything outside a corner grocery store.

The man said, "Ain't no thing man. Just trying to get my dues. That's all. I ain't worried bout it."

Axe spat at the man's face and waited a few seconds for a reaction, to which there wasn't one. The man by the pay phone seemed to know he would get hurt if he responded.

The men turned and walked south. As they walked, Axe looked at Declan, locked eyes with him, and spat on the ground. They crossed the parking lot of a catholic church. Then they turned onto busy Linden Boulevard and over scrappy grounds with about a dozen solemn-looking eight-story brick buildings scattered further ahead. A tatty wooden sign read, "Welcome to Louis H. Pink." Each building spawned weed-ridden, interconnecting pathways. The entrance to each building had a heavy door with bars over a small square window and two or three sets of locks. There were children all around, but, rather than playing, they were grouped in clusters and eyeing the other clusters of kids.

The three men led Declan to an open area in the middle of a group of four of the buildings. A set of benches circled the area, and they stopped at one set and sat down. "Who on watch tonight?" asked Dwayne.

"Me," said Axe.

Just then, a group of three other men walked by and nodded over towards Dwayne and the others. They nodded back. But then the group looked at them with curiosity and drifted over to Dwayne's group. The apparent leader, in a long raincoat, with a muscular build, tattoos on his neck, and what looked like a left ear with part of it missing, looked Declan in the eyes. Declan suddenly became overwhelmed with a sense of fright— he instinctively knew the man was dangerous.

"Who this white motherfucker?" said the man, turning his focus to Dwayne.

"He cool, he from Englan. Just a friend of ours we picked up. He no problem," answered Dwayne.

"Well, keep that motherfucker out of our bidness or else he'll be hanging off that motherfucking roof," said the man nodding to one of the tops of the building. He then said, "Who watching this area tonight?"

"Me," said Axe shakily.

"Then get your motherfucking Black ass over to your station."

Axe walked hastily to the intersection of the paths that went through the grounds in front of the four buildings surrounding the men.

The tough guy then turned and glared again at Declan before walking away with his cronies.

"Shit, who's that guy?" asked Declan.

"That's Commando. When he's not in jail he runs all the drugs outta the Pink Houses. No one can sell anything here unless it come through him. Not even a joint. He'll kill anyone who crosses him. I know for a fact he's killed four guys in this project. Rumor is he's killed at least ten people, including a baby. Although that was by accident," said Dwayne.

"Yeah, he even shot a crippled guy in a wheelchair coz he was selling dope to his neighbor," said Roller.

"There are some people you never ever mess with, and Commando is one," said Dwayne.

"I'm gonna get some food," said Roller and he walked off to a nearby store.

Dwayne and Declan continued to sit, drink and talk.

"You got these PJs in Englan?" asked Dwayne.

"Yeah, not as bad, but we do have 'em. I live in one, actually."

"Yeah?"

"Yeah, it's a row of ten-story flats called council flats. And they put all the social security people in them. Rent is usually free if you are unemployed or need social security help."

"You get murder and shit there?"

"Naw, not really. We get fights all the time. Maybe someone might get stabbed—usually not killed though. We get suicides too; people jump off the top floor and kill themselves."

Declan almost mentioned his brother's suicide, almost told Dwayne the horror of seeing his brother's broken body squashed onto the concrete—his head split open and blood oozing through his thick, hairy scalp. He took a large gulp of the Old English 800, and then another, and said nothing.

"We don't get that many suicides from jumps, coz they were smart when they built these projects—they made them just eight stories high and all the buildings are surrounded by dirt. You can see the paths leading into the buildings are narrow. They did that for a reason—wanted to cut down on suicide jumpers. Most jumpers survive—they did tests on it. People just shoot themselves now."

"The other difference is Russian bastards have taken over my estate and control all the drug selling. They've really fucked things up for the residents," said Declan.

"Shit. That don't sound right some motherfuckers from Russia running the operation. Should be homegrown like the way we do it here. We all from this PJ."

As they talked, two Black youths walked past. Dwayne looked them up and down then whistled a high-pitched note to Axe. Axe turned and whistled the same note to another man, apparently posted further up in the project complex.

"What's that about?" asked Declan.

"Well, they tweakers."

"Tweakers?"

"Meth users. Come here for a fix. Commando sells the shit from his post in the center of this project. Now, for those motherfuckers to get to the center of the project, they gotta come through one of these 'quarter areas.' So, we scope everyone out who comes in. Commando pays us to do it. If they look cool then it's one signal, if they look like cops, another signal, or if they look like motherfuckers from another project come to fuck with us, then a different signal. The project is like a fortress. No one can get to the core without coming through all us lookouts posted everywhere. We got a certain signal where everyone in on it will hang out their window and start shooting every motherfucker down here with AK-47s!"

"Jesus, that's some setup."

"Yeah, that's right. No one fucks with the Pink Houses. No one. We got over four thousand people living here—it's a goddamn fort built perfect for this kind of stuff."

"How come they aren't painted Pink?"

"They named after some dude who helped build them, Louie Pink or some shit," replied Dwayne.

The men continued to drink their beer and talk. Declan was unnerved to hear the background sounds of domestic fights, crying babies, windows being smashed, and occasional shouts and screams. Dwayne seemed unmoved by the noises.

The first two youths left, and within a couple of minutes, two more white youths wearing New York Mets sweat-shirts walked by. Dwayne gave the same signal to Axe. Roller then returned with six hot dogs covered in Ketchup. "Thanks man," said Dwayne.

The men ate the hot dogs, and as they did two female residents came by and sat on the edge of their bench and began to smoke.

"Why don't you give me some dat 45?" said the first, who was wearing a strange wavy afro haircut Declan had never seen before, with a comb stuck in the back.

Roller handed over his Colt bottle and the girl took two swigs and handed it to her friend.

"Who dis white boy?" asked the other girl.

"He our homie. We showing him how we operate," said Dwayne.

"He like Black women?" the girl replied.

With that Dwayne and Roller laughed and hooted and clapped their hands. Declan felt his face redden.

"Maybe he need to see some Black titty if he come all this way."

And again more laughing.

"No, thanks, just visiting my mates right now," said Declan.

"Shit, and he from another country too. I'll give him double helpings."

"Now come on, ladies, you gonna have to move on. We here doing our business. If Commando come by he gonna beat shit outta me," said Dwayne.

"OK, we going, but bring that white boy over sometime," said the second woman who took another swig of the beer, handed the bottle back to Dwayne and then inhaled on her cigarette before turning with her friend and walking away.

After having seen about twelve people walk past on their drug treks, it approached one a.m. and Dwayne told Declan, "Since it's a weeknight, things will get slow now. We might only see one more customer."

"You want me to get another beer?" asked Declan.

"Sure, but give me the money, you won't make it there and back this time of night," said Roller.

Declan gave Roller a twenty-dollar bill, and he walked off towards the store they had passed earlier on the way from the subway.

About an hour later, as the men were drinking the beer, they heard a scream, followed by a loud thudding noise. They ran to the quarter just north of their station and found a Black man lying face down in the grass. His body had made at least a six-inch impression into the soil. He was groaning, but did not appear to have any blood coming out of his body except a small trickle from his nose. His hands had been tied behind his back with duct tape.

"Shit, Commando did this," said Dwayne, "it's his specialty. Done it all the time. Does it to anyone who tries to rip him off. Usually they don't die, so it ain't no murder."

"Jesus Christ," said Declan.

"OK, let's get back," said Dwayne.

"Shouldn't we help him?" asked Declan.

"You want Commando to see you? If he does he'll haul your ass up there too. He carries the duct tape around with him, you know," said Roller.

The men quickly returned to their posts. Axe said, "I'm done. Nothing doing now. People scared off by Commando."

"Shit, attempted murders are always bad for business," said Dwayne.

Then wailing sirens could be heard, and a couple of minutes later two paramedics came walking by, almost casually, with equipment bags and a stretcher. Declan thought of Sean and the way he had died from jumping off their block of flats. He wanted to cry, and had to force himself to take deep breaths to avoid crying out loud. But that is all he wanted to do at the moment: cry.

"OK, I'm outta here," said Axe, and then turned to face Declan and mockingly pointed his finger at his chest and pretended to fire a pistol.

"Me too," said Roller.

"You can crash at my place if you want," said Dwayne to Declan.

"Thanks, I bet it's probably a bit dangerous for me to get up to the subway at two a.m.," said Declan, looking at his watch.

"Well, it closed anyway," said Roller, and the men started laughing.

***

WITH THAT, DWAYNE AND Declan made their way into the building just behind where they had been sitting. The sturdy door with the bulging locks and metal bars covering the window had been broken into and didn't need a key. The elevator was not working, so they walked up piss-ridden steps to the third floor where Dwayne unlocked his door.

"Just me, mom," shouted Dwayne.

A girl, probably only seventeen, appeared from the living room with a baby in her arms. "Who this white boy?" she asked.

"Friend of mine. What of it?"

"Nothing," said the girl.

"Declan, this is my sister."

Dwayne then popped his head behind a bedroom door and told his mother he was home and asked if she needed anything. She didn't, so Dwayne led Declan to his bedroom. There were two small beds with the walls covered with posters of 50 Cent.

"You can have my brother's bed. He's in prison," said Dwayne.

"Thanks."

"Does your mum mind me coming here?"

"Naw, she got cancer of the brain so can't move outta bed—probably only got a few months left. I don't need to worry her about visitors," said Dwayne.

"Sorry, mate," said Declan.

"It's OK."

"Shouldn't she be in hospital?"

"No insurance."

"My brother died a little while ago. So I know a little how you feel," said Declan.

"Yeah, well, life is just one bad thing after another. It's just a fucking jungle. Sometimes I wonder what the hell point of it all is," said Dwayne.

"Keep going, mate. You can break out, that's why I'm in America. I'm trying to break out of my situation. You can do it too. I know you can."

"Yeah, thanks. I'm glad you can see how we live. I knew there was something about you. That's why I invited you here—I kinda knew you would understand."

"Yeah, I understand, mate. It's the same shit but just in a different place."

"I lived in this project my whole life. I never been anywhere else—never even known anyone from another country. So, when we bumped into you, I just thought you could see my life and so at least someone else out there knows how we are living here. Maybe I'll be dead tomorrow, but at least you can go and tell people in Englan how we living here."

"I will," replied Declan.

Dwayne gulped the rest of his beer and lay back on his bed and fell asleep. A small table light was left on in the room. Declan laid on the bed with his hands under the back of his head. He thought of his life on the English council estate: as bad as that had seemed, life in the Pink Houses projects was far far worse. In fact, it almost felt as if the whole complex was one big prison for Black people. Declan wondered if slavery had really been abolished in America. It was as if the American Government had created prison complexes to house the Black people. The murder, violence, drugs, and deprivation seemed inevitable to Declan. He remembered, too, walking with Dwayne, Axe, and Roller and watching the looks on people's faces as they saw a group of Black men walking together—a mixture of fear and revulsion. As socially encumbered as Declan was, in England, he realized he by no means had the restrictions of Black people in America.

He then felt incredibly sad. He felt like crying. He didn't know exactly why he wanted to cry. He looked over at Dwayne and thought he almost looked like a boy—just a boy. And he realized, too, that the world was a cold, bitter place, and he wondered just why it was that way. And he wondered, too, if anyone in this life was happy. Declan felt overcome by what he had seen that day, and he wasn't sure what it all meant. But he did know he had to absolutely keep pushing forward; at all costs, he had to keep pushing forward.

Chapter Eight

Declan found it challenging to sleep in Dwayne's apartment in the Louis H. Pink projects. Harder, even, than sleeping in Central Park or at the Waverly Theatre. During the night, Dwayne's sister's baby constantly cried, there were heated arguments between residents that could be heard throughout the courtyards, dogs barked, police sirens wailed, and at one point, a gunshot rang out. By six a.m., Declan was ready to leave, but saw Dwayne was still in a deep sleep. He carefully dressed, straightened out his bed, and then began writing a note when Dwayne stirred and asked if he was leaving. "Yes, mate. Gotta get back to the city for my job. Sorry to leave so early. Thanks so much for inviting me over. I'll do the same for you one day once I get established somewhere."

"You too Declan. You're welcome in my house anytime. Anytime man. Hey, write down my number: 718-453-3200."

"What's your surname?"

"Jefferson."

"Well, Dwayne Jefferson, I will see you again, my friend."

"You bet," said Dwayne as he sat up in bed, rubbed his eyes, and then shook Declan's hand.

Declan made his way to the door, unlocked the bolts, then quickly went down the steps at the end of the hallway, and with his head lowered, made his way out of the projects and onto Euclid Avenue and north to the subway station. As soon as he caught the subway, he felt increasingly safe as he closed in on Manhattan. He was able to take the

"A" train to 81st Street and Central Park West, which was a short walk over to Artie's Deli. "You are a little late today," said Nancy.

***

AFTER DECLAN'S USUAL ROUTINE of visiting the library and then catching some sleep in the park, he made his way to work at The Boathouse Café. His shift went smoothly, and he again was able to sleep in the storage room thanks to Sanat's kindness.

Just after five a.m., he was woken abruptly from his sleep by Louie screaming, "What the fuck are you doing here, motherfucker?"

"Urmmm, well, I was tired and it got late, so I thought I'd just rest. But I fell asleep. I'm sorry. It wasn't anything to do with Sanat," said Declan, scratching his head.

Sanat, hearing the shouting, came running from the kitchen.

"We could lose our license from the city if anyone found out about this shit."

"Sorry," said Declan.

"Get the fuck out! You're fired!"

"Hold on. What about my pay?"

"Stop by the hostess stand tomorrow afternoon. I'll leave an envelope with them."

Declan snatched his backpack and left through the back entrance. Outside, he tried to compose himself, tried to pat down his wayward hair. It was almost five-thirty, so he still had an hour before Artie's Deli opened. Almost sleepwalking, he made his way to John Lennon's Strawberry Fields memorial and lay down on a grassy bank next to the "Imagine" mosaic. Flanked by fragrant and bright spring flowers, he used his backpack as a pillow. For some reason, it felt reassuring to lie by the mosaic.

Within an hour, Declan felt a wet lapping sensation on his cheek. He sat up and found a German Shepherd looking at him curiously.

Declan gently stroked the back of the dog's head. The dog lifted his head up and then down as if to indicate he wanted more. Declan continued to stroke the dog for several minutes. The dog's coat was clean and the dog seemed healthy—as if it had an owner. But it had no collar or tag. Declan wondered if it was possible for him to keep the dog. However, as soon as the thought crossed his mind, the dog abruptly turned and trotted from the park and out to the street. Declan stood up stiffly and decided to walk to the Deli.

***

ARTIE'S DELI HAD JUST opened as Declan arrived. Nancy unlocked the door and said, "You look pretty rough today, Declan."

"Yeah, well I just got fired and didn't sleep well."

"Wow, you certainly make things interesting for yourself. I'll get your tea, babe. You'll feel better soon."

Declan noticed his hands were shaking.

Sitting at the table, he became depressed. It had only been six days since he arrived in New York City, but he felt exhausted—absolutely and completely physically and mentally exhausted. He wondered if he would be able to keep it up. It occurred to him that even if he made it through the summer, he would not survive a New York winter on the streets. It suddenly all seemed too much for him. He felt he had only one option left: he had to call Isabella. She was the only person he knew here in New York. Maybe she could help him in some way. He decided he would phone her immediately after breakfast.

***

WALKING TO THE TRUMP Tower, Declan wondered what he would say to her. *Should I pretend everything was fine and I was just checking in? Or should I come clean and tell her the whole sordid story and ask for suggestions?* He wasn't sure, but he knew he couldn't go on in this manner.

"Hello, could I speak to Isabella, please?" Declan asked the polite voice on the phone.

"Of course, who's calling please?"

"Her friend Declan, from England."

"Oh, yes. She told us about you. Hold on."

Declan felt happy Isabella had told her family of him.

"Declan, is that you?" said Isabella. Declan was relieved to hear Isabella's voice.

"Yes. I thought I'd give you a ring to see how you were doing."

"I'm doing great. Was wondering if you would ever call me."

"Here I am."

"So, what are you up to? Got a job? Place to stay?"

"Not exactly. I had a job for three days but it didn't work out. Plus, accommodation has been tricky."

"Well, come over to my family's house. I can at least help you look for accommodation."

"I really wouldn't want to impose."

"It's no problem at all. I'm bored—don't start college again until September and all my friends are busy so I'd be happy to see you. Hold on a second."

Declan could hear as Isabella covered the receiver and shouted to her mum, "Hey mom, can Declan stay for dinner tonight?"

"Yeah, sure," came the muffled reply.

"OK, we are good for dinner at my house. You might as well spend the night here since it's a bit of a trip."

"Sounds wonderful. Thank you so much, Isabella."

"It's nothing, really. I know what it's like being overseas on your own."

Declan took a deep breath in relief.

Isabella told Declan to catch a Long Island Railroad train from Penn Station to Great Neck Station. She said the journey would take about thirty minutes and cost twelve dollars. She said to call her once he was about to board the train. Declan told her it would be in the afternoon sometime, after he had a chance to clean up.

****

DECLAN MADE HIS WAY to the library to find out where all the local public swimming pools were located. The closest was on 54th Street at the public "Recreation Center." He immediately walked there, stopping on the way to buy shampoo and soap. He swam in the pool, wearing his underwear, to curious looks from other swimmers. After ten minutes, he used the showers to clean himself with the soap and shampoo. Then he put on his clean change of clothes from his backpack: shirt, jeans, underwear, and socks. He felt better as he left the public swimming pool and headed to Penn Station.

He bought a train ticket and called Isabella, who answered excitedly, "Great. I'll see you soon, Declan. I'll be waiting out front with my mom's white Mercedes."

The train sped straight out of Manhattan and through Queens without stopping. The scenery changed dramatically as the busy cityscape transitioned to more suburban views. As the train neared Great Neck Station, Declan felt a lump form in his throat and started to get a little nervous about meeting these apparently wealthy people. He then imagined what Chris would tell him: "Bollocks to it, mate. They're just people like you and me. Remember—we used to run that country."

The Great Neck Station would not have been out of place in England with its brown bricks and steep-pitched roof. It had character straight out of a Dickens novel, and made Declan feel a tiny bit at home. Clutching his backpack, Declan hopped from the train as it stopped at the station. Outside, he saw Isabella waving her hands extravagantly, as if there were hundreds of people exiting the station, when in fact there was only Declan and an old lady with a walking stick leaving the lobby.

Declan approached Isabella and intended to shake her hand, but was instead greeted with a modest hug, which embarrassed him slightly. He noticed, too, that Isabella no longer wore the thick-rimmed glasses she had on the airplane. Declan cleared his throat and said, "I like your mom's car."

"Yes, we call it the 'boat' coz it just bobs along the road," replied Isabella with a wide grin. "Well, let's go!" she continued.

Isabella seemed in a hurry and quickly exited the station, driving north through Great Neck and into an area called Kings Point. The houses continued to increase in size the further they drove from the train station, many with Grecian-style columns at the front and spacious grounds surrounded by wrought-iron fencing. "This looks like a really nice place to live," said Declan.

"Yep, it's pretty nice here. Lotta rich Jews—like my mom and dad."

"What do your parents do?"

"Well, dad runs his own private finance company, and mom stays at home."

"You have brothers and sisters?"

"One older brother, but he's graduated college and works down in D.C. now."

"Oh right. Sounds good."

Declan felt uneasy hearing all of this. The all-too-familiar queasiness in his stomach reappeared, and he felt the palms of his hands get clammy.

Within five minutes, Isabella pulled into the semi-circle driveway of a large house. Declan imagined he could play a full-sized football game on the spacious grass at the front, back, or sides of the property. He thought the house could easily pass for an English stately manor—even though it was in the suburbs of one of the most expensive cities in the world.

As they entered through the thick wood front doors, Declan noticed the mezuzah on the side of the doorframe. He recalled Isabella's request, from the plane ride, that he be on his "best behavior." As he entered the hallway, Declan saw Mr. and Mrs. Ber were standing ready to greet him. "Well, hello, Declan. We are so glad to finally meet you. We have heard lots about you," said Mr. Ber with both of his hands outstretched to shake Declan's. He was a short, wiry man with a balding head and wire-rim spectacles. However, he made up for this with an infectious smile that seemed to be permanently on his face. He instantly put Declan at ease, and he immediately liked the man. Mrs. Ber was next, and she approached Declan, held both his shoulders, and then kissed both his cheeks. Declan's face flushed bright red. He was not used to being kissed by anyone—let alone strangers—and looked down and away from Mrs. Ber. However, he had managed to see enough of Mrs. Ber to know she was one of the most beautiful people he had ever seen: long, flowing blond hair, a perfectly slim body, and a flawlessly shaped face. But, more than that, she just seemed to radiate a healthiness that he was unused to in adults her age. He wondered if she was an athlete of some kind.

"Come, Come, Come. Come into our home, Declan, and please make yourself comfortable. We are so glad to meet you after all we have heard of you from Isabella," said Mr. Ber.

Declan was taken aback. It seemed Isabella had been talking about him a lot. But they had only known each other for eight hours on a plane flight—*why are they making such a fuss over me?*

Declan was led through another large hallway with a dining room to the left and a music room with a concert-sized piano to the right. In the central area was a wide, open, two-story area with several sofas facing a vista of Manhasset Bay.

"What a fantastic view," said Declan.

"Thank you," said Mrs. Ber.

"You hear his accent Dad, a real English accent!"

"Yep, sounds like it to me."

"Dad left work early so he could meet you in person," said Isabella.

"Mr. Ber, there really was no need for that. I'm nothing special. Really."

"No, no, no. It's no big deal. We've been hearing about you all week, so I had to make sure I found out right away who this Declan character from England is."

Isabella looked at the floor as Declan looked over at her. He felt a heavy burden press on his shoulders as he considered the situation. He wondered exactly what Isabella had told her parents. Whatever it was, they seemed keenly interested in getting to know him. Declan knew he had to get Isabella aside to find out what was going on.

"Show Declan the house, we'll have dinner in an hour," said Mrs. Ber.

Isabella walked Declan around the seven-bedroom house. He noticed the thick hardwood planks that spread throughout the main area; the huge two-story velvet curtains; the decadent use of European art sprinkled throughout the rooms; and the sheer size of everything. All the furniture, windows, doors, and fixtures seemed to be twice the size of normal-sized items. It was like he had entered a giant's castle.

Lastly, Isabella showed Declan her bedroom. He felt uneasy, but she left the door open and he could hear her mom cooking in the kitchen below, which relaxed him a little. They sat on her large, soft bed. On her walls were framed pictures of scenes from Israel, along with pictures of her family. She also had a scroll of her family tree in a gold leaf frame. She had an electronic keyboard in the corner and next to that a writing bureau with a Sony VAIO laptop sitting on top. Bookshelves filled the wall above her bed, holding many works of classical English Literature in hardcover. Everything was neat and tidy. It seemed to Declan that Isabella spent a lot of time in this room; there were so many books, and although they were the expensive kind, he had a feeling they were not for show but had been read. There were two books on her bedside cabinet: Shakespeare's *The Merchant of Venice*, and Jonathon Swift's *Gulliver's Travels,* and several more books were poking out from beneath her bed. There were what appeared to be journals, too, all neatly lined along the top shelf of her writing bureau. Her plush bed was wrapped in thick sheets, heavy blankets, and topped with deep pillows, with six furry animals lined along the top. Declan could imagine Isabella spending hours and hours in this room, reading and writing.

"So what's happened, Declan?" asked Isabella, leaning over wide-eyed toward him in anticipation of his answer.

"Well, to be honest, it's not been easy. I'd been sleeping rough in Central Park for a few days until I got a job as a waiter at The Boathouse Café. The night worker let me sleep in the storage area of the Café, which I did for a few days, until I was discovered by the manager and then fired. That was this morning. Also, I spent an evening in a Brooklyn project and witnessed an attempted murder. A few other things have happened, but that's the general idea."

"Are you serious? That's unreal," replied Isabella as she leaned back in a sort of shock. Declan looked at the floor and said nothing, glad only that he had not mentioned the incident at the Waverly.

"Well, I think what you need is information. Tomorrow morning, I'm going to take you to the local bookstore and get you a book with information on cheap accommodation in New York for students. I have one for England called, *Let's Go England,* and it lists all the cheap places to stay for international students. You'll be fine in no time. I already looked it up on the computer, and they have one in stock."

"Isabella, you don't need to do all this for me. I'll be fine. I just wanted to come over and say hello."

"I want to help you. And besides, my family thinks you are really cool with what you are doing. You see, all the kids around here just leech off their families and do nothing with their lives since they don't need to. So, my family thinks it's great that you are creating a new life for yourself."

"Well, I'm really just taking a year off and will see what happens. If I wind up staying, then so be it."

"Yeah, exactly," replied Isabella with a smile. "Do you want some wine? My family is fine with me having a glass even though I'm not twenty-one yet."

"Sure, sounds good."

"Oh, and you are staying here tonight. It's all set. We have a guest room set up for you."

"Thank you so much, Isabella. You and your family are brilliant. But, I do have to ask you something."

"Sure."

"How come your parents are making a big deal out of me visiting you? I don't understand it. They seem like very nice people but I feel they are making some sort of special effort."

Isabella blushed, then stood up and stepped over from the bed to the window, looking out through the net curtains. "My visit to England wasn't that great," she replied. "In fact, it was totally miserable. I spent most of my time in my room reading. I'm not good at making friends, and I just got a little intimidated being on my own. So, I stayed in my room when I wasn't studying."

"Surely some of the other students were on their own too, and invited you out?" replied Declan.

"They did at first, but after a few weeks of turning them down they stopped asking. So, when my family asked me how it went I made up this story that we were dating in England and you made a special trip here to see your friends in the city so you could be with me longer before you started travelling."

"I see."

"I feel so dumb," replied Isabella, who then dropped her head into her hands and began to cry quietly.

Declan sprang to her side and held her in his arms.

"I understand. I've felt like that myself here sometimes. That's why I spend a lot of time in the library—it keeps me away from people."

Isabella rubbed her face into Declan's chest and held him tighter. Then slowly she pulled away and said, "We should probably go downstairs now."

"Yes, right."

Isabella went to the bathroom to compose herself and then led Declan downstairs. Isabella's father was sitting on a stool at the large breakfast bar area overlooking the kitchen, where her mother was busy at the stove mixing ingredients in a pan. Declan sensed Isabella's father had been waiting for them. He also guessed Mr. Ber probably didn't really spend much time sitting at that breakfast bar reading the newspaper. "Come, come sit down and talk with us," said Mr. Ber with a big smile and nasally voice. "What do you think of New York, Declan. Are you having a good time?"

"I like it here. There's so much going on it's hard to take it all in. I've only just been here a week but already I've seen so much—all kinds of things," Declan replied with a grin as he sat on a stool next to Mr. Ber.

"Well, you shouldn't judge all of us by what you see in the city. There's a lot more to the United States than New York City."

"That's right, Declan, don't think this whole country is full of those crack-heads you see down in the city. There are lots of good people here, too," said Mrs. Ber, turning from the stove.

"Yes Mrs. Ber, I have met some nice people here already. There have been several individuals who've been quite kind, actually. Of course, including Isabella."

"Now Declan, please call us David and Barbara," said Mr. Ber.

Isabella came to the bar and gave her father and Declan a glass of wine. "Let us have a toast," said Mr. Ber, holding up his glass.

"Oy vey! Wait for me!" cried Mrs. Ber as she reached for her wine glass.

"Good luck to Declan on his journey here in America!"

Declan suddenly felt panicky, as he did from time to time, as he took in the grandeur of the Ber's kitchen: its tall custom-made mahogany cabinets, its large marble central island, and the thick, dark hardwood floors. He gulped on his wine and almost finished the glass in one go.

A few minutes later, the doorbell rang. "Did you invite someone else?" asked Isabella.

"Yes, your Uncle Larry and Aunt Sarah wanted to drop by. We haven't seen them in ages, so we thought we'd have them over," replied Mrs. Ber.

Isabella looked at Declan and rolled her eyes.

"Now don't go worrying about them, they'll be on their best behavior since we have a guest," said Mrs. Ber, turning from the stove.

Suddenly, the house was filled with Uncle Larry's loud voice. "Hey, David, how've you been? The guy from England here?"

Declan stood up and was introduced to the lively, aging couple who both seemed to have boundless energy. Again, he received a two-handed handshake followed by a hug.

The questions continued before dinner, and as Declan drank a second glass of wine, he became more relaxed and appreciative of the kindness the Bers were showing him as the house filled with the aroma of the baking Challah bread. The dinner cooked by Mrs. Ber was quite fantastic to Declan: stuffed fish for an appetizer, glazed chicken barbecue, potatoes, asparagus, and finally a mousse pudding. Even more surprising was that Mrs. Ber was able to prepare and cook the meal with just a few hours' notice. Declan felt quite inadequate after realizing he hadn't often shown such kindness to others. At this moment, he decided that even though he had little, he would try in his own way to show some of this sort of kindness to others whenever *he* could.

At one point during dinner, Uncle Larry turned to Declan and asked, "So, Declan, how long yer been dating Isabella?"

"Larry!" cried Mrs. Ber, "will yer stop it! They're just friends, you know!"

"Sorry," replied Larry, "but Isabella would be a real good catch for a guy like you, you know."

Aunt Sarah elbowed Uncle Larry in the rib cage and said, "Stop it, Larry. Can't you see poor Isabella is embarrassed?"

Isabella's face turned pink, and the color seemed to flow down her neck. Mrs. Ber raised her hands in the air and exclaimed, "Oy Vey!" once more. Declan smiled and tried to ignore the fuss. Mrs. Ber tried to deflect Isabella's embarrassment and asked Declan, "So, Isabella tells us you are from the southern part of England, and it is nice there. Do you think you will stay here in the States for a while?"

"I'd love to, Mrs. Ber. But right now I'm still trying to get my footing, so to speak. I'm hopeful things will move in the right direction, and I'll get to stay and maybe even start a new career."

Mrs. Ber turned to Isabella and gave a slight nod.

The fullness of his stomach and the alcohol made Declan daydream. He thought of his mother and wondered what she had eaten for dinner today. No doubt the fridge would have been empty of food, and she most likely would have scrounged up enough money from here and there to buy a bag of chips from the local fish and chip shop, where she might also have had enough for a battered sausage. Most of her social security money would have been spent on cheap vodka and orange juice, and, inevitably, she would fall asleep before nine p.m., then wake at three a.m. and start watching the late-night TV shows. If it were a few days before the bi-monthly social security check, the house would be darkened and cold since, indeed, his mother would have run out of money and be unable to put any coins in the electric meter. And then he thought of the Russians—Declan hoped they were not causing his mother any trouble.

For Declan, the evening went too fast. Soon dinner was over, and the guests were leaving. Both Aunt Sarah and Uncle Larry kissed Declan on both cheeks and said, "Shalom." The last thing Declan remembered was sitting on the sofa before being shaken awake by Isabella who said, "It's OK, you fell asleep. Come, I'll take you to your room."

As he was led upstairs by Isabella, he heard Mrs. Ber say, "The poor boy hasn't slept properly all week."

***

THE NEXT MORNING, DECLAN was woken by a knock on his bedroom door. He leapt out of bed and heard Isabella say, "It's nine o'clock, Declan. Are you OK?"

"Yes, sorry, I'll be right out."

Declan quickly packed his backpack and made his way down the winding staircase. "He's here Mom!"

"OK. I'm making his breakfast now."

Again intimidated by the attention, Declan tentatively made his way into the main den area where Isabella was watching the news on the television. She stood up, and Declan hoped she would not hug him or anything like that. Thankfully, she didn't, but instead waved her arm over towards the kitchen bar and said, "My mom has your breakfast nearly ready."

"There's really no need for that. Just some milk or orange juice will do me fine," said Declan.

"No, no, no. I will make you a proper English breakfast," said Mrs. Ber. "Eggs, bacon, sausage. No?"

"Yes, that's brilliant. Thanks so much."

Isabella went into the kitchen area and said, "Coffee?"

"Do you have tea?"

Isabella and Mrs. Ber looked at each other. Mrs. Ber said to herself, "Tea?" and after a rummage in the pantry came out smiling with a box of "Lemon Ginger Tea." Declan smiled and said, "That'll be just fine. My favorite."

Isabella made the tea for Declan and told him, "After you've eaten, we'll go to the bookstore."

"Thanks, sounds great."

"David said to tell you, 'Good Luck. And drop by anytime,'" said Mrs. Ber as she placed the large plate of breakfast in front of Declan. Declan looked at Mrs. Ber and was reminded of how beautiful she was. He ate quickly and was soon ready to leave. Mrs. Ber handed him a sandwich wrapped in tin foil, "Lunch."

Declan didn't blush this time as Mrs. Ber kissed him on both cheeks and said, "Shalom."

He wanted to reply with so much more, in order to express his appreciation, but thought he might sound foolish so he simply said, "Thank you, Mrs. Ber," before he and Isabella made their way to the Mercedes. Declan was sad to leave The Bers, but at the same time relieved to be away from the attention. He wondered if he could make some kind of advantage out of the situation with the Bers, even if he didn't love Isabella. But he quickly dismissed the idea and committed to keeping them purely as friends.

***

AT THE BOOKSTORE, ISABELLA knew precisely where the travel section was and quickly found the book she wanted: *Let's Go USA*. "This book is written by students and has all the info you need to find a cheap place to stay," said Isabella. "Look here, there's a youth hostel in the city for thirty bucks a night—you can't beat that!"

"Yeah, that sounds great. What kind of place is that—a *youth hostel*?"

"You don't even know what a youth hostel is?"

"No."

"Well, you'll share a room with some other guys. Sometimes the rooms are mixed, but usually they split them between men and women. Also, there'll be a shared kitchen, so you can make cheap meals. Some of them have a social room where you can hang out and watch TV."

"That all sounds right up my alley!" said Declan, smiling. "I better get going over there. Don't want to arrive too late."

"Yes, I guess you should," said Isabella with a tinge of sadness in her voice.

"Thanks so much for telling me about this book, I feel like a right idiot not knowing about this stuff before I came over," said Declan.

"Yeah, it probably would have saved you a lot of trouble."

"Yeah," replied Declan, feeling even more foolish.

Isabella dropped Declan off at the Great Neck train station and seemed to sense Declan did not want an extended hug. They embraced quickly before Declan stood back, adjusted his backpack, and said, "I'm so grateful for you and your family. You are such fantastic people. Thank you so much Isabella."

"It's nothing. Just be careful and give me a call once you find a place, and let me know where you are."

Declan shuffled his feet and adjusted his backpack again. He then leaned forward and pecked Isabella on the cheek. Isabella stood still with her mouth slightly open and an expectant look in her eyes. Without thinking, Declan leaned in again and kissed Isabella on the lips, then quickly turned and walked toward the station entrance. Isabella called from behind, "Be safe, Declan. And please call me soon. Bye."

***

On the train ride back to Manhattan, Declan read the inside cover of the *Let's Go USA* guidebook:

> For fifty years, *Let's Go* has published the world's favorite budget travel guides, written entirely by students and updated every year. With pen and notebook in hand and a few changes of underwear stuffed in our backpacks, we spend months roaming the globe in search of travel bargains.

Within the book, he found a wealth of information detailing cheap lodgings, cheap restaurants, cheap travel methods, and a host of other valuable details for navigating America on a budget. The book, along with the visit to Isabella's family, felt like a turning point for Declan. He closed the book and leaned back, reflecting on his journey so far. It occurred to him that he had a multitude of excuses to return home now, if he wanted. But he had now also experienced the kindness from several people who genuinely seemed to want to help him. It was as if he had entered a doorway and knew there was no turning back. He would only move forward from now on.

Chapter Nine

From Penn Station, Declan made his way north on Broadway and directly to the youth hostel at 210 West 55th Street. The guidebook said the hostel was located on the fourth and fifth floors of the Woodward Hotel. Surrounded by scaffolding, the hotel bustled with dusty workers, several of whom were walking out with buckets of debris as Declan approached. Inside, the small check-in desk encased an old man watching a small TV lodged under a set of empty pigeonhole mail slots. "Youth hostel?" asked Declan.

"Fourth floor," said the old man without looking up.

The elevator door had a scribbled sign stating "Broke" on it, so Declan made his way up the uncarpeted stairs.

The door to the International Youth Hostel office was open and as Declan entered, two young Scandinavian-looking females left. A young man looked up from watching the backsides of the females and asked, "Yes?"

"Got any rooms?" asked Declan.

"No. But we have beds," came the curt reply.

"I'll take one, please."

"How long you staying?"

"Two months—at least."

"We have a two-week limit, cash up front."

"That's fine, mate," said Declan as he realized the man was English and so felt at ease using "mate."

"How much for one week, please?"

"Two hundred dollars, which includes the weekly discount," said the hostel manager.

He turned away from the man, fumbled under his jacket and shirt for his money belt, and pulled out, as gracefully as he could, two one-hundred-dollar bills.

Declan handed the man the money and said, "Cheers." The man replied, "You'll be in bed two in room five-fifteen."

"All right, thanks mate," said Declan.

"Here's your key. Just pick up two sheets, one pillow, and one blanket by the door there," replied the man.

"Right then."

Declan waited a few moments, hoping for more conversation, but the man picked up a newspaper and began to read. A pang of loneliness pierced Declan's stomach as he realized not even one of his own fellow citizens was interested in him. He quickly turned and left the office.

***

DECLAN REALIZED HE WAS getting desperately short on cash. He now had two weeks in which to find a job or else he would have no money and no place to stay. He walked up one flight of stairs to the fifth floor and entered room five-fifteen. Inside were three beds. The first, numbered "2" on the headboard, was next to the door. Then on the other side of that bed were two heavily chipped small cabinets, and then, bed "1" in the corner. On the other side of the door in the far corner of the room was bed "3," which had a large chest of drawers next to it. There was a small bathroom with tiny, grimy tiles on the floor and wall, and underwear and shorts hanging from a rope strung from wall to wall. Next to the bathroom was a large window overlooking a small courtyard littered with builders' debris.

Declan put his backpack down on the floor and made up the piss-stained gray mattress with the sheets and blanket. After going to the bathroom, he left the room and made his way to the library, where he read a newly translated version of *Beowulf*.

***

LATER THAT EVENING, DECLAN arrived back at the Woodward Hotel. He walked up to the fifth floor and entered his room. Inside on bed "1" sat a Chinese man reading a book. The man looked up and Declan nodded to him. He half-nodded back and continued reading his book. Declan washed himself and then sat in bed and read his George Orwell book: *Down and Out in Paris and London*. He felt awkward sitting in bed reading a book so close to a man also reading a book with whom he had been unable to start a conversation. He wished he were able to just blurt out, "Hello, I'm Declan," to break the silence. He knew Chris would have done that. Chris would have sat down and interrogated the man for half an hour. But Declan wasn't the sort to do that, so he read his book instead. By ten p.m., he was tired and decided not to make a fuss over the light but just turn over and go to sleep.

A few minutes later, the door close to his head burst open and a man flew by, slammed the door, and dove over into the corner onto bed number "3." He lay spread-eagled and executed a loud fart. "Oopsss, sorry lads. Should've ripped that one on the way up the stairs." After a few moments of silence, the man turned over on his back and said, to no one in particular, "Fuck me, I could do with a cup of tea."

The man then pulled a cell phone from his pocket and tried to type in a text message. "Fucking internet is down again. For Christ's sake!" said the man who then looked up, saw Declan, and continued, "Well, looks like old Froggy bastard's gone. That's good."

Declan sat up and made eye contact with the wiry, dark-haired, energetic man, who looked to be in his mid-twenties. "I'm Zane Harris, mate—from Oz. Good to meet yer."

"Declan O'Neill from England."

"England ay? Poor bastard. Well, I won't hold that against yer!"

Remembering what Isabella had told him, Declan replied, "Well, I was born in Ireland."

"Well, that's it then. No worries there. Glad to meet you, for sure! Not that I really 'ave anything against the poms anyway. 'Spose you met old Jing Jang over there?"

"Well, sort of. Just nodded to him."

"Yeah, don't speak hardly any English. Poor fucker. Just does his work, comes back here, reads his books, probably has a wank or two, and then goes to sleep," replied Zane before laughing.

Declan grinned.

"Well, he's better than the frog that was in your bed. Right miserable bastard. I nearly gave him a slap once or twice just coz the way 'e looked at me. Typical French bastard, if you know what I mean," Zane continued.

"Yeah right."

Zane lowered his head and whispered, "I wouldn't trust that sneaky bloke over there either. Keep yer stuff safe, mate, if you know what I mean."

"Right," replied Declan softly.

"So, where ya been before this?" said Zane back to his loud voice, not seeming to care if he was disturbing the Chinese man who was trying to read.

"Well, slept in Central Park. Got into some trouble there. Also got a job, then was fired after a few days since they found me kipping in the storage room. So, now I'm 'ere and looking for some work."

"Fuck me, you've 'ad a time. Well, no worries there. I can get you fixed up with a job with my blokes. We clear asbestos. Good money, but hard work."

"Is it dangerous?"

"Naw, just wear the masks and a suit they give ya so it's no problem at all. I'll get you in if you like. There're Irish bastards like yourself. Just tell 'em you're Irish but grew up 'against my will' in England. You'll be right in," replied Zane, grinning.

"Well, cheers mate."

"Yeah, no worries. We're on a job at Riverside Drive, so you can tag along with me in the morning and I'll introduce you to the boss. Bit of a gruff old fellow, but nice enough, all the same."

"Yeah, thanks Zane. Appreciate that. Is it legal work?"

"Course not. All under the table."

"Nice."

"What else you been up too? Any sheilas yet?"

"Naw, not me, mate. Just trying to get on me feet right now. Been going to the library on any downtime."

"Well, bollocks to that—with your looks and accent you could be shagging all week. Christ, if I weren't so tired I'd take you out now. I know the best clubs. Just sneak a small bottle of vodka in and buy a coke and you're golden—no need to pay ten bucks for a drink. Shit, if I didn't have to get up at six a.m. I'd be out with yer now. Anyway, I've just 'ad a few on the way back, if you know what I mean."

"No problem mate, I'm tired meself. Be nice to get some kip in a decent bed."

"Yeah, too right mate."

"Well, you know I have this bottle of rum in my backpack if you want some?"

"Yeah, good on yer. Hold on, I'll go down to the kitchen and get my Coke—as long as no bastard's nicked it."

And with that, Zane sprang from the bed, left the room and returned within five minutes carrying a plastic bottle of Coke. He then produced two tea mugs from his chest of drawers. By this time, the Chinese man had turned over, switched off his bedside light and was attempting to sleep. Under the glow of Zane's small bedside lamp, the two men talked and drank rum and coke.

"So, 'ow long you been here, Zane?"

"About half a year."

"At this youth hostel?"

"Mostly—you 'ave to check out every now and then to keep 'em happy on the stay limit."

"Yeah, they told me I could only stay two weeks."

"That's bollocks! You must have spoken to old wanker-boy Johnny—tall, blonde-haired pom?"

"Yeah, that's 'im."

"He's a right cunt, that one. Don't worry; just come down with me on Saturday. Julie's on the desk and can sign you up for two months at a time. They get touchy when they are swamped, but you can just check out for a week and come back later."

"Do you like it 'ere then?"

"Well, price is right. But, honestly, it's filled with a load of middle-class backpackers travelling in groups who think they are really cool staying here for a couple of days then pissing off somewhere safe like the theme parks in Orlando. They're playing on their mobile phones all day. Don't usually meet any of your hard-core traveler types in this place."

"Oh right."

"So, what you doing here?" asked Zane as he took a deep gulp of the rum and Coke.

"Well, just wanted to take a year away from England. So, thought I'd come over here for a while and check it out. And you?" replied Declan, hoping Zane would not probe too much more.

"Fiancée dumped me a few weeks before our wedding. It turned me upside down. I knew a mate here in New York and fucked off over here to see him. But he left a couple weeks after I'd got here, so I've mostly been living 'ere and working with the Irish on the asbestos job."

"Like it here?"

"It's all right. Lots going on. But, it's not like home, you know."

"Yeah, I know exactly what you mean. Great place, but there's lots at home that I miss."

"Yeah, my problem is, I don't have much to go back to now. So, I'm not sure what I'm going to do. Maybe make a go of it here. I'll give it a few more months and then decide if I want to be here over the winter," replied Zane.

"Good thinking. I've got sod all to go back home to, either—just some bad memories. So, I'm hoping to get stuck in over here and see what happens."

Zane filled both their cups with Coke and the last of the rum and then raised his glass. "A toast to us both in New York. May we both find what we are looking for."

"Here, here!"

Chapter Ten

The next morning, Declan was woken at six a.m. by Zane, "Come on mate, we gotta get going if we want to get to the site on time. Ray likes us there by seven."

"Yeah, right, no problem. Just clean me teeth and I'll be ready."

Zane took a small backpack with him and explained that it contained his work clothes, "I like to look a bit normal going to and from work. Don't want to look like some skivvy waiting for the subway."

Zane took Declan's backpack and stashed it at the back of one of his drawers, "Should be safe there, mate." Then the two men left and caught the subway to 72nd Street. They then walked two blocks towards the Hudson River and a tall red-brick apartment building at 5 Riverside Drive.

Outside the building in the street were two dumpsters—both covered with large blue tarpaulins—each the length of two cars, back to back. Waiting under the building's entrance canopy was a short, fat, balding, hairy-armed, anxious-looking man, smoking a cigarette. "Decided to show today, eh Zane?" said the man with a thick Irish accent.

"Yes, mate. I'd never want to let you down, Ray."

"Right," replied the man.

"Ray, I wanted you to meet a good friend of mine. A very hard worker over from England—although he's actually Irish."

"Oh, yeah? What part of Ireland you from then, sonny?"

"Lurgan, in County Armagh," replied Declan, noticing the man had a set of brilliantly white and perfectly shaped teeth. He also noted he had long black sideburns that contrasted with his mostly bald head.

"Up north eh? Lots of trouble there. I'm from County Mayo in the Free South. Family still there?"

"Yeah, all my aunts, uncles, and cousins. Only my mum left."

"Want to work then?"

"Yes."

"It's hard graft and messy. You'll be filthy every day, but we'll supply you with a mask and goggles."

Just then, two men, covered in white dust and wearing goggles and mouth masks, walked out carrying large pieces of wallboard. One of them threw back the tarpaulin on one of the dumpsters, and they both lofted the pieces of wallboard into the dumpster before returning the tarpaulin.

"That is what you'll be doing," said Ray, "ripping off the wallboards, roof boards, and floor tiles, and bringing all the stuff down here to the dumpsters. It's pretty straightforward but hard graft. There are twenty floors in the building. We started at the top and are down to the fifteenth. Lots of work left – probably six months' worth. Still interested?"

"Doesn't this stuff cause cancer?" asked Declan.

"Only if you don't wear the safety gear."

"What's the pay like?"

"We'll start you off at fifteen bucks an hour. Once you've been here a month, I'll raise it to twenty."

"I'm in," replied Declan as he quickly calculated that he would be earning six hundred dollars per week—much better than the $8 per hour minimum wage he was earning as a dishwasher at The Boathouse Café. It would accelerate his savings, allowing him to return to help his mother more quickly.

"OK, you'll be working in Zane's team. We've got three teams of three lads. Zane will find you some goggles and a mask. Keep track of your time and we'll settle up each Friday."

"Thanks, Ray," responded Declan.

Zane led Declan inside the building to a utility cupboard. Inside, he found the cleanest-looking mask and pair of goggles and handed them to Declan. "If you think you'll be doing this more than a couple of months, you're best off buying your own mask and goggles. These won't fit right and you'll be coughing like a bastard in no time. You'll also need boots and overalls, as well as a cap. We can get that stuff after work; you'll be OK for today."

Wearing their masks and googles, they made their way up to the fifteenth floor in an elevator caked in the white, fibrous asbestos. From the elevator, they entered a hallway drenched in a fog of suspended asbestos fibers. Dust spilled from three of the rooms; banging, tearing, and ripping noises emanated throughout the hallway. They made their way to one of the rooms, and Zane shouted out to the men inside, "New bloke 'ere. Declan from England."

The men stopped working and courteously waved and nodded towards Declan. Already, the workers were covered in dust, although they could only have been working for an hour or so. Zane and Declan said hello to the second team and then went to a third room where a man was hosing down the ceiling and walls with water. "Seamus, this is Declan. Gonna be on our team."

"Right oh, nice to meet you."

"Thanks. Why are all the windows closed?" asked Declan.

"Regulations," said Seamus, "we can't allow the dust to get outside. Neighbors would sue us in a heartbeat. Technically, we should tape up the windows with plastic. But, old Ray won't waste any time or money on that."

"Seamus is hosing down the ceiling and the walls with water to try and cut down on the dust," said Zane. "That's a regulation too—helps a bit, but not much. Supposed to hose it down with a special binding agent, but Ray won't pay for that either. Anyway, once it's all washed down, we get to work and start ripping down the ceiling. That's the worst part. When that's done, we start on the walls. We work in three-man teams—two blokes are the 'grafters' who rip down the walls and ceilings, and the third keeps the surfaces damp with the hose. He also picks up the large bits of board and puts them in the barrow outside the room. Plus, he gets any tools we need—sledges, crowbars, et cetera. Then, after we've done a room, we switch positions and someone else is the 'support' guy. Gives everyone a turn."

"Right, good idea. 'Ow many rooms do you get done each day?" asked Declan.

"A typical two-bedroom apartment like this would take us around two days. Ray wants us to work faster, but you'd really risk burning out if you push any harder. If anyone on this job tries to move faster, they'll get kicked off pretty quick by us," explained Zane.

"Right," said Declan.

The men got to work and allowed Declan to be the "support guy" for his first day so he could get familiar with the work. Seamus and Zane went to work on the ceiling—ripping and pulling large swaths of the material, which, on breaking, would spill large plumes of white dust into the air. Declan hosed down the untouched sections and quickly handed either man a "sledge" or "crow" whenever they asked for it. Most of the time, they used a long, thin-bladed rip saw to cut into the boards. Declan would pick up the large pieces ripped down and place them outside the room, and then shovel up the small debris into the wheelbarrow. Once a large area had been finished, the men would all take a hand in getting the material down the elevator and into the dumpster outside, taking care to cover the debris in the wheel-barrow. "Technically, we should individually wrap these big pieces in cellophane," said Zane.

"Bollocks to that," said Seamus, "the quicker we can get out of the dust into the fresh air the better."

After dumping the first set of material into the dumpster, Declan started to brush himself down. "Stop that Dec," exclaimed Zane, "you can't do that out here. Against the environment code—neighbors will call the city. You've got to brush off inside to keep the dust from spreading. Technically, we are supposed to change clothes every time we come outside."

"No way," exclaimed Declan.

"Yeah, it's the law. This stuff is dangerous. That's why Ray gets the contracts—he underbids everyone, pays us half the going rate, and doesn't give us any of the proper safety items: full body overalls, proper full face ventilators, fully sealing rubber boots and gloves. Plus, he's supposed to have a shower on-site with special cleaners for us when we finish up our shift. The city turns a blind eye to it since they are getting a great contract deal from Ray. We're the ones that get shafted, and the neighbors here. Also, I know for sure he's not dumping the stuff in the proper controlled location—he's shifting it over to his brother's property in New Jersey and they bury it in a landfill."

"Shit," said Declan.

"Don't worry Dec, as long as you wear a decent respirator and goggles, and have a good shower each night, you should be safe as houses," said Seamus.

By one p.m., Declan was tired. "Lunch time, lads," shouted Zane.

"I have to ring my friend in Long Island to tell her I found a place to stay," replied Declan.

"No worries, just meet us back here by two," said Zane.

***

DECLAN WALKED ACROSS THE street, a small cloud of dust blowing from his hair, and on into Riverside Park, then continued north and found an area with a café and an outdoor phone. Using his AT&T number, he dialed Isabella's phone. "Hello. Mrs. Ber? Is that you?"

"Yes, this must be Declan. How are you?"

"I'm doing well."

"I'm so glad to hear that. Wait, I'll call Isabella down from her room."

"Hello, Declan?" asked Isabella a moment later.

"Yes, it's me. I just wanted to let you know that your book worked wonders. The youth hostel is perfect, and I even found a job."

"Doing what?"

"Well, it's in the building game," replied Declan sheepishly.

"What do you mean by that?"

"We do conversions. Fix up old apartment buildings."

"So what do you do—are you a carpenter or something?"

"Well, no. I'm sort of in the demolition crew. We take down the asbestos walls."

"Asbestos?"

"Yeah."

"Declan, you're crazy. Why put your health in danger?"

"We have all the right equipment and it's good money. Plus, I won't be doing it forever."

"Well I hope not."

"Anything new with you?" asked Declan.

"No, not really. Just doing some reading."

"Oh, right," said Declan.

There was a pause; Declan didn't know what else to say. But then Isabella asked, "Declan. Do you think that sometime, you'd want to do something together?"

"With you?"

"Yes. Of course with me!"

"Well, yeah. Sure, that would be nice."

"Well, how can I get hold of you?"

"Just call the International Youth Hostel on 55th Street. Leave a message for me, and they'll get it to my room. Then I can call you back."

"I have my cell phone switched back on, too, if you want to take down the number."

"Crap. I don't have a pen on me. I'm in my work clothes. I'll have to get it from you next time."

"OK, that sounds good," said Isabella, a little unsure.

"Well, I just wanted to thank you and tell you I'm doing well now. Tell your family I really liked meeting them."

"They enjoyed meeting you, Declan."

"OK. I'll say goodbye then."

"Bye, Declan," said Isabella.

Declan stood by the phone for a few seconds, staring at the receiver. He thought about Isabella, her family, and her life. He was unsure how he should handle things with Isabella. He then remembered Sir Roger de Coverley. *He realized that as long as he did the right thing, he had nothing to worry about.*

***

HE MADE HIS WAY back to the pathway and walked south from the café. A strong breeze from the Hudson River helped blow much of the dust from his head. He stood by a rail and looked out over the river, and then dusted down his jeans. As he turned to walk back to Riverside Drive, he realized a girl sitting on a bench just twenty feet away had been watching him the whole time. He felt embarrassed and continued to walk in her direction. He looked over at her again and saw she was looking after a baby in a pushchair. The girl, in her early twenties, was wearing a Union Jack t-shirt. Declan wondered if she was really from England. He gathered up as much courage as he could and walked over to the furthest side of the bench, sat down, and started to light a cigarette, but suddenly stopped and turned to the girl and said, "I'm sorry, I should have realized you have a baby. Do you mind if I smoke?"

"It's OK if you can blow the smoke to the side."

"Sure," replied Declan. Not being able to tell completely if the girl had an English accent, he continued, "By the way, I couldn't help noticing your t-shirt. Are you from England?"

"Ha! Well, no, not really. I like British bands. Listen to them all the time. Got this t-shirt at a Coldplay concert."

"Oh, Coldplay. Yeah, love them. I have most of their CDs."

"Yeah, me too," replied the girl.

"What about Radiohead and Arctic Monkeys?" asked Declan.

"Oh yeah, I love 'em both."

After a brief pause, Declan snatched a quick look at the girl—she had long black silken hair, a clear bright complexion, sharp cheekbones, tender lips, and a body shape that in his mind was the perfect balance of slim and curvaceous. Her manner, too, was calming to him. She sat on the bench with a slight smile on her face, legs crossed loosely, and one hand resting over her lap while the other gently rocked the baby carriage. She seemed elegant and nonchalant, exuding a confidence that Declan was unfamiliar with. But he was confused about the baby, since the girl couldn't have been much older than himself.

"So, do you live around here?" Declan asked awkwardly.

"Sort of. I nanny for a family on Riverside Drive, and I walk their baby down here a lot."

"Oh right. That's nice."

"What are you doing here—you look a little dusty?"

"I'm with the construction crew over there at Five Riverside Drive."

"Oh, yeah, I've seen that mess going on. When will it be finished?"

"Well, we'll be done with our bit in about six months. So, it will probably be at least a year until it's fully refurbished."

"Oh, OK."

Another pause came into the conversation, so Declan politely said, "Well, it was nice to meet you. I have to get back to work now."

"Nice to meet you too. My name is Marie by the way. I come down here most days."

"I'm Declan. I'll keep a lookout for you then. Cheers. Bye!"

"Goodbye, Declan."

Declan's step felt lighter as he returned to the construction site. All he could think about was the girl—Marie. And he felt mad at himself for not staying longer and getting more details about her. But it was his first day of work, and he didn't want to jeopardize the new job. He absent-mindedly walked straight across the busy road, forgetting that the cars in America drive on the other side of the road, and just missed getting hit by a large van hurtling along Riverside Drive.

At work, the day went quickly as Declan continued thinking of the girl by the river. *Why was such an elegant girl working as a nanny?* He gathered she wasn't a foreigner since she had a Southern American accent. He kept coming up with all sorts of scenarios that would have led her to where she was now. He sensed something was not quite right with her—but he didn't know why he felt that way. All he hoped was that he would see her again.

***

At five p.m., Declan and Zane made their way to the building's lobby. They approached Ray's makeshift office and heard a baritone voice singing, "Love Me Tender." Zane and Declan tentatively poked their heads around the door and saw Ray singing out of the window, his left arm outstretched into the sparkly asbestos dust, his right fist mimicking a microphone by his mouth. He suddenly stopped as he sensed he was being watched.

"Elvis fan then?" asked Zane.

"Oh yeah. Used to be a part-time impersonator. Reason why I came to America."

"Oh. Don't do it now?" continued Zane.

"No. Left County Mayo to make it big in Vegas. Gave up a lucrative tree-trimming business. But when I got there, I found out there are thousands of bastards in the Elvis game. That's why I'm now in the asbestos business."

Zane and Declan looked at each other and smiled.

"Righto lads. How did it go for you young Declan?" asked Ray.

"All right, really. Takes a bit of getting used to. Be better when I get some proper work gear."

"Yeah, you'll get the hang of it in no time. Well done. I'll see yers both tommorra."

"Cheers, then," said Declan.

Declan and Zane walked along past Lincoln Center and then onto Broadway and stopped off at several stores to buy Declan a pair of boots, several long-sleeved shirts, thick workman's gloves, a cap, a towel, decent goggles and mask, and a backpack.

"Like I said, keep all your kit in this bag along with a garbage can liner. Then each day, change out of your regular clothes to your work clothes, and put the clean regular clothes in the plastic bag to keep the dust off them."

"Thanks mate."

"No worries. Pub'll be open, so let's go get a beer, or two," Zane said, smiling.

By the time they had arrived at The Fiddler's Irish Pub on 47th Street, Declan was exhausted, "I think I can only manage one pint, mate," he said dejectedly.

"I can understand that—took me a couple of weeks to get used to the job. Don't worry—you'll get the hang of it. Once you see that first wad of cash Ray will hand you on Friday, you'll think of it differently!"

Declan enjoyed the pub—they served real Guinness and the surroundings resembled what he was familiar with in England. A large, bright bar, friendly staff, and lots of plush seats around the perimeter, along with Irish and British music playing over the sound system, made him feel at home. Zane introduced Declan to the Irish barman, Brendan, who oddly reminded Declan of Heathcliff from *Wuthering Heights*. Declan shook Brendan's hand.

"We've made Zane an honorary Irishman for his services to Irish pubs," said Brendan to Declan.

"You find the best conversations in a pub," said Zane.

As good as his word, Declan said goodbye to Zane after just one pint and walked north on Broadway to the youth hostel. The alcohol made his thoughts swim together in his mind: Isabella, Zane, and Marie. It was too good to be true. He wanted to save this moment forever, knowing that something important had just happened.

Chapter Eleven

On entering his youth hostel room, Declan saw the Chinese man sitting in bed reading. Not wanting to feel any awkwardness as he had the previous night, Declan put his bags of new clothes on the bed, looked directly at the man, and said, "Hello, how are you?"

The man looked up and replied, "Good, thank very much."

Declan smiled and said, "My name is Declan."

"I am Junjie."

"Are you from China?"

"Yes, from Fujian Province—city called Fuzhou. I here on Christian Exchange Program."

"Oh nice. I'm here to work for a while. Not sure how long I'll stay. I am from England."

"Yes, thought so. Hear you speak with Zane."

"You know Zane?"

"I try but he speak too quick and not really interested. So I mind own business. He crazy guy!"

"Yeah. He's a good bloke, though. I suppose if you didn't know him you'd find him a bit hard to deal with at first."

Junjie nodded.

"So, what do you do here? Do you go to a college or school?" asked Declan.

"Yeah, community college in Greenwich Village each morning to learn English. Then work Chinatown in afternoon in restaurant."

"Sounds like you keep busy."

"Yeah. It tough, but better than China—no future there. I learn English and save money from job and maybe buy a car when get home."

"That's nice. Good plan. I'm working with Zane now. Asbestos removal. Hard work but fifteen dollars an hour."

"Be careful. That stuff bad. Sometime Zane come home and take off jacket and dust go in room. Can't even see it but make me cough."

"Yeah, I know. I won't be doing it forever. Just want to build up some savings and then find something else."

"If you need job in restaurant, let me know. I can get you job in Chinatown. Pay not good but least not get sick."

"Thanks, Junjie, I'll keep that in mind."

Declan looked at the man's face and was taken aback by how smooth his skin looked. It was as if he had the face of an infant but the body of a man. Junjie put his textbook down on the bedside cabinet, and as he did so, Declan noticed the book waver. Declan sensed a weakness in the man.

Declan sat on the window ledge, lit a cigarette, and blew the smoke out the window. He then looked over to Junjie and asked, "What is that book you are reading—ESL?"

"English as Second Language. It for foreigners like me want learn English."

"Oh, right. That's nice. What other courses do they have at this community college?"

"Lots. Engineering, Nursing, Computers, Music. You name it."

Declan inhaled deeply on his cigarette and thought about the possibility of going back to college. Another pang of sadness struck him as he realized he might have missed his chance at a real education and a good job.

"Declan, you ever want free dinner you come my restaurant and I get you big dinner for free. No problem."

"Thanks, Junjie."

Declan finished his cigarette and suddenly decided to phone Chris. He knew it would be late at night in England, but he had the urge to find out if Chris had any information on his mother. "I'm going to phone a friend of mine. I'll see you later, Junjie," said Declan as he made his way out of the hotel room.

***

DECLAN SETTLED INTO ONE of the plush chairs at Trump Plaza's phone bank. Using his AT&T phone card number, he called Chris, "'Allo," answered Chris.

"Chris, mate. It's Dec. 'Ow are ya?"

"D'you know what bloody time it is? It's after one a.m. over here. I'd just fallen asleep!"

"Oh, sorry mate. I had to work all day, then pick up some new work gear. Didn't have time to call earlier."

"That's OK. So, how's it going? Still doing the dishwashing in Central Park?"

"No. They fired me 'coz I was kipping in the storage room at night. I was only there three days. But, now I got a job clearing asbestos. Excellent pay but hard work."

"Don't that cause cancer, that stuff?"

"Yeah. But the gaffer is very safety conscious," said Declan, smirking into the phone.

"Found a place to stay yet?

"Yeah, at a youth hostel. Sharing a room with students. Met some decent blokes and getting good tips on how to get by here. Hopefully things will get a bit better from now on."

"Yeah, I'm sure they will. You can't go wrong over there in America—it's all handed to you on a plate. Not like here where you 'ave to fight for everything."

"Well, it's not been exactly that easy. I haven't had people come up and throw cash at me or anything. You have to put the effort in."

"Yeah. Fair enough on that."

In the background, Declan could hear a bark. "Is that a dog?"

"Yeah, that's my new dog—Death Row."

"Death Row?"

"Yeah. He's a Doberman. Got him for defensive purposes since I got beaten up the other night coming home from the pub. Couldn't believe it. Two Russians—the ones that are after you—beat the shit out of me. Kept saying something in Russian, too, but not sure what it was. Sounded like they said your name."

"Shit."

"Yeah. I don't get it."

"Have you seen my mum? Is she OK?"

"Yeah, saw her the other day. Seemed OK to me."

"Well, tell her I will write in the next couple of days and I'll send her the youth hostel address. Christ, I wish she would get a phone."

"Yeah. It would be handy."

There was a pause.

"I'm sorry mate, but the Russians want me. That's probably why they did you over," said Declan.

"I don't understand—why *exactly* do they want you?"

"Sean. He ripped them off for over a hundred thousand quid and they are after me for the money."

"Jesus. So that's the real reason you went over to America? It makes sense now. I couldn't understand how you had the bollocks to get on that plane."

"It's part of the reason. You know me, I've always wanted to come over here. So all this business just gave me the extra push I needed to do it."

"Right."

"I'm sorry they jumped you, mate."

"Don't worry about it. I'm sorry about Sean."

There was a pause. It was as if both men had come to some sort of understanding.

"Right, I'll get going so you can sleep. Sorry I woke you. I'll call in a few days."

"OK Dec. Take care of yourself."

After hanging up, Declan stared at the receiver. He suddenly felt cold as he realized that there was no escape from the danger waiting for him in England.

***

BACK AT THE YOUTH hostel, Junjie was asleep, and the lights were out. Declan crept into bed as quietly as he could and fell asleep almost instantly. Later, he was woken as the door slammed. He looked up at the clock that read two a.m. He wondered how Zane could drink so late during the week and still be up for work the next day—he knew he couldn't do it.

***

THE NEXT DAY AT work, it was Declan's turn to be one of the "grafters" rather than the support person. Zane showed him how to cut through the wallboard, "If you hold the saw at about a forty-five degree angle, it's like cutting through butter." He showed him that the first step was to cut a "section" with the saw and then use the claw hammer, or one of the crowbars, to pry the board from the wall studs. "Why don't we use one of those electric saws?" asked Declan.

"Well, this ain't no demo job—it's a restoration. So, we have to keep the wall studs, wiring, pipes, and everything in top condition. Ray gets docked money for repairs that have to be made to the substructure. So, he checks on each room once we've cleared it out. We'll get a right bollocking if we mess up any of the wall frames."

Wearing his new overalls, respirator, and goggles, Declan felt a little more comfortable being around the asbestos. However, he soon realized he was getting hot and sweaty within minutes of working. The goggles would often have to be defogged, and the respirator would frequently have to have the outside cleaned off due to the buildup of white, fibrous dust around the filter.

As Seamus and Declan were carrying two large pieces of wallboard to the dumpster, Seamus mentioned that they needed to spend as little time as possible outside the building. "Why's that?" asked Declan.

"Technically, we are supposed to hand this stuff over to another crew who haven't been contaminated inside with the asbestos. Trouble is, Ray won't pay for the extra crew or extra time and money needed to wrap this stuff up and transfer it properly. This is a bloody two-year job being done in six months!"

"I see."

"But somewhere down the line, someone will have to pay."

"Seems like life in general—there's always a price to be paid," responded Declan.

Declan helped Seamus with a large piece of wallboard. He threw back the tarpaulin on the dumpster, then helped throw the pieces in, causing a small cloud of asbestos dust to waft around the street.

"Hey, you guys!" shouted a short, stocky, old lady with bright blonde hair and a barking Pekinese accessory dog. "You are supposed to put all that crap in bags. D'you see the god-damn dust blowing everywhere? That stuff could kill my dog!" she shouted.

"Sorry misses. Just doing what we are told, like," replied Seamus.

"Well, you tell that Irish asshole in there that if he doesn't start bagging up this cancer material, I'm gonna call the City Health Department."

"We will missus. We will."

Declan and Seamus went immediately to Ray's office to give him the bad news. "Oh, for fuck's sake! Now we're really in the shit!" said Ray.

"What we gonna do, Ray?" asked Seamus.

"Well, we'll have to just bring the boards and materials and dump them in all the first-floor rooms for now. Then we'll sneak them into the dumpster at night. I'll have to pay for another shift of guys to come in and move it when we get full up. I'd seen this coming, to be honest. Don't worry lads. Get back to work—and tell all the others we need to stack all the materials on this floor as tight as we can."

"Right you are, Ray," said Seamus, and he and Declan returned to the fifteenth floor to tell the rest of the workers.

As soon as lunchtime arrived, Declan rushed toward the elevator with his backpack. "Where are you going, Dec?" asked Zane.

"Gotta make a phone call. I'll see ya in a bit."

Downstairs in the small bathroom, Declan took from his backpack the plastic bag containing a pair of trainers, a clean shirt, aftershave, and a comb. He carefully took off his overalls, trying not to cause any dust to float in the room, then washed his hands and face, wetted down his hair, and combed it. Next, he put on the clean shirt, trainers, and finally, packed his backpack with his overalls, mask, and goggles. He left the backpack in one of the vacant rooms and rushed out of the building and across the street to Riverside Park.

***

DECLAN HURRIED TOWARD THE bench close to the small marina and felt a rush of adrenaline through his body. As he closed in on the bench, he was saddened to find no one sitting there. He stared at it for a second or so, then turned and walked over to the railing overlooking the marina. He pulled out a Benson and Hedges and lit it. He realized he now only had one cigarette left and would need to find some more—and from what he had seen in the stores, it would be difficult to find Benson and Hedges.

He began to wonder about his future. For now, he knew he had no option than to endure the asbestos job. It was difficult, but others were doing it too—people like him. But what of his mother and Chris? Surely he had an obligation to help protect them from the Russians? Yet he knew there was not much he could do. He reassured himself that being away safely in America, and building savings so he could move his mother back to Ireland, was the best thing he could do right now.

"Got a light, me old mate?" asked an American female voice mockingly.

Declan turned to see a smiling Marie holding up a cigarette. She held on to the baby buggy with her left hand as the toddler slept comfortably inside.

"Oh, of course," replied Declan as he fumbled for his cheap BIC lighter.

He was entranced by Marie's long eyelashes as she brought her face towards his hands. Her skin looked exotically soft and slightly brown, not pale white as an English girl's, and her hair was beautifully full and silky. She exuded healthiness and beauty. As she lifted her head, Declan could not avoid looking at her ample, firm breasts beneath her black sweater.

She exhaled to the side of Declan's face, smiled, and asked, "Well, how you been Englishman?"

"Not too bad. Just working. On me break again. Nice to be outside and get some fresh air."

"I bet. Must be full of that disgusting dust in there."

"Yeah, too right. Good to come out here and breathe in some cigarette smoke!"

They both laughed.

Declan noticed, too, that Marie—instead of wearing clothes that might further show off her figure and beauty, perhaps a summer-type dress, or a blouse and skirt—chose to wear a black sweater, jeans with tears in the knees, Adidas trainers, and a fake-looking pearl necklace. He had the feeling he could tell her the story of his punk band without reproach.

"What are those cigs you are smoking?" asked Declan.

"Camels. Never had one?"

"No, never seen 'em."

"Give mine a try."

Marie handed Declan the cigarette, and he slowly put his lips to it. Not really thinking about the cigarette, Declan was more interested in knowing the taste of Marie's lips on the filter. As he inhaled on it, he could sense the softness of her lips; he could taste her deep red lipstick. He wanted to smother the filter with his lips, and, right then, he realized he wanted more than anything in the world to kiss Marie.

"Well?"

"What?" replied Declan.

"What do you think?"

"Oh. Oh. I'm sorry, yes, it's very nice. In fact, I may change to them since I can't get hold of any B and H here."

"B and H?"

"Benson and Hedges."

"Yeah—you won't find them here. They sound very regal to me—sort of like the royal family's favorite smoke."

"No, everyone smokes 'em over in England. Want one?"

"Sure."

"It's my last but you are quite welcome to it."

"Thanks. I'm sure I'll enjoy it."

They exchanged cigarettes. Marie lit the Benson and Hedges and spun around and leaned back on the rail as she exhaled the smoke.

"Yeah, I like it. Smother than the camels, but not quite as strong. Good though."

"Thanks. Well, that'll be my last one for a while. I'll start smoking Camels now, I think."

"Good for you!"

"So, you don't seem to have a New York accent. Are you from somewhere else?" asked Declan.

"Yeah, I'm from North Carolina. A town called Raleigh. It's kind of quiet there. Not much happens. You've probably never heard of it."

"Well, no I haven't really. But, I do know of Sir Walter Raleigh, of course. Is it named after him?"

"Don't know. Could be. You know it probably is, considering the Brits landed in North Carolina way back when."

"Yeah, sounds about right. I'll have to look it up in the library when I'm down there next."

"Yeah, you do that, mister!"

This woman entranced Declan as she leaned back with her elbows on the rail of the fence and puffed on his Benson and Hedges cigarette, blowing smoke towards the New York City skyline as her long, silky black hair swung across her cheeks in the soft breeze.

"So, how come you are up here in New York, then? Didn't like Raleigh or something?"

"Yeah, basically. I was in college studying music. But I wasn't doing too well, so I decided to take some time off and visit an aunt of mine who lives in New Jersey. Anyway, I got this job so I could live in the city."

"That's a good idea. Rent free?"

"Yeah, but I'm on call all the time. Except when they go out of town—I get the place to myself then, which is good."

"Yeah. I bet. Well, I'm doing the same sort of thing as you. Taking time off from my degree program in England to travel about. I like it here a lot."

"How long do you think you'll stay in New York?"

"As long as I can. Maybe up to a year, hopefully."

"Good. What part of England are you from?" asked Marie.

"Brighton. On the south coast below London."

"The town from Quadrophenia?"

"Yeah. That's right. I love that CD."

"Me too. I've seen the movie tons of times. So, all those places are real? And the mods and rockers fighting?"

"Oh yeah. It's all real. The places and everything. Though there's not so much fighting these days."

"I'd love to go there."

The baby started to cry. Marie immediately threw the cigarette to the ground and tried to console the baby girl with a small rattle. She settled down a little, but Marie turned to Declan and said, "I need to get her home. It's her feeding time."

"OK. Well, thanks for the Camel."

"You are quite welcome."

"I suppose I'll get back to work too," Declan said as he and Marie looked at each other solemnly.

"I usually get off at seven p.m. and sometimes walk to Lincoln Center for ice cream. Do you want to come tonight? We could even get a beer if you like," said Marie.

"Yeah. I'd love to. Thanks very much."

"No problem," smiled Marie, "just look for me on the plaza. I'll be there about seven-fifteen."

"OK. I'll see you there, then."

Declan started his walk south on the Greenway, then suddenly stopped and turned to look again at Marie. She was walking north, pushing the baby buggy. He couldn't take his eyes off of her—it was as if he wanted to make sure she was real. He couldn't believe he was able to spend two lunchtimes with such an exquisite human being. She was simply perfect in his eyes. He had never been so close to such beauty, and more than that, he sensed there was something else about her that somehow bonded them together. What that was, he just couldn't grasp. But he knew it was there.

***

BACK AT WORK, ZANE asked Declan if he wanted to come to The Fiddler's for a "couple" after work. "No thanks, mate. Gonna meet up with someone, actually."

"You what? You're meeting someone? A sheila?"

"Yeah, as a matter of fact. But just friends. We're going for ice cream. That's all."

"Well, 'ave a listen at this Seamus! Old Decky got 'imself a girl! How the bloody hell did you manage that? I've been 'ere nearly a year and found nothing decent."

"Luck, I suppose. Met her at Riverside Park yesterday. Just got talking and found we had a few things in common."

"Yeah—like you both want a shag!"

Seamus and Zane laughed loudly.

"Very funny. It's not like that at all. Friends—that's all. Just going for some bloody vanilla ice cream!"

"Yeah, that's how it always starts," said Seamus, "then you're married with three kids and a mortgage."

"Is she a yank?" asked Zane.

"Yeah."

"Well, there ya go. Marry her and get the green card. After two years you get permanent residence alien status. Then you can get divorced, and they can't kick you out."

"Bollocks, Zane—it's not about that for me. I hardly know her. Anyway, I don't need a green card. I can always go back to England if I want to."

***

AFTER WORK, DECLAN ENTERED his room and found Junjie curled up in the corner of his bed, reading his ESL book. "All right there, Junjie?" asked Declan.

"Hello," replied Junjie.

"Good day for you?" asked Declan as he lay back on his bed.

"Yes, good. Easy day in college and not busy in restaurant."

Declan rose from his bed, opened the window, and sat on the window ledge. He lit a cigarette from a pack of Camels he had bought on the way back from work.

"So, what's it like in China?"

"I quite lucky. My father is Secretary of Municipal Party Committee. He help me get here. Only two people in China get on this exchange program with ICYE."

"ICYE?"

"International Christian Youth Exchange. Two Chinese come here and two Americans go China."

"So, do they pay for all your expenses?"

"Yeah, college paid for, youth hostel paid for, plus get a three-dollar voucher each day for McDonald's. And whatever I get from restaurant is mine. So, I don't spend any money, eat McDonald's, eat restaurant, save everything. If I make enough money for mobile phone, motorcycle—even car—I be very happy!"

"Just buying a mobile phone or motorbike would be that good for you when you return?"

"Yeah, see my dad send me here so can't go back with nothing. Look idiot if go back with nothing. Have go back show I did something. My dream to walk out airport with mobile phone and then next day go buy car."

"Well, I hope you get to do that, mate."

"What 'bout you. Here make money?"

"Well, kind of. I'm here more to sort of make a new start. Life's not that great for me in England right now, so I'm over here to hopefully find something better. Maybe I will or maybe I won't. We'll see. Do you know what I mean?"

"Yeah. I know. But England not like China. England good place right?"

"Yeah, I suppose so. When you compare it to China or somewhere like Ethiopia, then it does sound like a great place. But for me, I just wanted to try something different."

"Yeah. I think I know," replied Junjie. "But, think you crazy leaving England for here."

***

BY SEVEN P.M., DECLAN had showered, changed into his one clean shirt, and was walking north on Broadway towards Lincoln Center to meet Marie. He was excited—more excited than he could remember. This wasn't just a lunchtime chat in the park—this was a planned meeting between Marie and him. However, mentally, he tried to play it down; *it's just a chat between two people who want a bit of company instead of staying indoors for the night*. But the mantra failed to calm his fast-beating heart, and he felt sure he would blush and stammer the whole evening or make a fool of himself in some other regard.

Declan crossed Broadway at 63rd Street and stepped onto the Lincoln Center Plaza. It had a magical look as the grand structures of the performing arts center, theatre, and philharmonic buildings lit up against the dusky-blue New York skyline. However, even more impressive was the central fountain, with its dozens of jets cascading plumes of frothy water high into the air, lit in a bright mauve. Declan passed several groups of people dressed in evening suits and gowns and drinking cocktails from plastic cups. Feeling out of place and thinking he would be turned back at any moment, he, nevertheless, made his way to the center of the plaza and immediately laid eyes on Marie who was sitting on the fountain-side bench.

At first, he felt like turning and running—she looked so relaxed, as if she was an invited guest, and again sat with her legs crossed and her wrists limply crossed on her thigh. She wore a long black gypsy-looking crepe skirt, short black boots, and a long-sleeved white blouse that perfectly set off her deep-black silky hair. As he approached her, he saw the outline of her bra, and he noticed she was wearing the same deep red lipstick. He knew he was about to make a complete fool of himself, but didn't care. As he approached her, he noticed her fingers were trembling, which surprised him and belied her casual demeanor.

"Hello, Marie," Declan said, tentatively.

"Hi Declan," said Marie as she turned with a broad smile.

"Looks like some sort of show going on tonight."

"Yeah, Placido Domingo is performing."

Declan sat next to Marie.

"Nice. What a night to be here. What is he doing, Carmen, Tosca?"

"No, La Traviata. You like opera?"

"Yes, a bit. I would listen to Radio Three—that's a classical radio station we have in England—all the time back home."

"Sounds as if you like all types of music."

"Yeah, I do. I used to be in a band myself. Mostly Green Day covers and a few of our own works."

"What was your own work like?"

"Well, it was a little bit on the punk side. I tried to move us more to a Coldplay-type music, but our gigs always ended up rowdy in the places we played, and so we always reverted to our punk tunes. What about you? What do you plan on doing with your music background?"

"I always dreamed of being a piano virtuoso and playing a piano concerto in front of an orchestra. But, you know, I realize now that the most I can expect is to become a piano teacher."

"Well, at least you could get to do the thing you love every day. You know, be around music. Better than clearing asbestos—that's for sure!"

"Yes, I guess that's a good way of looking at it!"

They walked towards an ice cream vendor, and as they did, Declan looked at Marie and was overcome with an almost primeval urge. He tried to act normal, tried to concentrate on just walking, but at every step, he wanted to grab Marie and kiss her. Not only kiss her, but bite and lick her all over and then make love to her as hard and as fast as he could. He felt quite mad. He felt he didn't deserve to be anywhere near her. He didn't deserve to be at the Lincoln Center amongst these fine people with Placido Domingo who was, no doubt, in his dressing room at that very moment rehearsing. But, that's how he felt: he wanted to take all her clothes off, lay her on the ground, then feel his body on top of her—and inside of her. How he would survive the whole evening, he did not know. And he realized that it was more than physical attraction. He couldn't quite comprehend it, but he just felt a closeness to her as if they had always meant to be together.

As they started to eat their ice creams, Declan was almost relieved to hear Marie had to leave early. Her employers had unexpectedly decided to meet with friends, so she would have to babysit. They finished their ice creams and walked north on Broadway, then across to Riverside Drive. As they approached the intersection with 85th Street, Marie turned to Declan and said, "I better say goodbye here. If the doorman sees you he may say something to my employers. They are all so petty in this area."

"Yes, I understand," replied Declan.

And before he could think of how he should say goodbye, Marie quickly pecked him on the cheek and said, "I'll see you in the park tomorrow afternoon," then she turned and hurried off towards the elegant building of 140 Riverside Drive.

Declan watched her enter the building before turning and walking back towards Broadway. He stopped off again at Lincoln Center and smoked a Camel. He decided that the Lincoln Center fountain was his favorite place in the entire world.

Chapter Twelve

For the next week, Marie was all Declan could think about. He hardly spoke to Zane or any of the other men while at work—his thoughts were wrapped up in Marie. Everything now for him had changed. His priorities were no longer to find a new life away from his past—that didn't matter as much anymore—all that mattered was being with this woman. The more he thought about her, the more he determined that she was probably the most perfect woman in the world. But he had to keep tempering his thoughts; he realized they'd only known each other for two weeks and those mainly were cordial meetings in the park, an ice cream date at Lincoln Center, and last night, a few glasses of wine at the semi-posh, Upper West Side, Bin 71 wine bar where Marie had kissed him on the lips—a kiss he couldn't stop replaying in his mind.

It was at Bin 71 where Declan revealed to Marie a little bit more of himself—told her that one of the main reasons he came to America was in the hope that there might be a better life for him here, and that he wanted to make some money to help return his mother to Ireland. He told her that England was not a bad place, but he wanted to find a better place where he could escape his past and live a better life. Marie had replied, "I know how you feel. That's sort of why I'm not in Raleigh. Being away from some bad influences and negative people makes it easier for you to move on and live your life and be free."

"Yeah, that's it exactly," replied Declan.

Declan had asked what these "bad influences and people" were, to which Marie had simply replied: "Oh, just some people I knew who liked to have fun at other people's expense." Declan didn't probe any further. He knew from the way Marie turned her head away from him and then lit a Camel that she didn't want to talk about the subject. But none of that mattered to Declan—he just couldn't believe how much his luck had changed in just two short weeks in New York City.

"I love that New York City is so packed with people and always changing. You meet so many different people that it seems these random encounters will almost certainly point you in the right direction sooner or later," said Declan.

"Yeah, I know what you mean. I think you have to be open to it. Open to meeting new people and taking on constant new opportunities until you hit on the thing you are looking for. Or didn't even know you were looking for."

"Yeah," replied Declan, deep in thought.

***

THE NEXT DAY, DECLAN and Zane arrived at work to find all the Irish workers waiting in the lobby area, sitting on overturned buckets or leaning against the walls. Most were smoking. "What 'appened?" asked Zane.

"That fucking old granny next door complained to the city about the dust coming out the windows. Inspector was 'ere this morning and has given Ray twenty-four hours to get it sorted or he'll 'ave his contract pulled," said Seamus.

"Fucking old slag," replied Zane.

Just then, Ray came barging in the front entrance, his arms full of plastic wrap and tape. "Right lads, put yer cocks away and get to work. All the windows and doors have to be shut. Starting on the top floor, start taping up all the windows and doors with this plastic wrap.

Especially the ones on the front of the building—that's the ones that old cunt can see."

The men got to work. Within minutes, the three teams were ripping, cutting, and tearing down the asbestos wallboard, and within half an hour, the entire twelfth floor was covered entirely in suspended asbestos, floating menacingly as it flickered through the filtered sunlight.

"I can't see a fucking thing!" shouted Zane.

"This is bollocks!" said Seamus.

"It's impossible to work! Let's get out of 'ere before we die of asbestos poisoning!" cried Declan.

The men fumbled their way to the elevator and met up with the other crews who were of the same mind to evacuate immediately. Declan felt almost in awe of these men. They, including himself, seemed to be of the same substance, same mind. Willing to risk everything to try and make a better life for themselves. It comforted Declan that he was not the only person who was willing to do these things to hopefully have a better future.

Outside the building, the men gathered, took off their respirators, dusted themselves down, and lit cigarettes. Ray came out and announced, "All right, lads, I've been up there. It's a fucking disaster. Take the rest of the day off. I'll pay yer each a couple of hours for this bollocks."

"What we gonna do, Ray?" asked Seamus.

"I'm gonna pick up some extraction fans, and we'll have to seal each room we're working on. Then we'll run the dust out with ducts to a filtering system. Gonna cost me a packet, but I've got no choice. It's either that or close up shop."

"Right lads, pub's open, so I'm off down The Fiddler's if anyone's interested," said Zane, unsurprisingly.

***

At the bar, Declan was not able to keep up with Zane and the Irishmen—within two hours, the Guinness was making his head spin, and he left to return to the youth hostel. Junjie was in bed reading his ESL book. "All right Junjie, me old mate?" asked Declan drunkenly.

"Yeah, good Declan. You good too?"

"Yeah, mate. Down the pub. Drank too much. Sorry bout that. You good Junjie. You work your arse off and study all day. Never 'ave any fun."

"Yeah, but I look to future. I lucky you live here now. You good guy too."

"Well, I want to take you out sometime so you can 'ave some fun too, mate. It's the least I can do."

"Yeah, thank Declan. You good guy."

"OK mate. I'm falling asleep. Cheers mate."

Later that night, Declan was woken by the slamming door that seemed just inches from his head. Zane performed his usual swan dive onto his bed, belched loudly and said, "Oh yeah. Nice one, nice one." Within two minutes, he was snoring.

***

The next day, Declan was surprised to be woken by Zane already showering. "I don't know how you can drink all night and be up and ready for work the next day!" said Declan as a naked Zane came out of the bathroom, scratching his crotch.

"Practice makes perfect!" grinned Zane.

The two men caught the subway to work and, as they approached the building on Riverside Drive, were surprised to find everyone working industriously. "Got the extraction system set up. Each room door is sealed with an extractor fan that sucks all the shit out of the room through big ducts to a filtering system at the rear of the building," said Ray, standing by his office entrance.

Zane and Declan walked to the twelfth floor to inspect the "filtering system" and found it to be a simple extractor fan hooked up to large silver duct pipes that were routed to the end of the hallway, out the rear window, and dropped down towards the courtyard below. The ducts were spewing huge clouds of asbestos dust down the back of the building. However, the enclosed courtyard system of the building's rear made it impossible for anyone to see the dust being ejected if they were outside the building. Ray walked up behind the men and said, "That old slag won't know what's going on. If I had to pay for a real filtering system, I'd have to buy more equipment and hire another crew to keep bagging up the dust all day. I can't afford that. We'd all be out of a job, lads."

Declan and Zane looked at Ray suspiciously.

"Back to work then," ordered Ray.

Ray sang "Love Me Tender" as he made his way to the elevator.

Declan did, on the surface, like Ray very much. But there was something about him, cheating the system and making way more money than he deserved. It seemed that other people would have to pay for all these shortcuts. Most likely, the residents who had probably worked hard over many years to build their wealth. Ray's "Love Me Tender" singing did not help Declan's view of him.

***

THAT EVENING, DECLAN HAD planned to see Marie at The Fiddler's so she could meet Zane and some of his fellow Irish workers. At the youth hostel, Declan and Zane took turns showering. Zane lent Declan some "Stetson" aftershave. "Splash some of that on and she'll be all over yer, mate," said Zane.

"Steston? Never 'erd of it. Is it American? Sounds like it's a sort of cowboy or John Wayne product."

"Dunno, mate. All the rage in Oz. Decent price too."

"Cheers, I'll give it a go."

Declan splashed on the aftershave and reached for his alternate shirt that was hanging on the rope strung across the bathroom. He had hand-washed it in the bathroom basin the previous night.

***

DECLAN AND ZANE WALKED the eight blocks south on Broadway and into the bustling, smoky bar of The Fiddler's Irish Pub. Declan arrived thirty minutes early so that he could have a pint or two "to steady his nerves" before Marie arrived. This was the first time he had introduced Marie to the people he lived and worked with, and it made him nervous to think what she would make of these immigrants trying to create a new life for themselves. To Declan, Marie was a fine, intelligent, confident woman—and he wondered if he was enough for her.

After his second pint, Declan told Zane and Seamus he would wait outside for Marie so she wouldn't have to enter the bar alone. "What a gentleman you are, mate," laughed Zane.

Outside, Declan smoked nervously, and it was just a few minutes before he caught sight of Marie walking elegantly down Eighth Avenue wearing jeans, high-heeled shoes, a tight leather jacket, and a cream sweater, all the while ignoring the glances of most of the passersby who, no doubt, were admiring her. She was smiling as she gave Declan a quick peck on the cheek. Declan didn't know what to say. "Shall we go in?" asked Marie.

"Oh yeah, right," replied Declan as he fumbled for the door.

She strode into the pub as if she had been there a hundred times. Declan caught up to her and guided her to the far end of the bar, where Zane, Seamus, and several other members of Ray's crew were drinking. By this time, Marie had caught all of their attention, and none of them spoke.

"Marie, I'd like you to meet a few of my mates. There's Zane from Australia, Seamus from Dublin, Fin from Limerick, and Michael from Londonderry. And the barman here is Brendan from Belfast. Sorry about Michael and Fin, they didn't have time to brush off the asbestos before they came down."

"Sorry, love, I'd forgotten The Fiddler's was going to 'ave yer company. Else I'd have cleaned up fer sure," said Michael.

"It's no problem for me. I'm sure you like to get down here quickly to clear out the dust from your throat," smiled Marie.

"Well, how about a drink, Marie?" asked Zane, himself clutching a pint glass that never seemed to leave his hand when in the pub.

"Yes, I'll take a Bud please, in the bottle," replied Marie.

"I've got it," replied Declan, "anyone else ready?"

"Guinness for me Dec."

"Me too mate."

"Aye, I'll take a Guinness."

"Yep, Guinness."

"Very predictable, aren't they?" smiled Declan.

"I guess so," laughed Marie.

"I'll tell you, though, you never get better conversation than in a pub."

"I bet," replied Marie.

Declan ordered the beers and then turned to Marie, "Fancy a Camel?"

"Sure, but we'd have to go outside wouldn't we?"

"Yes."

"Let's stay inside for a bit so I can get to know everyone."

"Sure thing," replied Declan.

Zane turned to Marie and asked, "So, Declan tells us you work up the road from where we are on Riverside Drive. Who do you work for?"

"I work for a couple who have one of the penthouses at the Normandy Building at one-forty Riverside."

"Hmmm. That sounds posh."

"Yes, it's nice. However, it's not all glamorous for me. I'm at their disposal all day. Their baby is a good kid, though. So, I'm lucky with that, but I can't say they're the nicest people to work for."

"Bastards," said Zane.

"They're British, by the way," said Marie.

"You never told me that," exclaimed Declan.

"Sorry, didn't think it was that important."

"So, you like the British types. Is that it?" asked Seamus. "You should try an Irishman, one of these days!"

"Leave it out, Seamus! Sorry about him, Marie—had a bit to drink already, I think."

Marie laughed and gulped her beer.

The men kept snatching looks of Marie, and everyone was prepared to buy her a beer as soon as she was ready for her next. Declan felt it was a sign of respect for most of the men that an exquisite woman was happy to be in their company. It was as if she made them feel a little bit better about their lives. Within an hour, the music in the bar had been turned up and the din elevated further as the customers had to almost shout to each other—Marie had drunk three beers. Zane turned to Marie and asked, "Marie, do you like Irish music?"

"Yeah, I played some back in college—enjoyed it."

Zane turned to the barman, Brendan, and asked, "Brendan, why don't you sing the lady a song?"

Declan noticed Marie looking closely at Brendan. "Fancy him?" joked Declan.

"No. Of course not. Just thought how much he looks like you. Except older."

Declan looked at Brendan and thought him good-looking. But found him to be much more muscular and fit than himself. However,

Brendan had a weary look about him. Declan wondered if he would have that same weary look one day.

Brendan finished wiping a pint glass, turned off the sound system, sat on his stool in the corner of the bar, then began to sing, in perfect tone, the first two verses from "Rambling Irishman":

> *I am a rambling Irishman*
> *In Ulster I was born in*
> *And many's the pleasant day I spent*
> *Round the shores of sweet Lough Erine*
> *For to be poor I could not endure*
> *Like others of my station*
> *To Americae I sailed away*
> *And left this Irish nation*
>
> *The night before I went away*
> *I spent it with my darling*
> *Three o'clock in the afternoon*
> *'Til the break of day next morning*
> *But when that we were going to part*
> *We linked in each other's arms*
> *For Americae we soon set sail*
> *A journey without no charms*

The men applauded vigorously. Brendan swiveled from his stool, smiled, and busied himself cleaning more glasses. Declan asked Marie, "Did you like that?"

"It was wonderful. He's a great singer."

"Right. You would know with your piano background."

"Yep. I had to study one Irish song called, 'Molly Bawn.'"

"Did you sing it or play it?"

"Both."

"Would you sing us a bit?"

Marie gulped some more beer and replied, "Sure."

The bar hushed. Brendan turned down the stereo again and then sat back on his stool. The rest of the men stood about the bar expectantly. Marie sang the song in almost a perfect complementary tone:

Oh come all you young fellows
That follows the gun
Beware of night's rambling
By the setting of the sun
Beware of an accident
As happened of late
It was Molly Bawn Leary
And sad was her fate

She'd been goin' to her uncle's
When a storm it came on
She drew under a green bush
The shower for to shun
With her white apron wrapped around her
He took her for a swan
Took aim and alas
It was his own Molly Bawn

Oh young Jimmy ran homewards
With his gun and his dog
Saying, "Uncle, oh uncle
I have shot Molly Bawn
I have killed that fair female
The joy of my life
For I'd always intended
That she would be my wife"

The bar erupted in a unified cheer, the men clapped and hollered. Declan approached Marie and kissed her with vigor. Oblivious to the surrounding noise in the bar, Declan understood that at this moment, in this bar, in this city, in this country, on this planet, he had just fallen completely and irretrievably in love with Marie. He embraced her. Their mouths pressed hard and open against each other, teeth grinding, tongues exploring. Declan pulled her body closer and felt her breasts against his chest. Finally, they broke free as they both realized that most of the bar was roaring in appreciation of the spectacle.

"Your tab's on us tonight," said Brendan.

"Thanks," said Declan.

Marie looked at the floor. "I think I'd like to go now," said Declan.

Marie looked up, smiled, and said, "Me too."

"See ya lads!" shouted Declan to his friends and quickly left with Marie, both trying not to listen to the remarks and heckles that followed them out the door.

***

THEY HELD HANDS AS they walked east on 47th Street and then north on Broadway. Declan stopped and pulled Marie close to him and said, "Marie I want to make love to you. You move me so much I just can't help it. I think I love everything about you."

"Declan, I want that too. But where can we go? We can't go to my room at the Normandy—I'll get fired."

"Well, we can go to the youth hostel. I can ask my other roommate—a Chinese bloke—to leave for an hour."

"Yeah, that's fine with me."

***

THEY RUSHED TO THE hostel, and as was normal, Junjie was sitting in bed reading his ESL book. Marie waited at the end of the hall. Declan tentatively approached Junjie. "Junjie, I was wondering, I have this girlfriend, and we have nowhere to go. I was thinking perhaps I could bring her here for a little bit."

"Oh yeah no problem. Just let me know when and I'll go out."

"Well, it's now actually."

"Right now? Oh. OK. No problem. I can go for while."

"Let me pay for you to go to the Cinema."

"No. Is OK. I'll go bookstore and read. No problem. Glad help out Declan. You good guy."

"Thanks Junjie. You good guy too."

After Junjie left, Declan waved Marie in. "This is my bed here," said Declan, pointing to bed number "2." Marie wasted no time, grabbing Declan and continuing with their kiss. They undressed in a chaotic flurry and fell onto the bed, with pieces of clothing flung awry. Declan kissed and sucked Marie's firm, round breasts. Marie pulled his head hard against herself.

"Do you have rubbers?" asked Marie.

"Rubbers?"

"Trojans?"

"Oh, jonnies. No, I don't, sorry."

"Declan, you have to get some. I'm sorry, but I won't do it without them."

Declan felt the surge of his blood suddenly slacken, and he felt deflated.

"Oh, OK. I'll run across the street to the drug store and get some."

"Thanks."

Declan was back in just a few minutes and felt relieved to find Marie lying in bed, still naked. He fumbled a condom onto his penis. She spread herself for Declan, and, inexperienced as he was, he instinctively thrust himself into Marie, who groaned and then seemed to push Declan back. "Are you OK?" asked Declan.

"Yes, it's just been a while."

Declan quickly found his rhythm and, unable to control his lust, thrust harder and harder, faster and faster. Marie shouted "Yes!" as she grabbed Declan's ass. Within a few short minutes, it was all over, and Declan rolled over onto his side. "I'm sorry," said Declan.

"Why?"

"I was too fast. I got carried away. You are so beautiful in so many ways, I just couldn't control myself."

Marie wiped a long strand of sweaty hair away from Declan's cheek and said, "That stuff doesn't really matter. We have lots of time to practice. But tonight, I think it was the way it was supposed to be."

Declan leaned over and kissed her on the cheek and said, "You are so wonderful. I just can't get over you."

"Declan, you are wonderful too. You are certainly so different from anyone I've known. I do love being with you."

They rested for a few minutes, shared a cigarette, and then dressed before Declan walked Marie home to Riverside Drive. This time, their goodnight kiss was passionate. On his return walk to the youth hostel, Declan understood for the first time that the world could be tremendously fulfilling and joyous. So many new feelings were giving him reason to believe that it was possible to find happiness—an idea that had not occurred to him before.

***

BACK AT THE HOSTEL, Declan climbed the stairs to the fifth floor and just as he approached the hallway, found Zane slumped at the top of the stairs with his head turned to the side and vomit spilled on his jacket and around his chin. Declan also noticed a large dark stain down the front of Zane's jeans. "Come on mate, in we go," said Declan as he lifted his friend and carried him from behind. He dragged him into their room and kicked the door shut. Junjie got out of bed and said, "What's up?"

"Zane got sick. Gotta throw him in the shower and get him clean."

"Sure. No problem."

Declan dragged Zane into the bathroom. Then he sat him on the toilet, turned on the shower, undressed him, and then lifted him into the shower and poured some shampoo over him, quickly rubbing it on as many areas as he could before rinsing him down. Not wanting to think about what he was doing, Declan quickly dried Zane and dressed him in a pair of shorts, and then lifted him up. Zane was then able to stagger to his bed and flop onto it. Declan tucked him in and said, "Get some sleep and you'll be fine mate."

"Dec," said Zane, as he twisted his face to the center of the room.

"Yeah?"

"Dec, you struck gold mate. You really struck gold. That bird is the greatest thing in the world. You struck gold. You found your princess."

"I know mate. I got very lucky."

"Yeah, and I've got fuck all. Fuck fucking all. All this way for nothing. I'm just a fucking big loser. I don't deserve fuck all."

"Now don't say that. You are a great bloke—one in a million. You're a brilliant guy. It's just a matter of time, and you'll meet your princess. I know you will."

"Yeah, mate. But, there's something else. I can't go back 'ome. I'm stuck 'ere."

"What do you mean?"

"I fucking did over my fiancée—that's why we're not getting married. We got in an argument over nothing really. I goes out, gets drunk out my 'ead, come home and she started on at me and then I went crazy. I don't know what I did but coppers wound up coming to the apartment. She was taken to 'ospital with concussion, cuts, bruises. I was arrested and then let out on bail. So, I skipped out and came over 'ere."

Tears rolled down both of Zane's cheeks.

"Bloody hell. You 'ave got a bit of a mess. Christ."

"Yeah, you see what I mean?"

"But, we can fix it up. It's not the end of the world, mate—I can help you out."

"Well, I'm not sure."

"How's your fiancée now? Doing OK?"

"Yeah, last I heard there was no lasting damage—'cept psychologically. She's seeing a psychiatrist now. Thing is, I really love 'er. I just have some mental problems. I don't deserve her. I just hope she is OK."

Declan instinctively wiped the tears away from Zane's cheeks. He then looked down and took a deep breath and said, "Look mate, I 'avent told you everything about me either. See, my brother was mixed up in some drug gang and then killed himself over ripping off this Russian mob who were about to take him out. I had to leave England since the gang is trying to find me to get their drug money back—even though I had nothing to do with it. They've already done over my mate and they could 'ave a go at my mum. And I escaped over here, like a total bastard. But as soon as I get enough money, I'm going back to help get me mum home to Ireland."

"Jesus. You have got yourself a bit of a story too," replied Zane.

"Yeah. Seems like everyone has a cross to bear in this city."

Zane breathed a deep sigh, closed his eyes, and lay back on his pillow. Declan pulled the blanket closer to Zane's chin. Declan wasn't surprised to hear of Zane's tale. He seemed to be hiding something by drinking and being excessive in general. But Declan felt that Zane really did love his fiancée and needed help himself so he can hopefully move forward and deal with his situation back home.

As Declan made his way to his bed, he found a note from the youth hostel office resting on his pillow. It read, "Isabella Ber called. Wants you to call her back."

Chapter Thirteen

The next morning was a Saturday. Declan invited Zane to eat breakfast at Artie's Deli. "Haven't seen you in a while, Declan," said Nancy with a smile, "and you brought a friend with you, huh?"

"Yes, this is my mate Zane. He's from Australia."

"Good day, missus," said Zane.

"I guess he likes hot tea as well?" she smiled.

As soon as Nancy left, Declan asked, "So, mate, were you serious about your predicament back in Australia?"

"You mean the fiancée? Well, yeah, I have a Domestic Violence charge against me. The coppers said I could get a year for it."

"Christ."

"Yeah, not only that, her brother is a professional rugby player—plays for the Souths. Bastard said he's gonna string me up by the balls when he catches me."

"Have you tried writing a letter? Apologizing?"

"Yeah, sent several. I phoned her one night, but I was on the piss at The Fiddler's and she could tell, so told me to 'Fuck Off.'"

"Hitting her though—gotta say that's well out of order, mate. Was that the first time?"

"Absolutely the first time. I think the pressure of the wedding sent me over the deep end. I know I've got problems. I curse myself every night. I drink just to blot out the whole thing."

"Zane, I know you're a good bloke. You've made a bloody terrible mistake, for sure. But I really think you can fix it up. I could help, if you like, and be your intermediary."

"Would you do that, mate?"

"Of course. Maybe if you can straighten things out with her a bit, it'll be better for you when you face the court."

"Face the court?"

"Yeah, you've got no choice, I think."

"Yeah."

"Is there any chance at all you'll get back with her?"

"No. None. She's seeing some other bloke now. I don't blame her. I deserve it for sure." Zane's lower lip started to quiver.

"Don't worry, I'm with you on this one. Together, we will sort this whole thing out. I promise you that Zane."

They both sipped their tea and Zane asked, "And what about you? Your mum being around those Russian drug dealers? It's got to tear you up."

"Yeah. I gotta make some money and get back over there and take her home to Ireland. I want to get her a fresh start close to her brothers and sisters in Ireland. England's gone right down the toilet these days."

"Sounds like it, mate. I thought Oz was looking like shit these days but at least we don't have the Russian mob taking over our drug scene."

***

LATER THAT MORNING, DECLAN met with Marie at a bookstore just a few blocks from Marie's residence. Shakespeare & Co. Booksellers had quickly become a favorite place for Declan. Much of the stock was dedicated to classic writers: Shakespeare, Hardy, Dickens, Joyce, Fitzgerald, and Woolf, among others. Almost all their modern books catered to literary readers. There were some popular paperbacks, but the staff seemed to frown on anyone buying such books. In fact, the staff seemed almost arrogant in the manner in which they surveyed what their customers were reading. Declan bought *The Trial* by Franz Kafka, and he and Marie left after receiving a nod from the cashier.

Marie worked a second job on weekends at the apartment of Lady Sophia Parsons, the mother of Marie's boss, Elizabeth Morton. Lady Parsons lived at 1040 Fifth Avenue—on the opposite side of the park from her daughter. Declan and Marie walked together through Central Park on a warm Saturday morning. "What do you do for Lady Parsons?" asked Declan.

"She has a maid work for her during the week, so on the weekends I come in and do some clean-up, cook her lunch or dinner, and run any errands she may need. Even go for a walk with her. Lizzie Morton just likes me to check on her mother, basically—she's too busy to do it herself. I'm sort of their go-between now. They are not the closest family, so I fill in."

"Is she nice to work for?"

"Oh yeah, I really like seeing her. She lives in the same building where Jackie Kennedy lived, opposite The Met. She's the daughter of the Earl of Warwick. Studied at the Sorbonne. Moved over here after her husband died. There was some sort of scandal she wanted to get away from."

"That's interesting."

"Yes, it is. I told her you were coming with me today. She can be a bit short-tempered, so be careful."

"No problem."

As they approached the rear of The Met, Declan realized that they were coming up on the tree and bushes where he had slept on his third night in New York City. He slowed his walk and stared into the bushy area. "Everything OK?" Marie asked.

"Yeah."

"It looked as if you had seen something weird or something."

"Well, I suppose I should be honest. I slept behind that bush by the tree when I first arrived here."

"Are you kidding me?"

"No. I got woken up in the middle of the night by someone screaming. So I ran around the front of The Met and sat on the steps by the main doors. There was a security guard inside who didn't bother me the rest of the night."

"Goddamn! Why the hell were you sleeping outside?"

"Well, I didn't know about the youth hostel when I arrived, and all the hotels were expensive."

"Wow. You sure are resilient. Lady Parsons' apartment overlooks The Met. I'll never look at the view the same again—thinking of you sleeping behind that bush and someone screaming."

***

THEY SAID NOTHING MORE until they arrived at the entrance to 1040 Fifth Avenue. A doorman, in a uniform that looked as if it had been cleaned and pressed that morning, opened the door for them both and said, "Hello there, Miss Marie. Taking a friend up to see Lady Parsons?"

"Yes, that's right Felix. Lady Parsons knows Declan is coming."

"Well, have a nice visit then," he replied, tipping his hat.

They took the elevator to the 14th floor. Inside Marie said, "Felix is a nosy bastard. He knows the name of just about everyone who comes in this building, including delivery people. I guarantee he'll remember your name if you come again. He always has to know what's going on. It's a pain but it's what he's paid to do."

"Yeah, makes sense. Can only imagine how they advertise for those sorts of jobs: 'Nosy Bastard wanted for high-rise apartment block.'"

They laughed, then embraced with a kiss. Declan pushed Marie against the elevator wall, pushed his groin into her and said, "I could do you right now. You look so bloody luscious!"

"Well, now, you will just have to wait!"

The elevator bell rang and the door opened. They walked out, and Declan saw only two doors on the whole floor. "Lady Parsons owns half the floor," Marie said.

"And she lives on her own?"

"Yes."

Marie rang the doorbell and Declan suddenly became nervous. He had never been in an apartment building with a doorman, never met any British Nobility, and had never been in the same building where a person as famous as Jackie Kennedy once lived. He felt a little unsteady.

The door opened and Lady Parsons stood there, gazing at them both. Declan noticed she wore furry pink slippers. This put him at ease. She wore a long, beige pleated skirt and a flower-patterned long-sleeved blouse. Her hair was light grey and pulled back in a bun. She had on light red lipstick and light touches of white powder on her cheeks. She was stern as she looked Declan up and down. Her eyes stopped at his, causing Declan to freeze. "Well, have you shagged her yet?" asked Lady Parsons.

Declan's face turned bright red.

"Sophia. Please," cried Marie.

Lady Parsons burst into roaring laughter and said, "Come in, darlings, come in!"

Inside, Declan saw that the halls were lined with old books, long velvet curtains draped the window frames, antique oil paintings dotted the walls, and interesting knick-knacks that looked to tell a story from a far-off time were sprinkled about on each piece of wooden furniture. It looked to Declan like a colonial retreat from a time gone by—a place where a person could come and be at peace; a place where the time of day didn't seem to matter; a place that Roger de Coverley would almost certainly approve of.

Lady Parsons sat on a large leather reading chair near the window. Declan and Marie sat on a big sofa in front of one of the many bookcases.

"So, Marie, tell me all about your week. Any news from my selfish daughter and idiot son-in-law?"

"No, Sophia, nothing new there. They went out a couple times with friends. But, that's all."

"How's that lovely granddaughter of mine?"

"She's doing great. Happy as can be. I took her to the zoo again on Tuesday. You should meet us over there sometime."

"I'd like to, but I don't want to stray too far from home these days. I look forward to you bringing her up here. And what about this man here, Derek, is it?"

"Sophia, it's Declan," said Marie, frowning.

"Yes, Lady Parsons. I'm Declan from England."

"Call me Sophia, for Christ's sake. I don't need all that Lady malarkey anymore. That's only good for getting you into a decent restaurant, anyway. It's just the Yanks that piss themselves over titles anymore. The good old days are gone when a title actually meant something."

"I see," said Declan.

"You know I met a chap the other day—a yank—said he was the 'Earl of Cornwall.' I said there's no such bloody thing as the 'Earl of Cornwall.' He said he bought the title from a company in London. Showed me his credit card that read 'Abe Jackson, Earl of Cornwall.' He was from Kentucky and ran a long-distance lorry driving company. Needless to say, he was a complete idiot. There are a lot of them over here in the colonies."

"Would you like me to make some tea, Sophia?" Marie asked.

"Oh, yes, darling, please do, with a dash of gin, of course."

Marie left for the kitchen and Lady Sophia sat back in her chair, crossed her legs and lit a cigarette. "So, young Declan. Where are you from in England—you sound like a southerner?"

"Yes, that's right," said Declan as he sat on the edge of the sofa with his hands folded together, "I'm from Brighton."

"Ah, Sussex. I love Sussex—have lots of fond memories of my days at Roedean School. Couldn't care less about Brighton though—that's another place gone down the shitter. Full of bloody foreigners."

"Yes, that's true. Lots of foreigners there. Many of them come to learn English and wind up staying."

"That's the trouble with England—ever since they opened up the flood gates to the Blacks in the sixties, everyone from all over is coming in now. You'll never stop 'em. And you know what? You can never get rid of 'em. They're there for good now. Anyway, what about you? What line of business are you in?"

"Well, I'm just doing some temporary work with an Irish construction company. We're over on the same street where your daughter lives, renovating an apartment block. But, like I said, it's just temporary until I sort meself out."

"Yes, well, it does take time to find one's proper vocation. God knows it did for me."

"What did you do then, Sophia?"

"I used to be artistic director of The Royal Ballet—until they kicked me out."

"They kicked you out?"

"Yes, said I was not compatible with the company's ethics."

"Ethics?"

"It's a long story, darling. I'll tell you about it one of these days."

"Oh," replied Declan, unsure how to continue.

"Where's that bloody gin?" shouted Sophia.

"Tea's here," said Marie as she came into the room and placed an ornate silver tray on the center coffee table. She handed Sophia her cup. Sophia sipped her tea with gin alternately while smoking the cigarette.

"So, Sophia, what do you need me to do today? Any laundry or groceries?"

"No, darling. I have a wonderful idea. Why don't you and Declan go to the shop and buy some salmon and a cucumber. Then you can make us a nice luncheon we can eat on the patio. We'll open a bottle, and I want you both to tell me everything you have done since you met."

"Sure, that will be great," replied Marie.

Declan and Marie spent the rest of the day at Sophia's, eating, drinking, and talking. Before she left, Marie made sure Sophia had taken her prescription pills and also checked that her bed was made. "I'll drop by and look on you later tomorrow morning," said Marie as she kissed Sophia on the cheek. Declan approached Sophia and extended his hand to shake hers, but she would have none of it and pulled him to her face to kiss him on the cheek. "He's good stock, Marie."

Marie smiled. Declan blushed.

Declan walked Marie back to Riverside Drive. Then, later, as he walked home to the youth hostel, he felt a warm feeling as he thought of Lady Parsons. He thought meeting her confirmed that his relationship with Marie was the right thing to do.

***

That evening, as Declan lay in bed resting, the door suddenly burst open, and Zane did his usual swan dive onto his bed. "All right, lads?" he asked.

"Yeah, you sound perky, mate. What's going on?" asked Declan.

"I met this sheila. Well, actually, I've known her for a while. She's the sheila in the hardware store I usually duck into to get supplies for Ray. I always chat with her and she knew I fancied her, but she's really quiet, so I had a hard time communicating with her. Anyway, today I finally thought, 'Fuck it,' and asked her out. And she said, 'Yes.' I couldn't believe it! We are going out tomorrow night!"

"Nice one, mate. Is she from here?"

"Sort of. Not sure. Her dad is Mexican or something. He runs the hardware store. She sounds American though. She's fucking beautiful. Best looking bird I've seen in New York. Huge tits and a big arse!"

"Well done, mate. Where you taking her—not The Fiddler's, I hope?"

"No, I don't want to show my cards too early. I'll take her to a movie, and then I thought I'd take her up the Empire State Building."

"Yeah, that'll be really romantic at night. Good idea."

"That's what I thought. Bloody good idea!"

"I hope this works out for you, mate. What's her name?"

"Lucia. Lucia Garcia."

"Nice."

Declan felt happy for Zane. But at the same time a little worried, for it wasn't long ago that Zane was an emotional wreck, and now he was apparently ecstatic.

***

THE NEXT DAY AFTER work, Declan decided to take a walk to get some fresh air near the Hudson River. After about thirty minutes, he found himself on Greenwich Street by an industrial-looking area filled with parking lots, warehouses, and other lifeless buildings. This was the first time he had been near this area, but he knew enough that if he walked north and east from the river, he would eventually reach the familiar Sixth Avenue or Broadway. He crossed over to the east side of the road.

He thought about his future. Wondered if he should dare to dream of living the rest of his life with Marie. Suddenly, Declan heard someone shout, "Hold it right there, buddy." He looked up to see two police officers rushing towards him—both with one hand on their holstered handguns. Declan asked, "What is the matter?"

"Stand against the wall, please, sir," said one of the officers.

Declan stepped backwards towards the brick wall and then said, "What is the problem, officer?"

One of the officers pushed Declan by the neck against the wall and pinned him there.

"Jaywalking, motherfucker," said the other officer.

"Just remain calm, and we can write you a ticket and you'll be on your way, sir."

"Jaywalking? What the hell is that?" asked Declan.

"Foreigner, huh? Don't know what jaywalking is, huh?" said the first officer.

"Are you a terrorist by any chance, sir? Come here to blow some more buildings, while we are still trying to rebuild the World Trade Center Towers?" asked the other policeman.

"No, I'm from England here on holiday."

"Exactly. Lot of those ISIS terrorists are from the UK. Maybe that's what we have here."

Declan felt a punch to the side of his face, then another punch to his face, and another. Then he felt what must have been a blow from a truncheon to his ribs. He fell to the ground and then felt three, four, five, six kicks to his body and then several more blows from the truncheon to his back. It was over quickly, but it left Declan unable to move. One of the officers said, "We are letting you go with a warning. Make sure you go and find out what jaywalking means and have some respect when you visit other people's country."

Declan's body was wrapped in pain. His head smelled of blood, and his mind was numb; he could hardly move—his rib cage felt broken. After what seemed like several minutes, he lifted his head from the concrete and felt a mix of snot and blood slide from his nose and off his chin. He managed to sit up and then wipe his face with his shirt sleeve. As he continued to wipe his face, a man nearby exclaimed, "Hey man, I saw the whole thing from across the street. I got it all on my cell phone. Not a great camera, but it'll do the job. We can sue those bastards and sell the video to The Mail or CNN. How are you feeling?"

"I'm OK. Can you just help me get up and find a subway, please?"

"Sure thing. Houston Street is just a couple blocks away. But stay still for a few minutes and think about this. Police brutality is out of control here. But with my video, we can make a big payday. One guy recently got a hundred thousand dollars."

"No, thanks, mate. Appreciate it, but if you could help me get onto a subway, I'd be grateful."

"Absolutely."

"Why did they do this to me?"

"Cops are assholes here since September eleventh. Plus, there have been a few break-ins in this area, and they are coming down hard on anyone who looks out of place."

Declan wondered why he would be considered "out of place."

The man helped Declan to his feet, then held him with one arm under his shoulders as they walked to the Houston Street Subway station. As Declan was about to pass through the turnstiles, he turned and thanked the man.

"Let me give you my name and number, and if you change your mind about the lawsuit call me. I know an outstanding lawyer."

The man scribbled on a piece of paper and handed it to Declan.

"Thank you for all your help, mate."

***

EVENTUALLY, DECLAN MADE IT to the youth hostel. Inside his room, Zane and Junjie were lying on their beds in their usual standoffish manner.

"What the fuck happened to you?" asked Zane as he observed Declan.

"Got done over by the old bill."

"Shit. What were you doing?"

"Nothing. Just walking home. They said I was 'jaywalking.' I don't even know what that is."

"Jesus Christ. They did you over for not crossing the road properly."

Junjie came over and said, "This bad, Declan. I help. Where it hurts?"

Declan pointed to the back of his head, his face, and his ribs.

"OK, I go buy medicine."

Junjie left for supplies while Zane made Declan recount the whole episode.

"Fucking cops. You should be in the hospital, mate. But since you don't have insurance, you're shafted."

"You mean I can't see a doctor?"

"Well, yeah, but you'll have to pay cash. It'll cost hundreds, if not thousands, to treat you. In America, if you don't have medical insurance, you live a very high-risk life. Not like the rest of the world, where sick people are treated for free."

"That is harsh. Really harsh."

"Yeah, too right. Harsh just about sums it up."

"Can you leave a note at the Normandy Apartment building for Marie? I can't phone her and she can't have visitors."

"Yeah, no worries mate. I'll take care of that."

Junjie returned with bandages, antiseptic, pain killers, and a small first aid kit. "We take care of you, Dec. No problem," said Junjie.

The men then stripped him down to his underwear. Junjie felt his major bones and joints for breaks. "I know bit about medicine. Learn be doctor in China."

Like an expert, Junjie lifted each of Declan's limbs and felt for anything unusual. He checked each of his ribs. This wasn't hard to do since Declan's ribs were already easy to see due to his lack of fat. As Junjie softly ran two fingers over Declan's right rib cage, Declan yelled in agony. Junjie quickly moved his hands back up Declan's body and reached his face, where he ran his fingers over his cheekbones and nose.

"OK, two broke ribs. Everything else just bad bruise. Ribs not broken badly. OK in four weeks. Need rest in bed several days. Ice on ribs and bruises. We need to clean up wounds now."

Declan started to cry, "I'm sorry guys. I'm sorry."

"Don't worry about anything," Zane said. "You've been done over good and proper—I can't believe you managed to get back here without help. I'd be crying too if I was in that much pain. You really need to get yourself a cell phone."

But Declan wasn't crying because of the pain; he was crying because of the kindness of the men. They had shown him a kindness he was not familiar with. He hoped he could be as good a friend to them as they were to him.

"How did your date go with Lucia?" asked Declan as his tears subsided.

"Bloody great. Fantastic. I think I'm in love. But, don't worry about that—just get yourself well."

Chapter Fourteen

Early the next morning, the men in room five-one-five were rudely awoken by a loud banging on the door. Junjie leapt from his bed, wearing only a pair of black underpants, and opened the door while Declan rubbed his eyes and Zane covered his head with his pillow. "Wanker Boy" Johnny from the youth hostel office walked in and stood by the doorway holding a laptop. "Right, boys. We're doing a head count. We're having to turn new people away, so we need to clean house."

Zane swung his feet onto the floor, rubbed his face, yawned, and farted. Declan tried to sit up but couldn't and let out a small groan. Junjie helped Declan sit upright.

"Chen Junjie. That must be you," said Johnny, pointing his pen at Junjie.

"Yeah, that me."

"Well, you're all right since you're with the ICYE. Declan O'Neill?"

"That's me," said Declan feebly.

"You've been here for a few weeks. You'll have to leave in two days."

"Hold on there, mate. Take a look at him. He nearly got killed last night. He's been told by the doctor that he cannot move for two weeks. Now you wouldn't want the youth hostel to be responsible for him relapsing and being taken to the hospital? How would that look if someone posted a blog about it online? What about the French and Germans up the hall—can't you give them the boot?" said Zane.

Johnny looked at Declan and winced as he observed the knots on his forehead, the black eye, the bulging purple cheekbone, and the ice packs around his ribs that Junjie was adjusting.

"Jesus fucking Christ. OK, he can stay until he's well."

"He needs me too, Johnny. Doctor told me I need to make sure he takes his pills and gets his therapy."

Johnny looked at Zane suspiciously. "All right, Harris. You can stay until he is well. But watch your step—you've been in and out of this hostel for six months now. You're starting to take the piss."

With that, he turned and left. "Wanker," said Zane.

Declan smiled and then groaned. "Shit, it hurts to laugh!"

"Just rest, I get food," said Junjie.

"Zane, can you remember to take that note to Marie's building?"

"Yeah, no worries. I'll drop it off on me way to work."

"Cheers, mate."

***

THAT EVENING, MARIE CAME to visit Declan. "Oh my God! Why did they do that to you!"

"NYPD accused me of being a terrorist because I crossed the street diagonally."

"Unreal."

Marie carefully hugged Declan, the pain in his body quickly subsiding as he experienced the soft crush of her breasts on his body—a feeling that seemed to absorb the pain from him.

"My poor English boy. Don't worry, I'll take care of you."

She had brought a bottle of wine and some English Cadbury's chocolate. "I love Cadbury's. But do you have a corkscrew?" asked Declan.

With a smile, Marie pulled a corkscrew opener from her pocket. "You think of everything," Declan said.

"I try."

Marie sat on the bed as they listened to the radio and ate the chocolate while Declan recounted his beating. Later, Marie told Declan she needed to visit her family in North Carolina the following week. "I haven't seen my sister for six months, so I need to go. I'd like you to come with me. You can meet my parents."

"But look at the state I'm in. They'll probably think I'm a football hooligan."

"Don't worry; you'll look a lot better in a week. Plus, I'll fill them in on what happened. They'll understand."

"Well, OK, if you're sure."

"We can fly down. It's only an hour by plane. I can get cheap tickets—consider it my treat."

"That's very kind. Thanks. How long will we stay?"

"Just one night. That's all I can stand."

"Why's that?"

"Well, I don't get along with my parents that well. Part of the reason I left. They are very Southern in their ways."

"Southern?"

"Southern. I'm not sure how to explain it."

"They're racist, you mean?"

"Well, that's part of it, but it's more than that. I have some issues with them, that's all."

Declan got the sense that Marie didn't want to say more, so he tried to change the subject.

"Oh, right. They like country music too?" asked Declan, trying to lighten the mood.

"Yeah, that's for sure! That's another reason I don't like living down there—I hate country music!"

They laughed and kissed, kissed and laughed, and finished off the wine before Marie left. She promised to visit Declan each evening.

***

Six days later, Declan was feeling much better. His face was no longer swollen, although his eyes and nose still had a yellow tint to them. His ribs still hurt, but he was able to walk without too much discomfort. He met Marie early in the morning, and they caught a subway train to JFK airport. Declan sensed an edginess in Marie he had not noticed before. Usually, she was relaxed and carefree—a reason he loved being with her—but today she seemed subdued. "Smoking a lot of Camels this morning, ey?" asked Declan.

"Yes, I always seem to smoke more when I visit North Carolina."

Declan was surprised she called it North Carolina rather than "home." He thought to himself that he would probably always call Brighton "home" no matter where he was in the world. On the flight, he tried to lighten Marie's mood, "So are there any bands from the south that are any good? I'm thinking most of the American bands I know about are from New York, New Jersey, or California," said Declan.

"There are a couple of decent bands like R.E.M. and the B-52s. They are both from Georgia."

"Yeah, I've heard of them. The B-52s are a punk band, aren't they?"

"You've never heard of them, have you?"

"No," Declan replied with a wry smile and a chuckle.

"Bastard," laughed Marie.

"What? I think you're a mean barrr-stoood," replied Declan, mockingly.

They laughed and then kissed.

The plane was nearly full, though probably only a quarter of the size of the Virgin Atlantic jumbo jet that had taken Declan to New York. It struck him how incredibly lucky he had been to sit next to Isabella. Of the hundreds of people on that flight, he likely sat beside the only person willing to help him. He wondered how she was and felt guilty for not reaching out after she left a message at the youth hostel. He imagined her lying on her bed, reading medieval English novels and jotting down thoughts in one of her many journals. As much as he loved Marie, he thought it would be nice to spend time with Isabella and discuss books. Unexpectedly, he missed Isabella.

Declan looked out the window as the pilot announced they had passed from Virginia into North Carolina. There was nothing but trees below. It seemed so remote. Strangely, he felt he was removing himself further and further from England. New York didn't seem so far away compared to this. Perhaps it was because there were dozens upon dozens of direct flights home to London each day from New York. Looking out the window at the endless skyline of trees, he felt a spike of loneliness. He turned to Marie, who smiled at him.

The plane touched down in Raleigh on a muggy, sweaty day.

***

As soon as they exited the plane, they headed to the baggage area. "My mom and sister are over there," said Marie.

Marie hugged her sister, who was virtually a carbon copy of herself, except that she was two years younger. She was skinny, tall, with long, thick, dark hair, and Declan thought she was possibly even more beautiful than Marie. Her sister giggled as she hugged Marie. Declan stood a couple of steps back as Marie then hugged her mother in a quick, courteous manner, with no apparent emotion. Her mother was short and skinny, with a dour, almost angry expression on her face. She asked Marie, "How are you?" to which Marie replied, "Good."

Her mother then looked over at Declan, who was hesitant to get any closer. "Mom, this is my friend, Declan."

"Nice to meet you, Mrs. Cooper," said Declan, forcing himself to extend his hand.

"Nice to meet you," she replied as she shook his hand.

"This is my little sister, Becky," said Marie.

"Hello, Becky," said Declan formally as he shook her hand.

"He really is from England!" said Becky with a beaming grin.

Becky and Marie then looked at each other and smiled, as if they were sharing some silly secret.

***

THEY ALL WALKED OUT of the airport, Mrs. Cooper in front, then Marie and Becky holding hands, with Declan behind. Several times on the way to the parking garage, the sisters turned, looked at Declan, and giggled as they whispered to one another. Declan was confused as to what the fuss was about. He wanted a cigarette but wasn't sure if Mrs. Cooper would approve, so he decided to wait until he saw Marie smoke.

Mrs. Cooper drove them to Raleigh in her white Cadillac. Declan and Marie sat in the back while Becky sat in the passenger seat, frequently turning and asking Marie questions about her job and life in New York City. "Are you still dating that football player?" asked Marie.

"No, he was too arrogant, wanted me to be his little cheerleader, so we broke up," replied Becky.

"Good for you. Seeing anyone else now?"

"Yeah, a guy called Austin. He's on the golf team. He's OK. Real nice and does anything I ask him."

"Bet Dad likes him," said Marie, then turned to Declan and continued, "My dad plays golf all the time."

"Oh, right," said Declan.

"You play golf?" asked Becky.

"No, never played it in me life. I played football for my high school—soccer, you call it."

"Oh, yeah. That's pretty big here in North Carolina. Well, bigger than in most states."

The car pulled off the main road and into a large housing estate, which Declan was told was a "subdivision." The houses were big—at least five times the size of his mother's flat in England. Looking at the grassy area around the houses, Declan calculated that it would be possible to play a full-sized football game on any side of the building with room to spare, thus making the grounds larger than the Ber's house in New York.

"These houses are lovely, Mrs. Cooper. I really like the red brick walls," said Declan, trying to coax something out of Marie's mother.

"Thank you. We sure like it," she replied.

***

ONCE INSIDE, MARIE AND Becky showed Declan around the house. His first impression was that everything seemed brand new: all the furniture, paintings, and decorations looked recently purchased—even the walls looked as if they had been recently painted.

"Did you grow up here, Marie?" asked Declan.

"Yes, moved here when I was about five."

"But, it seems so new – looks as if you moved in last year!"

"My parents keep it fixed up."

One thing he noticed was that the house seemed to be a showcase for Marie's father, with each wall displaying some award or photograph of Mr. Cooper's business accomplishments in the paper industry. There was one picture of Mr. Cooper with a group of men outside the Senate building in Washington, D.C. Golf, too, played a prominent theme in the house—multiple golfing trophies were dotted about, some encased in Perspex boxes. On the other hand, there seemed to be nothing to indicate any achievements of Mrs. Cooper. The few pictures of Becky and Marie appeared to be an afterthought.

Upstairs, Declan was shown Marie's old bedroom, which had been turned into a storage room for paper samples. They then walked further along the upper hall to Becky's room. Inside, Declan was enchanted—it was a labyrinth of pictures and items relating to horses and riding. There were framed photographs of Becky riding a giant horse and jumping small gates. There were medals and trophies strewn over bookshelves and dressers. Bridles and reins hung from hooks, and even a worn saddle sat on top of a bookcase. Declan looked at the pictures of Becky as the two girls sat on the bed with their legs folded while Marie quizzed Becky on her college applications. The images of Becky riding her horse caught Declan's attention the most. The reflection of beauty, grace, and privilege of Becky in her riding pants, boots, and with whip in hand, on top of a beautiful tamed beast struck Declan as something enormously special. Declan felt Becky could pass for a young Elizabeth Taylor.

Declan sat in a small chair at a writing table and looked over at the girls, and then noticed under Becky's bed a pile of discarded clothes, and prominently in front of the pile was a pair of yellow underwear. Declan's gaze locked onto the item, and when Becky realized what he was looking at, she jumped off the bed and scooped up the clothes, then threw them inside her closet.

"You must think I'm a real mess!" exclaimed Becky, flustered.

"No, not at all," replied Declan, smiling a little as he turned away.

He picked up one of Becky's books—a book on horse care—and tried to look busy while he thought of what a wonderful room it was. For some reason, just watching the two beautiful sisters talk on the bed, the brand new furniture, the pictures of horse riding—it all seemed like some sort of dream. It was a new world to Declan—a safe and happy, carefree world.

"Lunch is ready," shouted Mrs. Cooper from downstairs. Declan felt another intense need for a cigarette.

"Let's eat lunch and then show Declan around the neighborhood," said Marie.

"That'll be nice," said Declan.

Mrs. Cooper didn't eat and said nothing as the group quickly ate their sandwiches. Declan wondered, oddly, if there was a price to pay for all these luxuries.

***

THEY LEFT THE HOUSE quickly and got into Becky's small Honda Civic—Becky driving, Marie in the passenger seat, and Declan in the rear. "Fancy a Camel, Marie?" asked Declan.

"Yes!"

They made their way around the North Raleigh area, which seemed to consist of sidewalk-less roads and desolate-looking "subdivisions." Declan asked, "Where do you go if you just want to buy a newspaper or a sandwich?"

"You have to drive to the grocery store. It's about four miles away," said Becky.

"What about pubs? Well, I know you don't have pubs, but are there bars here?"

"No, not really. You'd have to drive downtown. That's about a thirty-minute ride," replied Marie.

"Are there buses?"

"Yeah, but no one rides them. I don't think they even come up this way."

"So, if you didn't have a car, how would you go and visit a mate of yours who lived in another subdivision?"

"Well, you'd have to get a ride from someone. Probably your parents. How does it work in England?"

"All my mates live in walking distance. There's a pub every few blocks, a newsagent's every few blocks, and corner grocery stores everywhere. You don't need a car, since buses and trains go all over. But we don't get the big houses you have, and we definitely don't have all the land around the house. I live in a council flat in England."

"What's that?" asked Becky.

"It's an apartment owned by the government that rents it out cheaply to poor people," replied Declan.

"Oh," replied Becky.

They drove to Marie's college, North Carolina State University. "It looks more like an athletic complex with all the sports fields around it. Can we take a walk around?" asked Declan.

"No!" exclaimed Marie. "Can we just go, please!"

"You OK?" replied Declan.

"Sis, what's the matter?" asked Becky.

"Nothing. I'm just not feeling good. Can we get away from here, please?"

"Sure. We can go and see Velvet."

"Yes, that would be nice," replied Marie.

***

THEY CONTINUED TO A small, farm-like area that housed a stable, just outside Raleigh. Becky guided them through the small stable complex and on to a barn that housed her horse, Velvet. "I named him after my favorite movie, *National Velvet*," said Becky.

"I know that film. Elizabeth Taylor. I thought you looked a little like her in your pictures," replied Declan.

"Oh, thank you."

Becky showed Declan how to groom Velvet's mane and tail and reminded him, "Never stand behind a horse; he could kick you where it really hurts!"

As she gently combed the horse's coat with a soft brush, Declan looked into Becky's face and saw the love she had for the horse. He realized he'd never known anyone to have such love for an animal. She was transfixed, and Declan understood Becky was lucky to have so much love for Velvet. He thought back to his council estate and realized he knew no one with a pet of any sort.

"We'd better get going soon," said Marie, "Dad's coming home early and is going to barbecue steaks."

Declan turned to Marie and said, "I really am happy you brought me here. It's certainly different, but I do appreciate you showing me your world."

"It's my pleasure," replied Marie.

***

BACK AT THE HOUSE, as they walked through the garage, Declan was surprised to see the exact same car parked next to Mrs. Cooper's. "Dad is friends with the Cadillac dealer, so he gets a good discount. I think they were doing great deals on white Cadillacs last year—so he bought two," said Becky.

Declan and Marie smiled at each other.

They walked out onto the back deck, where Marie hugged her father and then introduced him to Declan. "Nice to meet you, Mr. Cooper."

"You must be the foreign guy," replied her father, quickly looking at Declan, before turning and continuing to tend to steaks on the grill. Mr. Cooper was a short, rotund, yet firm, balding man with a certain intensity that seemed to cause him to block out everything and everyone around him.

"No. I'm not foreign. I'm English," replied Declan with an air of indignation.

"Come over here to take a job away from a hardworking American?" he replied with a smirk.

"No. I'm here to help this great country grow."

"Sounds like a crock. Our economy is in real shambles, and the main problem is because of all the foreigners in our country."

Declan's face reddened, and his upper body tightened. Marie sprang to her feet and stood in front of Declan, her arms wrapped around his. "Declan, let's go for a walk."

"No, I wanna hear what he has to say, specifically about me."

"Let's go," replied Marie. Then, she shoved Declan down the wooden steps from the deck toward the side of the house. As they walked, Mr. Cooper shouted, "These steaks are shit!"

Declan then felt the whoosh of a half-cooked steak that, apparently, Mr. Cooper had thrown towards Declan. It went flying by Declan's head and into the backyard, where it landed in a bush. The family cat instinctively sprang from his shady corner and into the bushes to search for the meat, as if it had happened a hundred times before.

Marie continued to guide Declan to the front of the house. "What the bloody-hell is wrong with that guy?" asked Declan.

"He's got problems. He always has. That's why I've been so worried about bringing you down here. I didn't want you to see this side of him. I was hoping he might have changed."

"Accusing me of being some kind of thief and chucking a steak at me? What kind of bloke does that when he meets someone?"

"I know, I know."

"And how can he be so rich and in charge of people? How can he get a job anywhere with that attitude?"

"He's different at the office—everyone loves him there. But he comes home and takes it out on us. Always has."

"What a wanker."

As they stood in the driveway, a light-blue two-door BMW pulled up to the curb of the house. The driver's-side door opened, and

Declan recognized the thumping bass and aggressive lyrics of Eminem blasting from the sound system. As if from a 1950s sit-com, a prep-school-dressed youth stepped out and said, "Hi, I'm Becky's boyfriend, Austin."

Declan thought Austin could have been straight from a Ralph Lauren advert. Marie guided him to the back of the house. She came back and said, "I'm glad he's here. It'll cause a bit of a diversion. Dad will be fine now. He'll drink his Jack Daniels and go to bed. Don't worry, we'll be gone in the morning."

"Thank fuck for that," replied Declan. "But why is he like that?"

Marie paused for a second and replied, "He is mixed up in some big financial crisis at work, so he has gotten worse over the last year or two. But he has always had a temper with us. And he really seems to have a problem with me lately."

***

DECLAN AND MARIE WALKED the neighborhood, smoked, and talked. When they returned and approached the Coopers' house, it was dark, and they could clearly see Mr. Cooper and Austin in the brightly lit garage taking practice swings with Mr. Cooper's new golf set. Mr. Cooper was laughing and drinking with Austin and did not notice Declan and Marie as they made their way to the back of the house. Mrs. Cooper had saved them both some food, and they sat down on the deck and ate hurriedly. After a couple of cigarettes, Declan and Marie heard Austin's car leave. Becky came out to tell them her mom and dad had gone to bed, and it was all quiet inside. The evening fizzled in a whimper, and Declan was glad when he was able to go to bed.

***

DECLAN FOUND IT HARD to sleep in the Coopers' guest bedroom. He was more than puzzled at the family situation at the Cooper house. In one respect, it was a privileged life; however, he couldn't help but think how desperately lonely it felt in the house, in this subdivision, in North Carolina. Marie's parents were cold and interested only in material things, and, of course, Mr. Cooper seemed nothing short of a psychopath to Declan. He conjectured that something was seriously wrong at the Cooper household. He had no idea what it was and why, but it seemed like the house had almost a sense of evil about it. Declan wondered if there might be some deep issues in Marie that he wasn't aware of.

North Carolina itself felt isolated to Declan—just filled with trees and pockets of existence in "subdivisions." He imagined himself in his mother's house and recalled hearing buses, trains, and lorries at night, as well as the elevated voices of people leaving the pub after closing time. That, together with dogs barking and occasional shouting matches between couples in neighboring flats, and the odd object being thrown from a balcony to the parking lots below. But the cold, deathly silence of the Coopers' house was very different and made it difficult for him to sleep. It occurred to Declan that there were likely tens of thousands of "subdivisions" like this all over America, in lonely states like North Carolina, and he imagined they must be churning out millions of young Americans with no idea of what lay beyond their country.

***

THE NEXT MORNING, DECLAN emerged from his room and smiled upon seeing the giggling sisters at the kitchen table. Mrs. Cooper wore her usual frown as she busied herself in the kitchen. Mr. Cooper had, thankfully, already left for work.

After breakfast and just before leaving the house, Mrs. Cooper held up two small remote control units from the kitchen counter and pressed each of their buttons. Declan looked at Marie and asked quietly, "What's that about?"

"Remote controls to open the garage and start the car," replied Marie.

"I like my car temperature just so, before I drive," added Mrs. Cooper.

***

AT THE AIRPORT, MARIE hugged her mother and sister, and Declan hesitantly shook Mrs. Cooper's hand, feeling relieved that a hug was not needed. Becky, on the other hand, seemed more mature than she looked and easily approached Declan and hugged him.

As soon as Becky and Mrs. Cooper left, Declan and Marie each smoked a cigarette. "Well, I'm sure you think I am crazy now," said Marie.

"Are you serious? You should meet my mother one day, then you'll know what crazy really means."

"I know you are being nice. I'm so sorry about my dad. It's not you. He does stuff like that to lots of people outside of work."

"The bloke's got serious problems. I feel sorry for him. I'm glad I didn't hit him or anything like that. And your house seemed like a shrine to your dad."

"Yeah, I never thought of that—but you are right."

"What about your sister? Do you think she'll marry that Austin bloke?"

"Maybe. But, she's going to college next year, and who knows who she'll meet there. I think she likes having Austin around just to keep my Dad in check. Especially with the golf—it keeps Dad calm."

"Yeah. Makes sense. Well, I know firsthand things change a lot once you leave home."

"Yep. I just hope nothing bad happens to her when she leaves," replied Marie.

"Huh?"

"I don't know. Anyway, I need to use the bathroom. I'll be right back."

***

LATER, AS THEY WAITED to board the plane, Declan used his AT&T number to call Chris, since he knew it should only be about six p.m. in England. "Chris, it's me Dec."

"All right, mate?"

"Not too bad. I'm in North Carolina at the moment, visiting my girlfriend's parents."

"Where's North Carolina?"

"Sort of between Florida and New York, in the middle of nowhere."

"What's it like?"

"Bloody boring. Just trees, strip malls, and misery."

"Yeah, too right. Sounds like a load of shit."

"And listen to this. My girlfriend's mum has these remote controls that open the garage and start the car up. She does it so the car is nice and cozy when she gets in!"

"Christ! Lazy bastards, those yanks!"

"Yeah—too right. Anyway, what about you? Anything new?"

"Not much. Should be able to pick up my unemployment check today. Just eating me egg and chips and I'll be off round the pub. Meeting up with Tony, we're seeing this new geezer to fill in for your, er...brother, on bass. If that works out, we'll keep an eye open for a lead guitar, unless you come back, of course."

"What about your amps. Are you going to the Legion to pick them up?"

"Probably, Tony said he'd come with me. If we like this bass player, I'll swallow my pride and go round there."

"Any news from my mum?"

"Haven't heard or seen her in over a week. I'm sure she's fine though, mate."

"And the Russians? Have they given you any more aggro?"

"I stay away from their turf, and when I pass along by the flats, I make sure I've got me dog with me. But the other day one of them shouted over to me from the parking lot, "Tell your friend interest is being added monthly to the hundred thousand he owes us.""

"Oh, fuck."

"I'm sorry, mate. Never have good news, do I?"

"It's OK. Well, I'd better go—they are loading up the passengers now. See ya, mate."

"Bye Dec."

CHAPTER FIFTEEN

BACK IN NEW YORK, Declan and Marie went directly from the airport to The Fiddler's. Declan had a heightened appreciation of the pub as he entered and looked at the Guinness signs, the huge map of the British Isles, the Gaelic Irish and British football shirts hanging from the ceiling, and the dart board tucked into the far end of the main bar. He smiled too, when the barman, Brendan, shook his hand and asked, "What'll it be, Declan?" He was in no hurry to ever return to North Carolina and have food thrown at him.

Declan finished his pint quickly while Marie worked on her first glass of wine. She too, was in a cheerful mood as she whispered to Declan, "Why don't we have one more and go back to the youth hostel?"

***

WITHIN HALF AN HOUR they were in Declan's room, where he locked the door and began to undress Marie—slowly at first and then with haste, almost ripping the buttons off her blouse and tugging at her underwear. They fell on the bed and Declan winced: his ribs were still not fully healed. Marie pushed him back, pulled his jeans and underwear off, caressed his penis slowly so he was ready for her, then stood up and temptingly finished undressing herself in front of him—leaving on just her bra.

"Where are your Trojans?" asked Marie.

Declan said, "They're in the bathroom."

Marie came back with a condom and helped Declan fit it to himself. Then, she mounted him slowly, rode him softly so as not to hurt his ribs, then teasingly unsnapped her bra and threw it to the floor. He caressed her breasts, pinched the nipples. She became more aroused, rode him faster, and then faster. He cried out—half ecstasy, half pain. His face tightened up as the pressure on his hurt ribs increased. "Are you OK?" asked Marie.

"Yes. Don't stop!"

Declan was understanding something strange and new: the sexual pleasure mixed with the pain he felt in his ribs seemed to heighten the experience. It was the oddest thing in the world to him that he could enjoy sex while enduring the painful pressure on his fractured ribs. Tears began to well in his eyes. "Are you sure you are OK?"

"Yes," he replied as tears rolled over his cheeks.

Marie rode him harder and harder still—thrusting her pussy deep onto his penis, her breasts bouncing to the rhythm. It was too much for Declan and he climaxed all too quickly while releasing a cry.

Marie gently lifted herself and curled up next to Declan. "That was something," said Declan, his body still straining under the pain, his cheeks wet with tears.

"I'm glad you liked it," Marie replied quietly.

"Oh. I'm sorry. Christ, that was selfish of me. I got carried away again, didn't I?"

"Yes. It's OK, though. You'll have to make it up to me next time."

"I will."

***

WEEKS LATER, DECLAN'S RIBS had healed and he was working as many hours as he could at 5 Riverside Drive. At the height of the summer and the end of a particularly grueling fifty-five-hour work week, Declan was happy to calculate that his savings had reached four thousand dollars. From the worksite, Seamus and Zane went straight to The Fiddler's while Declan went back to the youth hostel to shower and stash his new earnings. As he entered the room, he noticed a new person in Junjie's bed: a tall, dark-haired, European-looking man. "Who are you?" exclaimed Declan.

"I am Peter, from Germany."

"Where's Junjie?"

"Who?"

"Junjie, the Chinese bloke that was in your bed?"

"I don't know, I checked in this afternoon."

Declan panicked. He knew Junjie would never leave without saying goodbye. Only if he was in trouble or only if he...but Declan didn't want to think it. Quickly, he wrenched the mattress off his bed and felt inside the small hole he had cut in the rear of the box spring. His money was gone—all of it. He ripped off the bed spring lining completely. Peter the German sat watching in astonishment. The money was really gone. Declan sat down and put his head in his hands. He felt sick. He got up and ran down the stairs to the youth hostel office. "What happened to the Chinese guy, Junjie, in my room?" he asked Johnny.

"Gone back to China. Left in a hurry. Said he didn't want to complete the entire year program. Didn't give you a goodbye kissy then?"

***

DECLAN SAID NOTHING BUT turned and ran straight to The Fiddler's. The bar was busy. Friday happy hour was in full force as Irish and English accents mingled with American above the din of the sound system playing Irish folk music. In their usual place at the far end of the bar were Zane, Seamus, and several other men from Ray's crew. Zane looked up and saw Declan rushing towards him. "What's up with you? You look like the cops are after yer!" said Zane.

"Worse than that, mate. I think Junjie stole all my money from my hiding place in our room."

"What?" said Zane, "You mean you've been hiding your cash in the room! How much did you have?"

"Well, yeah. I'm not legal so can't open a bank account, can I? I had nearly four thousand dollars."

"Jesus fucking Christ! Four-thousand! There are ways around the bank account problem, you know—you just have to go to the right bank. I should have told you this stuff. Shit. I'm sorry, mate."

"Not your fault. You're not my babysitter."

"That fucking Chinese bastard. I never did trust 'im. Sneaky bastard 'e was," replied Zane.

"It all adds up now, don't it?" said Seamus.

"What a cunt. Are you sure he left? Maybe he's staying somewhere else?" said Zane.

"Youth hostel says he's gone. I could always try the restaurant he worked at in Chinatown. They might know something."

"I'll go with yer," said Zane.

"Me too," said Seamus.

Zane then shouted, "Who's up for doing over the restaurant?"

Michael, Fin, and a couple of other of Ray's men said they'd come.

"Right then, lads, one more pint and we'll get down there and sort this out!" shouted Zane.

***

THREE PINTS LATER, DECLAN, ZANE, and Seamus made their way from The Fiddler's to the subway on 50th Street and Broadway. The bravado of the other men had subsided, and they decided to stay in the comfort of the bar and watch a football game. Declan, Zane, and

Seamus arrived at the Canal Street subway station within fifteen minutes and quickly proceeded to Junjie's workplace. Without discussing exactly what their plan was, the men entered the small Oriental Garden Restaurant on Elizabeth Street in the heart of Chinatown. The restaurant was a moderately priced establishment with no host, tablecloths, or waiting line. Just three of the ten or so tables were occupied. The three men walked directly to the far side of the restaurant, where two cooks were preparing food behind a large open-backed food bar. Zane shouted to one of the middle-aged Chinese cooks, "Hey, you. Where's Junjie?"

"Junjie?" the man replied in a heavy Chinese accent.

"Junjie Chen," said Declan.

"Chen?"

Just then, a short wiry Chinese man dressed in a waiter's outfit several sizes too big for him, appeared from behind a bamboo door and said, "Junjie gone. Went back China today."

"Why did he leave?" asked Declan.

"Said enough New York. Made enough money so go home."

"Well, he stole four thousand bucks from my mate 'ere," said Zane.

"Nothing do with me. He gone, so you go too," the man said as he shook his hand at the three men.

Zane and Seamus, in particular, were not happy with the man's reply. They had been drinking Guinness for two hours and were not ready to be reasonable. Zane turned to Seamus and Declan and said, "Well, lads. I think we 'ave a bit of a situation here. Now, Junjie owes us four thousand dollars, and we don't know where he is. So, I think we need to transfer some of that debt to Confucius 'ere."

With that, Zane lifted a chair above his head and smashed it down on the food bar, causing glass, noodles, soup, and food dishes to fly in every direction. Seamus picked up a chair and shouted, "Fucking wankers!" And proceeded to smash the food bar too—whipping a chair several times over the glass enclosures. The three men turned to leave the restaurant, whereupon Zane picked up a small table and threw it through the large plate-glass front window.

They then ran north on Elizabeth Street. "We're Irish so fuck off!" shouted Seamus to a Chinese onlooker as the men ran down into the large Canal Street subway complex and quickly disappeared into the labyrinth of passageways. They jumped onto the first train headed north. Hearts pounding, breathing heavy, and with broad smiles, the three men laughed as the train pulled away from the station. Within thirty minutes, they were back at The Fiddler's, where they spent the rest of the night trying not to brag too loudly of their exploits.

***

THAT NIGHT, BACK AT the Youth Hostel, Declan was shocked to find a letter left on his chest of drawers that he had apparently not seen earlier. In it was a letter written in broken English:

> Declan. Sorry. Had no choice.
> Big trouble for me in China.
> I pay back one day.
>
> Junjie.

Declan lowered his head. He recalled Junjie helping him when the police had beaten him. He folded the letter and put it in his backpack.

***

THE NEXT DAY, ZANE told Declan to go to the Asian Photo Shop on 42nd Street and buy a fake photo ID. "Get the type with a Social

Security number on it. They charge an extra five bucks, but it's worth it."

"Don't they ask for any verification for the details you give them?"

"No. It's all just a load of bollocks. That's why they're on 42nd Street. There's a constant line of New Jersey teenagers walking from Port Authority to get a fake ID so they can take them back to Camden and buy Olde English 800 from their local gas stations."

"Oh, right. Got it."

***

DECLAN MADE HIS WAY to 42nd Street and to the Asian Photo Shop, which was directly in the middle of Seventh and Eighth Avenues at 246 West 42nd Street. In the window, a large sign read, "Personalized Color Photo ID cards, Typed and Laminated," and as Zane predicted, inside there were already three teenage girls with excessive makeup waiting for their ID cards to be laminated. A fidgety Chinese boy, no older than eight, sat by the door on a stool and asked Declan, "ID card?"

"Yes."

"Fill this out. Then sit on chair over there."

Declan filled out the information card with another of his fake Social Security numbers and the address of the youth hostel. He paid twenty dollars to a lady, who appeared to be the boy's mother, had his picture taken, and the information hand typed onto a card. Within five minutes, he walked out of the store with an "Official Identity Card" that stated he was now twenty-one years old and legally able to drink alcohol in America.

Walking back towards Broadway, Declan passed Ripley's Believe it or Not! and recognized a man with large, black-rimmed glasses, excessive acne, and a toothy grin. It was Josh Rubenstein, the man who sat behind him at the Waverly Theater on his first night in New York.

Declan slowed down and approached the man. "Looking for some action there, bud?" asked Rubenstein.

"No. Don't you remember me?"

"Not really. Were you the guy in the bathroom last night looking for anal?"

"No. It was nearly three months ago at the Waverly. You sat behind me."

"Oh yeah. I remember now. The English guy. Hey, so you changed your mind about checking out the scene here?"

"No, I haven't. But I owe you something."

"You do?"

"Yeah. Remember you were wanking behind me?"

"Wanking? What do you mean?"

"Jacking off. You jacked off right behind me."

"Oh yeah! That was probably me," replied Rubenstein, with a smirk on his face.

"Yeah, so I owe you this," said Declan.

Declan raised his right fist and thrust it square towards the man's nose—sinking his shoulder into the impact and leaning into the blow. Rubenstein fell onto the ground, held his bloodied nose and whimpered. Several people inside the foyer of Ripley's came out to see what was happening, looked on, and chuckled at Rubenstein. Others walked by as if nothing had happened. Declan left without saying anything else. Rubenstein called out, "Asshole!"

As he continued north on Broadway, Declan felt strong. He reflected on his three months in New York City. He had seen so much, had encountered many obstacles, but now, with his unexpected vengeance on Rubenstein, he felt empowered. Still hurting from the betrayal of Junjie, Declan nonetheless felt he would now be able to face almost anything. He felt he knew the system, had friends, had found love, and now could cope with life in New York City. However, his faith in people had been lowered, and he worried he might eventually turn into Louie from The Boathouse Café. Junjie had not just stolen his money, he had stolen his sweat and hard work over three months.

But that didn't take away how strong he felt physically. The months of hard labor on Ray's team of men had made him physically the strongest he had ever been in his life. His legs, arms, chest, and forearms bore muscles he had never had before, and he didn't appear to have an ounce of fat. With this physical strength, he walked proudly up Broadway, exuding confidence. He thought of his brother—his dead brother. The world had taken much from him, and now he told himself that *from this day forward, he would make anyone pay dearly if they dared try to prevent him from attaining his American Dream.*

***

THE FOLLOWING MONDAY, AS he lay in bed, Declan heard something being pushed under the door. He looked down and saw a note with his name on it. Inside, he found another message from the youth hostel office: "Please call Isabella Ber." He felt guilty he had ignored her first note. She had been good to him, she was a good person, and she was from a good family. He compared her family to Marie's, and the contrast was stark. The Bers had treated him as if he were one of their own, had shown him a kindness he had never known. On the other hand, the Coopers from North Carolina had been nothing short of hostile.

He thought of Isabella, too. She wasn't as attractive to Declan as Marie. Marie was simply sexy in a way Declan had never experienced. Little Isabella was not sexy, but she had a deep humanity about her that seemed to set her apart from anyone Declan had known. He wondered if it was possible he was making a mistake with Marie; he wondered if, perhaps, Isabella was the person he should be seeing. He certainly could imagine himself talking with Isabella about things Marie had no interest in—especially books. But it was Marie who excited him physically; she created a passion in him he had never known. When he was with her, he had not a care in the world—he was happier than he had ever been. In any case, he phoned and agreed to meet Isabella at Columbus Circle that evening.

***

LATER IN THE MORNING, Declan took time off work and opened a savings account at the Lower East Side People's Federal Credit Union. Zane had recommended it to him as a "bloody top-notch place with decent people and no red tape" where many Irish illegal immigrants banked. Declan was able to open a new account with his fake ID and the small amount of cash he had left. The credit union was mainly aimed at the local Hispanic population. Still, the young, striking Puerto Rican assistant (as indicated on her name tag) told Declan they were "happy to have him as a customer." Afterwards, when he arrived at 5 Riverside Drive, Ray called him into his office and said, "I heard what that fucking Chinese guy did to yer. So, I'm upping yer pay. You'll be on twenty-five an hour as of today."

"Thanks, Ray, that's really decent of you."

"No problem, just keep yer money in the bank. Right?"

"Yep. Got it all sorted out today."

***

THAT EVENING AFTER SHOWERING and changing his shirt, Declan walked north to Columbus Circle to meet with Isabella. He saw her waiting for him with an expectant look on her face. They said hello to each other, and Declan kept his hands in his jeans, not really knowing if he should hug her or not. She looked different from how he remembered. She wore tight black pants and a white long-sleeved blouse that easily exposed the beige, flowery-patterned bra that held up her small, pert breasts. They walked through Central Park, enjoying the cool breeze.

"It seems like ages since I've seen you," said Isabella.

"Yes, it does. I would have phoned sooner but I've been so tied up just trying to get a foothold here. But I haven't forgotten about you. If it weren't for you, I would have been back in England now."

"No. I don't think so. You would have figured a way out. You're that type of guy."

"I don't know. When I called you that first time, I was in bad shape. You sort of gave me renewed hope. You were so kind. I will never forget it. Never."

"I'm glad I could help."

They talked more about Declan's job, his new friends, and the theft of all his money by his roommate, Junjie. Isabella could not take her eyes off Declan as he described what had happened to him. "I just can't imagine going through that. Doing that job and then being deceived and robbed by that asshole. I never had to go through any of that when I was in England. I had it easy."

"Well. I just have to keep going. At least I had a full week's worth of pay in my pocket when I found out. If he had robbed me on Saturday or Sunday, I would have had absolutely nothing left."

"You really are something else. Looking on the bright side like that."

"Well, it's been a few days since it happened. You should have seen me on Friday," and he frowned as he recalled himself, Zane, and Seamus running through Chinatown, chanting, "Ireland," after having smashed up the Chinese restaurant. And then he thought of the Bers and their kindness, and he thought of Sir Roger de Coverley, and he felt almost ashamed. But at the same time, he knew enough about himself to know that he had an anger inside, and he felt it could be growing worse as he encountered more of these hardships. And it worried him.

They walked past the ice-skating rink, then the pond, and over to the Plaza Hotel. Declan wished he could afford to pay for a horse-and-buggy ride for himself and Isabella. If it wasn't for Junjie, he felt sure he would have done that small thing for Isabella. She seemed so fragile to him, and there was a part of him that wanted to hold her and reassure her. It was the same feeling he had felt when he left her at the airport. Instinctively, he knew she would not come all this way and dress the way she did just to pass the time. He looked at her face as they walked. He realized, too, that she wore more makeup than she had on their other encounters.

They found themselves at the Pulitzer Fountain, where they paused to look into the gushing water. Declan recalled himself crying at that very spot when he thought of his brother. Isabella looked up at Declan and hesitantly stepped towards him. Surprised and not quite knowing what to do, he nonetheless held her waist.

They looked into each other's eyes, and he leaned down to peck her on the cheek. Then he looked at her again and realized she wanted more. Her mouth was half open, her eyes had a dreamy, expectant look. She wrapped her hands around his waist. Declan leaned down and kissed her on the lips. Her mouth opened wider, and she pulled him closer. He pushed into her, falling into what she desired. He kissed her fully on the lips, pressed himself into her, and felt her small breasts against his chest. She wore a sweet perfume that he knew was for him, and it seemed to intensify his desire—he then understood that this girl, with her books, cuddly animals, and diaries lined up on her writing desk, wanted him to make love to her.

This aroused him, and he pushed his hardness into her belly, letting her know she was indeed wanted. He kissed her neck—her skin so pale and smooth, and he noticed the dark curly black hairs at the base of her neck. He had never been with a Jewish woman—back in

England, the Jewish community kept to themselves. He felt happy she had let him into her life, her home, her world. He nibbled her neck, ran his hand over her breast, kissed her fully on the lips again, and pressed his tongue onto hers. She groaned. He realized he really wanted her, but suddenly pulled away. "I think I better go," he said.

"No. Please don't."

"I probably should."

"Why? It's someone else. You've found someone else?"

"Sort of. I'm not sure where it's all going. I don't know. I just don't want to...let you down or anything."

"Does it really matter? I mean, we can just see how it goes, right?"

"I suppose so. Can we meet up again another time?"

"Sure," Isabella replied despondently.

They were both breathing hard. They sat down on the edge of the fountain, and after composing themselves, Declan said, "I'll get you a cab; you shouldn't ride the subway at night."

"I know," said Isabella.

"Of course, I'm sorry. I forgot you are from here," replied Declan, feeling foolish.

"It's OK," she giggled.

He looked at her face and realized she was still flustered. Then, oddly, he thought of Sir Roger de Coverley. And it occurred to him that this was not a way to conduct himself. He realized he needed to be honest with Isabella and Marie. But, he didn't know what to say. He felt confused, as if events were unfolding too fast. He knew Sir Roger would simply tell him to do the right thing regardless. And he knew Sir Roger would tell him he needed to think about Marie before he started any relationship with Isabella. However, Declan was still unable to say anything.

They walked to the edge of the pavement, and Declan hailed a cab. "Where are you going?" he asked.

"I'll go to the NYU library. I like it in there."

He said goodbye and gave her a short kiss on the lips before she stepped into the taxi. As he watched the cab pull away, Declan had mixed feelings. He felt committed and duty-bound to Marie, but still felt pulled by Isabella—he didn't know why. But he knew it was wrong and could hurt them both.

Chapter Sixteen

The next day, Declan and Zane began work at seven a.m. at 5 Riverside Drive, and by the time they caught a subway from work, it was dark. "I'm stuffed, mate. Let's get a couple of eight-hundreds and drink back at the youth hostel," said Zane.

They arrived at the youth hostel with a bagged bottle of Old English 800 each. Inside, they wasted no time drinking. Zane told Declan of a letter he received yesterday, "From my sister. She said my parents got a visit from the cops. My ex-fiancée no longer wants to press charges, but the cops are still pursuing my case and are in contact with the American embassy."

"Christ," replied Declan, "well at least your ex-fiancée seems to have calmed down a bit."

"Yeah, but my dad gave all the information he knew about me to the cops. Luckily, they don't have this youth hostel address. They only have my mate's address where I first stayed and my post office box."

"That's good—shouldn't be able to find you then."

"Yeah, but now I know that the cops are never going to give this thing up. Even without the help of my ex, they are still gonna try and lock me up."

"Can't you try and strike a deal with them? Negotiate?"

"My sister told me to do that. She even looked into it. I'd need to have a solicitor lined up before I return to Australia. Most likely, I'd be arrested at the airport, but I could have a legal rep with me who could get the ball rolling on some deal. But, it would definitely mean spending time in jail."

Declan took a large swig of his beer.

"Jeez, I am sorry to hear all those issues," replied Declan.

"It's OK."

***

DECLAN LEANED BACK AGAINST his pillow, and although he was concerned about Zane, he couldn't stop thinking that Zane's problems were all self-inflicted. He began to reflect on his own situation, worried about how everything would turn out for him in New York City. The nightly drinking with Zane and the Irish crew was becoming monotonous, and he felt he could be doing something more meaningful in both his work and social life.

"Dec, why don't you tell me a story or something about your hometown and your mates? I know I've been harping on about my problems in Oz ever since we met. Be nice to hear something different for a change."

"OK, I have a good one for yer," he replied.

Declan then shared the story of how, when he was sixteen and in high school, he and Chris were chosen by the local Department of Health and Social Services to take part in The Duke of Edinburgh Award. The award was established to "help develop young people—particularly those from disadvantaged backgrounds." Their school and the DHSS enrolled them in the program to "hopefully show how the most at-risk can gain confidence in a difficult activity."

Their first activity was to hike part of the South Downs Way—a trail that stretches one hundred miles from Eastbourne, just forty miles east of Brighton, inland to Winchester. "The walk was split up into four, fifteen-mile segments. We were supposed to do one section each day, starting outside Brighton, and camping for three nights—well, that was the plan. Anyway, we had to carry all our gear except for tents and food for dinner. So, we had smallish backpacks with just spare clothes, water and snacks, first aid kit, and other stuff. It was hard going, especially when it rained."

Declan lit a cigarette and inhaled deeply as he continued. "When it rained, it was a bloody disaster—the fields were like mud pits and there was nowhere to rest. By the end of the first day, we were completely knackered, but we kept up well with the hundred or so other people. There were a lot of groups well-trained for the event, but we just took it easy since we were only on it to 'ave a laugh."

"Yeah, too right, mate," said Zane.

"Well, the second day was hard but by the third we were feeling much better since we knew there was just a day left. We finished the day's walk in Petersfield in Hampshire, but then lost our map, which had the directions to the campsite. So, when we got into the town, we were dog-tired and weren't sure where to go. We asked a couple of people if they knew where the campsite for the Duke of Edinburgh Award was, and they didn't know, but one old codger told us where a local campsite was. So, we walked through the town center and took off down a street that had a sign pointing to a caravan park. We thought that might be it, so we kept going and came up on some football fields where we saw a school behind a load of trees. We walked off towards the school, thinking they'd probably help us out."

"Anyway, after crossing the football fields, we get to this clump of trees and saw something. It looked like a kid standing by a tree with his head tilted to one side. But it was odd since he wasn't moving. I looked at Chris and he said, 'Fucking weird, that mate,' and we slowly walked over."

"Oh shit, I think I know what you are going to say," said Zane.

"We got closer and saw this kid in his school uniform, and he had hung himself from the tree with his school tie. I'll never forget that tie—it was blue with red stripes. And it really dug into his neck. His eyes were rolled back into his head and his tongue was sticking out his mouth."

"Fuck me. How long had he been dead then?"

"He'd been dead all night they told us later. Anyway, that's not the end of it."

"No?"

"Well, the weirdest part was that his trousers and underpants were pulled down to his knees and his dick was sticking out like it was ready for action, if you know what I mean."

"You mean on the jack?"

"Yeah. Plus there was this gay porno mag on the ground by his feet. Also, his feet *could* touch the ground."

"What? So, he could have stopped himself choking?"

"Yeah. At first, I thought it was some kind of joke or a setup. But Chris and me talked about it and reckoned he did it to himself."

"What, so he wanted to kill himself and thought he'd have a wank on the way out?" said Zane, confused.

"Well, turns out there's a weird thing some people do where they wank off and also sort of try and hang themselves. But, they don't really want to die—just cut off the air to their lungs and it makes them feel harder."

"No fucking shit! I've never 'erd of that. Christ. Who the hell would have thought to do something like that?"

Declan went on to say they went straight to the private grammar school, Churcher's College, and told the headmaster. School staff went out and sealed the area off, then called the police. Declan and Chris were questioned for the whole day, then driven back to Brighton. They never got a chance to finish the walk.

"The worst part about it was we were told it was a suicide and we were not to tell anyone about the 'unusual aspects of the case.' We got kicked out the Duke of Edinburgh program and had to tell our headmaster we got lost and couldn't finish. Everyone took the piss, and

I got in several fights. Kept hearing people say, 'Need directions to yer next class, Declan?' If it weren't for the dead body we could have got back on course and finished."

"Sorry, mate," said Zane.

"Well, I actually did eventually finish the course," replied Declan.

He went on to say how the whole incident kept bothering him. Not just the boy dying, but the fact that they were stripped of the chance to finish. For weeks afterwards, he could not sleep well—kept thinking of the boy and wondering why it happened. Declan could not comprehend the whole thing, and so one weekend, six weeks later, he caught a train to Petersfield and walked to the place within the trees where the boy had died. There was no longer anything to suggest something unusual had happened—even the branch the boy hung from was still intact.

Declan wondered why the boy chose this location to do what he did. It had a clear view of the school, and the boy could easily have found a more secluded spot. He sat down on a fallen tree and smoked a cigarette. When finished, he stubbed out the cigarette on the ground and left it there. For some reason, he wanted to leave something of himself there. As he stood, he noticed something glistening in the leaves of a thick bush behind. He knelt and pulled a small object from the bush. It was a silver cufflink with Churcher's College sail ship emblem engraved on it. Declan put the cufflink in his pocket, then walked to the tree where the boy had hung himself and lightly stroked the branch where the boy had hung.

Declan left the wooded area, walked through the village and made his way to the South Downs trail to finish off the course he failed to complete the first time. It took him nine hours to walk the final seventeen-mile stretch to Winchester, where he made his way quickly through the dark to the train station.

"So, I eventually did finish the course, and I felt better for doing so. Not just finishing the course, but having a cig where the kid died. It finalized the whole thing for me," said Declan.

"Christ, that's some fucking story, mate," said Zane.

***

The following Saturday morning, Declan met Marie in the Shakespeare & Co. Booksellers and then made their way to the youth hostel. Declan already knew Zane would be gone, and Pete the German always seemed to be out. As soon as Declan locked the door, they embraced and locked in a kiss. It had been several days since they had last made love—they undressed quickly and Marie fell back onto the bed, causing her hair to spread across the pillow. Declan was ready for her, with a condom quickly fitted, and entered her slowly. He had learned to try and stay more in control of himself and proceeded in a slow, rhythmic pace, which brought a smile to Marie. They kissed as he continued this pace until he could no longer hold back and began to thrust harder and harder into her. She groaned and wrapped her legs around his back.

Declan increased his tempo and force, causing Marie to stretch her arms back and brace herself against the wall. He thrust harder and harder, causing the bed to rock and squeak loudly. It was soon over.

Lying side by side, Declan turned to Marie and asked, "Do you ever wonder how it is things happen?"

"What do you mean?"

"I don't know. It's just a few months ago, I would never have dreamed I would be having sex with a beautiful American girl. It never occurred to me as a possibility. I only imagined the future as pretty bad, actually."

"I know exactly what you mean. Life seems so routine, and then something happens, and you realize your life will never be the same again. It can be a shock."

"Yes, exactly."

After a few minutes of rest, they took swift showers, left the youth hostel and made their way toward Lady Sophia's on Fifth Avenue. They stopped off and Marie bought beef steak, parsnips, carrots, and leeks for one of Lady Sophia's favorite foods: Brown Windsor Soup. "She always complains that American restaurants never make it. So, occasionally I fix it for her."

***

Upon entering 1040 Fifth Avenue, Felix the doorman greeted Marie and said, "Good morning, Mr. Declan."

"All right, mate?" replied Declan.

Inside, as he pressed the elevator button, Declan said, "You were right about that guy already knowing my name."

"He's paid to know everything. There are a lot of rich people in this block, and Felix is part of the security," replied Marie.

The elevator door opened and a tall, feline of a young woman, with blonde hair wrapped in a bun walked out. She gave a slight nod to Marie and left the building. Declan stood staring at the lady.

"You know who she is?" asked Marie.

"I recognize her, but can't put my finger on who she is. Absolutely beautiful though."

"Kate Winslet."

"From the Titanic movie?"

"Yes, that's her. I've seen her in the building before."

"Nice."

Lady Sophia had left the door unlocked for them, and on entering the apartment, they found her reading a book and listening to Debussy's Preludes. "Come on in, darlings." They sat down and Marie said, "I've been to the store and I'm going to make Brown Windsor Soup."

"Lovely," said Lady Sophia, "but let's have a drink first before I put you both to work."

They drank: Lady Sophia a gin and tonic, and Declan and Marie vodka and Cokes. Marie had earlier told Declan that Sophia had a few jobs she needed doing around the apartment and asked if he wouldn't mind doing them. "She doesn't like the guys the apartment building sends her—she thinks they are 'common as muck' or something like that."

Declan was more than happy to help out and went to the store to buy supplies to replace several bulbs and fix a broken door handle while Marie made the soup. Later, in the afternoon, they all sat down at the kitchen table and ate the delicious Brown Windsor soup.

"We saw Kate Winslet getting out the elevator this morning," said Marie.

"Indeed, I heard she is giving a speech at the UN on women's rights," replied Sophia.

"Does she live here then?" asked Declan.

"I don't believe so. She stays with some chap right above me. Bit of a floozy these days, so I'm told."

Sophia lit a cigarette. Declan would have liked one himself, but didn't feel enough at ease to light one. Sophia inhaled heavily on the cigarette and continued, "But, I'll tell you one thing—every now and then I'll hear a scream up there in the middle of the night whenever she is staying."

"A scream?" asked Marie.

"Yes. Very loud and distinct. Then, usually crying. I can only just hear the crying, but sometimes I find it difficult to sleep and am just lying there. My bedroom is right under theirs."

"What, you think it's nightmares then?" asked Declan.

"Yes, darling. Must be. I don't know what her background was like. But something bad must have happened there. Plus, she needs to find a steady man instead of frolicking about with that fat old bastard up there."

"Maybe she's a prostitute on the side?" replied Declan.

They all laughed, and Lady Sophia said, "Well, young Declan. I'm finally starting to see your sense of humor! Mind you, I don't think you are too far from the truth, my boy. This women's rights stuff at the UN is complete rubbish—just a publicity stunt for the girl."

Declan helped Marie wash the dishes as the sun set over Central Park and shone a red hue on the west side of Manhattan. They decided they would go for a drink at Bin 71 before Declan would walk Marie home. They said goodbye to Lady Sophia. Marie kissed her on both cheeks and turned to Declan and nodded to him to approach her. Declan did so and received a kiss on the cheek from the old lady.

***

"She's a fascinating person," said Declan as they walked by the side of The Metropolitan Museum of Art.

"Yes, she's seen so much and lived in so many places and knows so many people here in New York. It's a shame, though, she doesn't get out much anymore. I can tell she really enjoys our visits. I know she likes you, too."

"Well, I like her. Maybe we should take her out sometime. To a restaurant, perhaps?"

"Yes, she would like that."

"Maybe The Boathouse Café. I could tell her how I got fired as a dishwasher after three days!"

Marie laughed and replied, "She already knows! I tell her everything about you now. She loves the stories I've shared with her. I think that's why she's taken to you so easily. She doesn't like many people—especially her own kids."

"That's unfortunate."

"Well, I haven't told her you're just really a vagabond from the projects," joked Marie.

With that, Declan turned to her and said, "Well, let me show you what I think of that."

Marie took the bait and ran onto the grass; Declan chased her and quickly grabbed her by the waist, pulling her down. He lay on top of her. She looked up at him with a grin and breathed heavily into his flustered face. He brushed her dark hair away from her cheeks. She looked into his eyes and said, "Declan. You know, I think I love you."

He wasn't surprised and replied, "Well, I think I love you too. Actually, I know I do."

"Since when?"

"Since that time in The Fiddler's when you started singing that Irish song. I'll never forget it. You looked and sounded amazing."

They kissed. Declan broke it off and said, "We better get out of here. There are some weirdos in this park at night."

"Yes, I've heard the stories!"

They walked out of the park and turned south on Central Park West. Declan felt that Marie was all he ever needed, all he ever wanted. He believed that his new life had now begun with Marie.

***

AT BIN 71, THEY had several glasses of wine and for the first time talked about a future together. They chatted about apartments in New York and the different neighborhoods. Declan told her more about his plan to attend Community College like Junjie, and that it was just a matter of time before he could quit Ray's job and find real security in stable work. Marie said she was going to start teaching, "I've always wanted to teach children how to play the piano," she said.

"You'd be great at it. You have so much patience."

Marie said it would be easy for Declan to get a Green Card to stay and work in the United States. "All you need is a good lawyer—anyone can get in here these days."

"Well, thanks!"

"I didn't mean it like that. Anyway, you could even do it the easy way and marry me. You'd get an instant green card."

"Would you marry me then?"

"Yes, I would. But you'd have to ask me first."

Declan paused for a few moments and then asked, "Marie, will you marry me?"

"Why do you want to marry me?"

Declan suddenly felt anxious, but said what he truly felt.

"Because I love you."

"Yes. Yes, I will marry you, Declan."

Chapter Seventeen

Several days later, Declan's AT&T phone card number was no longer working. "You're bloody lucky it lasted that long. Some only last a week," Zane told Declan.

After work that day, Declan walked to Columbus Circle, the location Sanat had recommended, and bought a new number from an African man who was easily identified as such by his shoulder-length dreadlocks. Declan then went to Trump Plaza and gave the front desk personnel a smile as he made his way to the bank of phone booths with plush chairs. As he sat down and began to dial the number, a man wearing a blue suit and holding a walkie-talkie appeared at his side and asked, "Sir, are you a guest here?"

Declan regretted not going back to the youth hostel and showering—it had been a particularly tiresome day at work. Instead, he had come to the hotel with his hair full of asbestos dust.

"No, I'm not. Just wanted to use the phone for a quick call."

"Sorry Sir, they are for guests only."

Declan said nothing and awkwardly walked past the front desk, head bowed, and out of the hotel.

He made his call from the pay phone near the youth hostel on the corner of 55th Street and Sixth Avenue—it was noisy and hard to hear as rush hour traffic stopped and started at the busy intersection. "'Allo Chris, it's me, Declan. How's everything?"

"All right, mate. Haven't heard from you in a while."

"Found any decent work yet?"

"No, still signing on the dole. But been picking up days here and there down at the Brighton Marina—they're doing a big expansion."

"Cash in hand?"

"Yeah, some Indian geezer is running a small mob down there. Trouble is I 'ave to phone him at six a.m. every morning to see if there's any work."

"Why?"

"Well, he never knows how much work he'll be given until early that morning, and if he needs me it takes over an hour to get out there. It's all a big hassle, and the neighbors go nuts when I leave DR barking here all day."

"Yeah right. Any news on my mum?"

There were a few seconds of silence and Chris replied, "I was hoping you wouldn't ask."

"What?

"Well, she's back home now. Let me say that."

"OK," replied Declan, nervously.

"She was in hospital for a few days. She got mugged going into your block of flats. She's OK now. Nothing serious. Just a few cuts and bruises."

"Christ. Gotta be those fucking Russians."

"That's what I thought at first, but she's saying she doesn't think it was them."

"Who else would mug my mum? It's pretty obvious she has no money."

"Yeah."

"Bloody hell. I've got to get back there as soon as I can to get her away from there."

"Well, hurry up, mate. I'm seeing more of these Russians moving into the area. It's like little Moscow here these days."

***

THAT EVENING, DECLAN WAS supposed to meet with Marie and one of her nanny friends she'd recently met in the park. Declan didn't feel like going—he felt like heading over to The Fiddler's with Zane. He wanted to get drunk and forget the harsh situation his mother was in, and the fact that there was nothing he could do about it until he had enough money to get her out—he felt frustrated, he felt angry. But, he had promised Marie, and so after showering, he made his way on the subway to the John Street Bar and Grill located in the heart of the Financial District.

The bar bustled with after-work get-togethers for financial district workers. Declan was surprised by how many people were there on a Wednesday evening—it was as busy as The Fiddler's on a Friday evening. "They all drink after work," said Marie, "it's the pressure of the job. They come in here to unwind."

"Oh right," replied Declan.

Marie noticed her friend, Stacy, and waved her over. Stacy was several years older than Marie. She had a rugged prettiness, with bleached blonde hair, long eyelashes, and large breasts that were accentuated by her low-cut dress. Everything about her seemed excessive.

"Glad to meet you, Declan," she said with a gleaming smile.

Declan nodded.

"Where's Mitchell?" asked Marie.

"He's over there," said Stacy as she pointed to a rotund man with slicked-back hair, wearing an expensive-looking grey-flannel suit. He was talking flamboyantly with several other men.

"Hey Mitch! Over here!" shouted Stacy through the noisy crowd.

Mitchell wandered over and looked Declan up and down, thrust his hand out, and said, "Mitch, how yer doing?"

"Declan, nice to meet you."

"Mitchell is my boyfriend and works on Wall Street. He does a lot of wheeling and dealing," said Stacy.

"Oh, that's nice," replied Declan.

"So, what do you do, Daniel?" replied Mitchell.

"It's Declan. Right now I'm just working in construction," replied Declan.

"Oh, you're a developer?" replied Mitchell.

Declan looked to Marie for help, but she offered none. "No, I'm actually helping to renovate an apartment block on Riverside Drive."

"OK, gotcha," said Mitchell who turned to Stacy and said, "I'll be right back. I just have to talk with this guy about the morning trades."

Declan quickly finished his drink and told the ladies he would go to the bar and buy more. He ordered the drinks but was in no rush to return to the group. He'd taken a dislike to Mitchell. He sat at the bar, finished his drink alone, and ordered another for himself. A few minutes later, Mitchell appeared at his side and said, "Need some help?"

"No thanks. Just about to take these back to the ladies. Do you need another?"

"Yeah, but it's OK. I'll order it."

"So, what exactly do you do on Wall Street?" asked Declan.

Mitchell looked bored and frowned.

"OK, buy me a drink and I'll tell ya."

Declan wondered if he was joking but realized by the serious look on his face that he wasn't. He ordered the man "bourbon on the rocks" and listened as he explained: "I'm a day trader. I buy and sell stocks on the same day. I make profits by leveraging large amounts of capital to take advantage of small price movements in volatile stocks."

"Volatile?"

Mitchell sighed, picked up his drink from the bar and took a mouthful. "Volatility is a measure of the expected daily price range—I look for big volatility since it can mean bigger gains."

"But, you could also lose a large amount?" asked Declan.

"Oh yeah. That's the risk. But, if you are smart you can make it pay."

"I see. That's interesting."

"Yeah, and you wanna know what's really interesting?" replied Mitch, suddenly appearing agitated.

"Sure."

"Well, I just lost two hundred K today due to you goddam limeys."

"What?"

"Yeah, I had a partner bet on an energy company in London. I dumped two hundred on it based on a tip. And guess what? Those lazy motherfucker limeys went on strike and caused the stock to tank! I could go over there and kick all their lazy asses myself!"

Declan's face reddened. He guessed Mitchell had been drinking for several hours since trading had stopped at four-thirty, but it did not help lessen Declan's anger. Since the phone call with Chris, Declan was already upset, and anger began to envelop his mind. He grabbed hold of Mitchell's lapels and pushed him against the bar. Quickly realizing how weak the man was, he forced him down further so his head was bent back on the bar. Declan's strength was such that he only needed his left arm to pin the man down by the throat onto the bar. The man clutched Declan's wrist and shouted, "Get this thug off me! Help!"

Declan raised his right fist and said, "I could break your fucking face, you wanker."

The bar quietened. Everyone was looking at Declan, including Marie and Stacy. The barman came over and said, "OK, buddy. Out!"

Declan dropped his fist and released Mitchell, then turned and walked out of the bar. He did not look at Marie.

***

FROM THE BAR, DECLAN just walked. He walked fast. Even though he was nearly four miles from the youth hostel, he wanted to walk to try and quell his anger. He was angry at many things, not just the man who insulted his country. He was angry at not being able to help his mother, he was angry at being robbed of all his money and, mostly, he now realized, he was angry that he had to leave his home because his brother had killed himself and, in so doing, left his mother to face the Russian thugs alone. It occurred to him that if his brother were not dead, he would not be in America, far away from everything familiar to him.

Suddenly, he no longer wanted to be in America. The alcohol had fueled his new opinion that most Americans were like Mitchell, in that they believed the USA was somehow superior to the rest of the world and no other country was worth anything. Just like Mitchell had said: the English were just, "lazy motherfucking limeys." He tried to think of all the positive things: Marie, Zane, Isabella, The Fiddler's Irish Pub, and Ray. But it was no good. He wanted to go home—he'd had enough of America.

He came to a bar and went inside. He sat at the bar, where four men were watching several TVs showing a baseball game. No one sat at any of the small number of tables strewn about the floor. Declan walked to the bar and ordered a vodka and Coke. "That'll be nine bucks," the barman said, holding out his hand distrustfully. Declan drank quickly, then ordered another, and another. The other men at the bar kept their eyes forward. Occasionally, one would comment on the television, but that was the extent of communication. The emptiness of the bar reminded Declan of his visit to North Carolina. The feeling of needing to return home to England intensified. He got off his stool and tripped slightly as he walked out of the entrance.

Declan felt himself stagger a little as he made his way from the bar. He wasn't quite sure where he was, but he knew all he had to do was keep walking north and he would eventually find his way back to the youth hostel. Keeping the Hudson River on his left would ensure he was walking north. Eventually, he found himself on Seventh Avenue and was relieved to be going in the right direction.

***

DECLAN STOPPED AT A small park to rest. Christopher Park seemed a pleasant haven from the street and was filled with benches. He chose a seat several feet away from a group of three men. Declan took out a cigarette from his jacket and lit it.

"Hey! Could I have a ciggy?" shouted one of the men who got to his feet and walked over to Declan. It was dark, but Declan was able to see quite clearly that the man wore tight-fitting spandex pants. Declan gave the man a cigarette and was irritated when he then said, "Well, how about a light?"

Declan gave the man his BIC lighter. The man sat down next to Declan and asked, "Who might you be then?"

"Declan. Just having a rest here, if you don't mind."

"Oh, English! That's nice. I love that Prince William—even though she's still in the closet. Are you just visiting?"

"No, not really. Doing some work," replied Declan, starting to feel irritated. He noticed, too, that the man had a faint layer of mascara on his eyelashes.

"Well, you seem a bit young to be all this way from home. If you like, my friends and I can show you around the bars here."

"Are you gay?"

"Yes, of course."

"Just wondering 'coz I'm not gay. I'm just sitting here having a cig. Is that OK?"

"Now, now. No need to get huffy."

With that, the man spun on his heels and walked back to his friends. Declan could hear them laughing. He quickly finished his cigarette and decided to light another before leaving the park. Then he realized the man had taken his lighter. It was just a cheap plastic BIC model that cost him fifty-five pence, but Declan had had it with him since he left England and wanted it back. He walked over to the three men sitting on the bench and asked, "Can I have my lighter back?"

"Oh, he wants his lighter back. Going to be nice to me now that you want something. Is that it?"

"I just want my lighter."

"Why don't you show us your little dick first and then we'll give it back to you," said another man, sitting languidly with his arm resting on the back of the bench.

"I'll even suck it for you if you like," said the third man, giggling.

"Just give me the fucking lighter. OK?" demanded Declan.

"Oh, aren't we the nasty one? Now, we could all be friends. We don't have to have the bru-ha-ha. We can go to the bar and have a few drinks instead, you know. Live and let live, that's what I say."

"Give me the lighter first. Then I'll think about it."

"No. You go to a bar with us first, and then I'll give you the lighter."

Declan felt himself get hot in the face again. He felt the anger surging up inside.

"Look, I just want the lighter back. OK? Just give it back and I'll be gone."

"Don't you know there are three of us and only one of you?" questioned the man with his arm over the back of the bench.

"I don't give a toss. I just want my lighter."

The third man then said, "Jackie, why don't you shove it up your ass and then give it back to him?"

With that, the three men started laughing. Declan felt the anger boil inside. He lunged at the man who had his lighter and pinned him against the bench with his elbow and began rifling through the man's pockets. "Help! Help! I'm being murdered!" screamed the man.

The other two men jumped to their feet and immediately pulled Declan away and down to the ground. Declan knew he had to get off the ground quickly, or he would be beaten as he was by the NYPD.

He swung his arms and legs about and got to his feet and promptly punched one of the men several times in the face. The second man picked up a fist-sized rock and ran at Declan and lunged towards his head. Declan stepped back and kicked the man in the stomach and then punched him twice on the side of the face.

"Help! Help! Someone call the police! We are being attacked by a savage!" screamed the man who stole the lighter.

Declan ran from the park and north on Seventh Avenue for several blocks before slowing to a walk. He was still without his lighter.

***

WITHIN FIVE MINUTES, A screech of tires rang out. Two car doors slammed, and a man shouted, "Stop right there. Don't move!"

He turned to see two police officers approach him with their right hands resting on top of their holstered pistols. The man closest to him then said, "Put your hands on top of your head!"

The second police officer withdrew his pistol and rested it against his thigh as if to signal to Declan that he had better do what he was told. Declan had never seen an unholstered gun before, and he instinctively put his hands on top of his head. The first police officer moved quickly and yanked Declan's hands behind his back, then snapped on a pair of handcuffs. The cuffs were tight and hurt his wrists. The other police officer stood just ten feet from him, put his pistol back in his holster, and spoke into a walkie-talkie, "Suspect in custody." The officer holding Declan then said, "You have the right to remain silent. Anything you say can and will be used against you in a court of law. You have the right to an attorney. If you cannot afford an attorney, one will be appointed to you. Do you understand these rights as they have been read to you?" Declan said nothing—still in shock. "Do you understand?"

"Yes."

Without another word, Declan was whisked into the back of the police car. "What did I do?"

"You are being charged with assault and battery."

"Those guys stole my lighter; I was just trying to get it back."

"Tell it to the judge."

"One of them came at me with a bloody big rock—what about arresting him?"

"We've had several independent witnesses say you attacked a man in Christopher Park."

"But they were all together—how can that be independent?"

"Like I said, tell the judge in the morning."

The car smelled of urine, the seats were torn, and the plastic dividing panel between the front and rear of the car was cracked and scratched. The vehicle turned south, and within minutes they were driving through Chinatown and towards a massive brick complex, then under the building via an electronic gate. Declan saw a sign that read "Central Booking," and then he was shuffled out of the car and told to sit on a bench in a small room with several other handcuffed men, all of whom were Black. A few minutes later, he was told to stand. The arresting police officer removed Declan's handcuffs while another fat, greasy-looking man attached a plastic zip-tie to bind his wrists.

The man then searched Declan and placed his few possessions in a plastic bag and placed a "voucher" in the back of Declan's jeans pocket. He was then told to sit in a chair in front of a computer. Declan asked, "How long will I be here?"

"If you are nice, keep your mouth shut, don't cause no trouble, you could be out in twelve hours. If you are a trouble-maker, you could be down in The Tombs for days," replied the greasy man.

"I see," replied Declan.

The man then asked for Declan's name, address, and occupation. He then asked, "Nationality."

"Irish," replied Declan.

"Are you a legal resident?" the man asked, while looking at Declan for the first time. Declan hesitated and replied, "No. Tourist."

The man continued typing with one finger from each hand. It seemed to take an excruciatingly long time to type in all the details. Declan was then fingerprinted, photographed, and had a DNA swab taken from his mouth—all this in front of a small gallery of Black men who were sniggering and whispering to each other. It appeared to Declan that the other prisoners were relaxed and familiar with the whole routine. Declan was then led down two floors and through a door and into a hallway filled with open-faced cells. The cells were approximately fifty feet by fifty feet, and each of them was full of men. Declan's wrist tie was cut off and he was pushed into a cell. Immediately, he realized two things: he was in a cell with over twenty Black men looking at him, and there was nowhere to sit. Not quite knowing what to do, he walked to a small, unoccupied area by the toilet. The area was covered in urine and small feces.

One man in particular took immediate interest in Declan and walked over to him. The man was tall, tattooed, extremely muscular, and had a crazed look about him as he stood just inches from Declan and said, "Who da fuck you?"

"Declan."

"What'd you do motherfucker?"

"Murder."

"Don't shit me—you ain't killed no motherfucker! Don't fuck me, man!"

Declan was scared. Scared for the first time since he had encountered Commando at the Pink Houses. He instinctively understood that this man could quite easily kill him with only his hands. Declan sensed the man was comfortable with violence, and Declan felt absolutely helpless as he stood in the corner by the toilet. Declan had always been bigger and stronger than most people he'd known in school, but this man exuded a power and strength unknown to him, and together with the man's anger and being locked in a cell with him, Declan felt weak with fear.

Just then, a man even more muscular than the first wandered over to Declan's side and told the other man in a calm, almost relaxing voice, "Now I don't want no trouble tonight. You hear? We all get processed in a few hours, and I don't want no-one to fuck dat up. OK?"

The first man looked at the larger man with irritation, then turned and walked to the front of the cell, where two men immediately made space for him. The man now standing next to Declan said, "You better stay close to me tonight."

"Thank you," replied Declan as he felt overcome with emotion: it was a mixture of relief, respect, despair, and thanks. Declan's legs were shaking as he realized he was not so tough. And, oddly, he thought that he didn't want to be that tough—it seemed the price would be high.

The atmosphere in the cell was tense for the next several hours, but at four a.m., several guards came and started calling people's names for their arraignment hearings. New York City processed so many arrests that there were arraignment hearings eighteen hours a day, 365 days a year. By five a.m., Declan's name was called. He turned to his protector and said, "Thank you." The man stood leaning against the wall, with his arms folded, and nodded. To Declan, the man looked like a gladiator.

Declan was led along a hallway by a guard to a small courtroom where he was told to stand at a table in front of the judge, who glanced briefly at him before reading what Declan guessed was his arrest paperwork. An overweight man with thinning hair approached Declan and said, "I'm your public defender. Just plead not guilty. OK?"

"Yes."

The man then gave Declan his business card and said, "Give me a call if you have any questions. I'll contact you when your next hearing comes due."

"OK."

The judge then looked up and said, "Declan O'Neill. You have been charged with assault and battery on Jack Kettling—also known as: Jacklyn Cunylarge."

Several other prisoners waiting on the bench in the rear laughed.

"Quiet in the courtroom. How do you plead?" asked the judge.

"Not Guilty."

"Bail set at one thousand dollars."

The public defender then said, "Your honor. Mr. O'Neill has no prior record, and this is a misdemeanor. We ask that he be set free on his own recognizance."

"Mr. O'Neill has no apparent community connections. Therefore, he is a flight risk. But, I'll set bail at five hundred dollars," replied the judge.

Declan was then led out by the guard to another small side room, where his public defender asked, "Can you get hold of five hundred bucks?"

"Not right now. I'd have to go to the bank."

"You can't do that. You'll have to call someone, and they'll have to come here and pay. A bail bond company can't help since you aren't a legal resident alien, so they won't cover you. You'll need to get cash."

"If I can get the money, when would I get it back?"

"Once the case is over, the bail money will be returned to you. Can you call someone for help?"

Declan thought hard. He couldn't call his closest friend, Zane, since Zane hardly used his cell phone, and when he did, he turned it off at night. He couldn't call Marie since her employers would be extremely unhappy. He had only one option: Isabella. The lawyer gave Declan a quarter and, using the payphone on the wall in the interview room, he dialed the number: 516-487-0900, hoping that Mr. or Mrs. Ber did not pick up the phone. Unfortunately, a sleepy-voiced Mrs. Ber did answer. Declan apologized and asked if he could speak with Isabella due to a "bit of an emergency."

"Declan? Is that you?" asked Isabella.

"Yes, unfortunately, it is. I've been accidentally arrested and need to borrow five hundred dollars to get bailed out."

"Oh, my God. Declan, what is going on?"

Declan tried to calm her and was ashamed to include her in this messy business. But, he told himself he had no choice unless he wanted to face an extra day or two in the holding cell until he could make other arrangements.

"Also, I hate to sound pushy but the public defender said he can keep me out of the cells if you can get here in an hour."

"I will. Don't worry."

***

WITHIN FORTY-FIVE MINUTES, A guard led Declan to the public waiting area, where Isabella stood with a look of concern. Declan signed a paper for his few possessions. Then, he approached Isabella, and instinctively they hugged. Isabella said, "You look terrible, and your hands are shaking."

"You got here so fast."

"It's early. There's no traffic."

They walked to a nearby coffee shop, and Isabella bought them both a coffee. Declan explained the whole ordeal. Isabella asked, "Who were the friends you were with at the bar?"

"Some friends of mine," he replied.

"Any girls?"

"Sort of."

Isabella looked sad. She did not ask any more questions.

As the sun rose higher and peaked above the Soho buildings on Broadway, Declan turned to Isabella and said, "I owe you so much. I really do. I don't know what is going to happen to me. But I know I will never ever forget how you have helped me."

Isabella looked at the pavement and replied, "It's nothing."

Declan realized that it probably sounded as if there was an air of finality in him saying, "I'll never forget..." Looking at her, he realized how lucky he was to know her. He realized he was causing her some pain. However, at that moment, in his shaken state, it was beyond him to understand how to comfort her.

But, more than this, he felt ashamed of himself. Not only had he acted with poor judgment that night and put his whole journey in jeopardy, but he was deceiving two women. He knew if he was to have a clear conscience, he needed to come clean with both Isabella and Marie. However, he felt fearful of saying goodbye to either one of them.

Chapter Eighteen

For the next several weeks, Declan focused entirely on his job—working as many hours as Ray would allow. The team of men had now made their way down to the seventh floor of the twenty-story building. Zane was busy seeing Lucia each night and since she did not like to drink, visits to The Fiddler's had tapered off. Declan mailed Isabella five hundred dollars in cash to repay his bail money. He was still confused about his feelings for Isabella—feelings he pushed away into the back of his mind. His engagement to Marie happened fast, probably too fast, in his mind. But he saw a new future ahead with Marie, and a way to help his mother, *and was determined that nothing would now stop his plans*. He wrote and re-wrote a letter to Isabella three times before settling on the following:

Dear Isabella,

Thank you once more for helping me out of a difficult situation. The whole episode is quite embarrassing, and I feel sure you think of me in a lesser light after having to pick me up from jail. It's not quite the thing you would expect of anyone who enjoys reading of Sir Roger de Coverley. I am sure Sir Roger would be appalled if he knew of my actions.

If it means anything, I must tell you that I am trying to

be the best person I can. I try to learn all the time, but sometimes my feelings or temper get in the way, and it's hard to prevent an outburst or ill-conceived action from occurring.

You are such a wonderful, caring, beautiful person. I will always be in your debt and forever your friend.

Yours Affectionately,

Declan

***

DECLAN CONTINUED TO MEET Marie once or twice during the week at Bin 71 for a drink or outside The Lincoln Center for ice cream. On the weekends, they were able to spend more time together—usually starting with a rendezvous at the youth hostel. Partly out of embarrassment—fighting three gay men over a fifty-pence BIC lighter—and partly out of not wanting to explain how he attained bail, Declan did not tell Marie of his arrest at Christopher Park.

However, on their first meeting after the Mitchell incident, Marie had asked Declan, "Why do you get so angry all the time? It seems every time I see you, there's been an incident or some drama. I don't get it. Ever since you landed here, it's been one fight after another. I am just worried it will get worse, and I don't know how it will all end up for us."

"I'm sorry. I let things get on top of me. I've always had that problem. I am doing my best to control it. But it sometimes seems the situations I get myself into force me into action."

"Maybe that's just it. Maybe you could think about not putting yourself in the situation in the first place."

"Yeah, I get it. I know."

***

A FEW DAYS AFTER his arrest, as Declan entered 5 Riverside Drive, Ray called him into his office, told him to sit down, and said, "Declan, I've been watching you. You keep yer head down and keep going. Even through all the bollocks you've come up against. Most of the boys here would have pissed off back to Ireland, but you've stuck it out."

"Yeah, well. What else can yer do?"

"Well, that's it. Isn't it? Most of these lads don't get it. That's why I guarantee yer in one year most of them will have nothing to show for their work except a coupla dozen nights on the piss."

"Probably so," replied Declan, wondering what Ray was trying to say.

"Anyway, I've got one or two more jobs on tap after this one and I'm going to need someone to run one of them. Would yer be interested in managing one of them?"

"Well, yeah. I would. Thanks for thinking of me."

"Well, you've a good head on yer shoulders. You can always find mugs to do the donkey work, but running the job to make a good profit needs a bit 'a brains. Know what I mean?"

"Yes, I think I do."

"All right then. Well, that's it for now. I'll get back with yer in a few weeks once this job winds down and we can talk about the new jobs coming up."

"OK. Thanks Ray."

"Oh. One more thing: don't tell any of the lads yet, will yer?"

"No. I won't."

Declan went back to work and realized his grand plan could still work, regardless of his latest problems. With the extra money a supervisor role could earn him, he thought he may only need to work a full year and then have enough savings to return temporarily to England and help get his mother safely back to Ireland, away from the Russian drug dealers. He became excited at this prospect—excited that his American Dream might come together much quicker than he had imagined.

***

LATER THAT DAY, A dump truck arrived outside the building and unloaded several tons of topsoil onto the front pavement. Minutes later, Ray came to his men and said, "Lads. Stop what you are doing. I want you to get down to the ground floor and use the wheelbarrows to move the topsoil and cover all the dust in the back courtyard."

"Are you serious there, Ray?" asked Seamus.

"Yes, I am. We have to cover up that fecking dust before the old granny gets wind of it all."

The men spent the rest of the day with wheelbarrows and shovels, leveling the, by now, huge mound of asbestos, and then covering the whole back area with topsoil.

"If the authorities find out what's going on here, Ray will be in deep shit," whispered Seamus to Declan.

***

THAT NIGHT, ZANE INVITED Declan and Marie to dinner at Lucia's family house. Lucia's family had taken well to Zane, and he had spent many evenings there with Lucia and her parents. Lucia was the youngest of six children, and the only one still living with them.

Declan was curious to meet the girl who had caused such a change in Zane. Not once since they had started to date had Zane come home late to the youth hostel. And not once had Declan seen him drunk—it was as if he no longer needed alcohol to prop himself up.

The Garcias lived above their small, 72nd Street hardware store, just a few blocks from 5 Riverside Drive. After cleaning themselves up, Declan and Zane met Marie at the corner of Broadway and 72nd Street, and they all made the short walk to the Garcias. The window of the hardware store was packed with all types of things: drills, trash cans, mousetraps, boxes of nails, and light bulbs. Zane led the way through a door to the left of the storefront. They walked up four flights of stairs to the Garcias' apartment. On the way up, Zane explained that Mr. Garcia now owned the entire building. "He came here with nothing and started off as a shop-hand twenty years ago at this store, but eventually bought the owner out of the business when he retired. Then, gradually over the years, he's bought each of the three floors above the shop. Now 'e owns the whole bloody building! How's that for the American dream?"

"Amazing. Bloody amazing," replied Declan.

As they reached the top floor, Zane coughed loudly and a strange wheezing noise seemed to come from deep within his lungs as he tried to catch his breath. "You all right mate?" asked Declan.

"Yeah, just give me a minute before I knock on the door."

"How long has this been going on?"

"Just started a few days ago."

Zane knocked on the door and Mrs. Garcia appeared with a bright smile. "Hola, Zane!" she said as she rose on her tiptoes to kiss Zane on both cheeks. She was a chubby woman with thick black hair pulled back into a ponytail. She wore large, dangly earrings and a bright-colored skirt and blouse. Zane said, "These are my very good friends, Marie and Declan."

Mrs. Garcia kissed both of them on the cheeks. "Zane tell me lot about you both," she said. "Please, come in my home."

Inside Mr. Garcia shook their hands firmly. He wasn't much taller than Mrs. Garcia. He was a stocky man who appeared to have known nothing but hard work all of his life. He made a point of looking both Declan and Marie in the eye and saying, "Welcome to my home." Lucia was standing in the background behind her parents. Zane introduced her to Declan and Marie and she quickly shook each of their hands before stepping back. She shared Mrs. Garcia's wonderful smile but appeared as shy as Zane had mentioned.

"Come, come. Sit down and let us drink a toast," said Mrs. Garcia.

Everybody walked into the living area, which was small and filled with photographs of the Garcia family. There were few decorations or books, and definitely no golf trophies, thought Declan — it seemed the Garcias were mainly interested in their children and extended family. The furniture looked well-used but was spotless and comfortable, and as Declan sat down, he remembered something from his grandmother's house in England: the couches both had pieces of lace draped over the arms.

Mrs. Garcia set a tray with a pitcher of lemonade on the coffee table and served everyone a glass.

"Marie, you American, no?" asked Mrs. Garcia.

"Yes, I'm from Raleigh, North Carolina. I've lived in New York for about a year and a half. Just a few blocks from here."

"North Carolina. Yes, I think I have heard of that place. You like New York City?"

"Yes, I do. It's hard to make a living here, but I like the people."

"You have to work for yourself in America," said Mr. Garcia, "you never make money work for other people. You have to have your own business. Plus a good accountant!"

"You are right there Mr. Garcia," said Zane.

"Declan, what you do here?"

"I work with Zane in construction, but I'm in the process of enrolling in the community college."

"That's good. Very good. I like that. Just don't give up. My only advice: never give up!" and with that Mr. Garcia laughed heartily.

As Mr. Garcia poured himself another drink, Declan looked over at Zane and Lucia and noticed them holding hands and looking into each other's eyes. Declan was taken aback by how infatuated Zane was with his girlfriend. It was the first time he had known Zane to act in such a way. Lucia, too, seemed happy to just stare at Zane and ignore the conversation. This seemed like a love Declan had not seen before, and he felt this may be the reason why the Garcias were so happy. Happy that their youngest daughter had found her true love. Declan looked at Marie, patted her hand, then looked down at the floor.

The group made their way to a small dining table, and Mrs. Garcia brought out an endless parade of tacos, burritos, and quesadillas, together with side dishes of rice, black beans, and salsa. The food was hearty and filling. Zane and Lucia hardly spoke at all—opting to watch each other eat. Mr. Garcia led the conversation with his talk on how he first came to America: "I had nothing: just the clothes I wore and a few dollars. Back then, you could walk across the desert and no one stopped you come to United State. I got job with a farmer. He helped me very much and I saved money. Then two years later come to New York."

"Why did you choose New York?" asked Declan.

"Well, everyone tell me, don't come to New York—too expensive to live. So, I come here since if it expensive then must have better pay. I don't care where I live—as long as I make good money."

"Makes sense," Declan replied.

"In this country, you make as much as you want. Just work—work hard—every day. Everyone can make it here. Except Blacks. America not like Blacks. They still are slaves to Americans. I feel sorry for them. They have no chance—none."

Declan felt sad. Mr. Garcia spoke of the plight of Black people so matter-of-factly and so honestly that it shocked him. Then he came to understand his friend Dwayne's life in the Pink Houses a little better. He sat back and pondered how his own trip to America would be different if he were Black. He quickly came up with a list of seven things that he felt certain would not have happened:

One: Would not have become friends with Isabella and her family.

Two: Would not have become friends with Zane.

Three: Would not have been offered the job at The Boathouse Café.

Four: Would not have been offered the job with Ray.

Five: Would not have dated Marie.

Six: Would not have visited the Garcias.

Seven: Surprisingly, he realized he probably would not have become friends with Dwayne.

The evening ended with tequila shots, and as the group left, there were hugs all around. Zane and Declan walked Marie back to her apartment. Zane asked Marie, "What do you think of the Garcias?"

"Wonderful people. Such a loving family. It was so nice to see how much the parents loved their children."

"Marie, there are tears on your cheeks. Why are you crying? What's the matter?" asked Declan.

"It's nothing. Really. Just something about them. The Garcias. So much love."

"Oh, come here. I didn't realize you were so sentimental."

Declan then put his arm around Marie and kissed her on the top of her head. They said no more about the subject.

Later, as the men walked back to the youth hostel, Declan said to Zane, "I hardly talked to Lucia. I don't think I know anything about her still!"

"She's sort of quiet. Takes a while to get to know her."

"Yeah, seems that way."

"Took me nearly a year just to get her to go out with me. But now we're inseparable."

"Good for you, mate. You seem like a great couple together."

***

THE FOLLOWING WEEKEND, MARIE had to go on a trip with her employers to Washington, D.C., and asked Declan if he would drop by Lady Sophia's on Saturday to check on her. Declan was woken early that morning by Pete the German slamming the door on his way out. Declan stirred and rubbed the sleep from his eyes. The asbestos removal work was beginning to take a toll. A few minutes later, he could hear Zane taking a shower. Declan sat up in bed and smoked a cigarette. Zane left to spend the day with Lucia so Declan locked the door and slept for another two hours—a daytime luxury he had not experienced in quite a while.

***

IT WAS RAINING AS Declan left the youth hostel. Making his way north on Broadway, the rain became heavier. He ran for cover under a canopy of bushy horse chestnut trees and was able to navigate his way across the park to Fifth Avenue under the umbrella of trees that lined the south part of Central Park's pathways: Blue Spruce, Lebanon Cedars, Saucer Magnolias, Eastern Hemlocks, and Hackberries.

"Could use an umbrella there, Mr. Declan," said a smirking Felix as he opened the heavy glass door to the 1040 Fifth Avenue building. Declan felt like telling him to "Fuck Off," but instead said nothing and made his way in the elevator to Lady Sophia's. "Good God, you are soaked!" said Sophia, "Come on in and I'll get you something to dry off with."

She shuffled away and came back with several towels. She also handed him a large shirt and said, "Dry off and put this on. I can put your clothes in the dryer."

"Thanks, Sophia."

Declan was standing in the living room, with Sophia close to him. She seemed in a sort of daze. Declan was not sure if he should leave and change elsewhere. As if sensing Declan's trepidation, Sophia said, "I'll just sit over here," and she walked with her cane and sat in her usual chair close to the sliding glass door. She kept her eyes on Declan as he slowly removed his shirt and dried his upper body with the towel. He wiped down his jeans and quickly mumbled, "No problem with the jeans, they're just a bit damp," and promptly put on the dry shirt. Feeling a little awkward, Declan asked, "So, is there much you need me to do today, Sophia?"

Sophia smiled, sat back, lit a cigarette, crossed her legs, and with her cigarette arm resting straight up on the chair arm, said, "Darling, I really don't need much help today. Just a tidy-up in the kitchen, and a hoover around in the dining area. No need to cook either—I can order in some Chinese take-out."

Declan quickly made himself busy: washing the dishes in the kitchen, cleaning the countertops, then vacuuming around the living room and surrounding areas. It didn't take more than an hour to do the work, and he wondered what Sophia would want him to do next—he felt out of place there without Marie and suddenly missed her.

"Since it's stopped raining, do you mind if we go for a walk?" asked Lady Sophia as she stood, hand on cane, in the kitchen doorway.

"Of course, I love to walk," replied Declan, relieved to go outside.

***

WITHIN A FEW MINUTES, they were walking from the apartment building. Sophia automatically wrapped her arm around Declan's elbow as they crossed Fifth Avenue at 85th Street. The air was humid as the sun shone through the thin gray dissipating clouds. They walked past the Metropolitan Museum of Art and along part of the reservoir pathway, then a short walk south to an area where several baseball teams were practicing. Sitting on a bench, Sophia said, "That's about as far as I can walk these days. Do you have a cigarette?"

"Camels?"

"That'll be fine."

Declan lit a cigarette and handed it to Lady Sophia, who inhaled deeply. Declan decided it would be proper to light a cigarette himself—the first time he had done so in Sophia's company. After a few inhalations, he felt more at ease with Sophia and said, "Do you know, I slept in this park a couple of times?"

"Marie said something about you not having a place to stay early on."

"Yes. It was quite an experience. It was when I first arrived—I had nowhere to go. Heard various screams during the night and made friends with a group of rats!"

"Good God. That's awful. What the bloody hell were you thinking?"

"Well, I was a bit stupid when I first arrived, didn't really prepare for anything. I left England in a bit of a hurry."

"Why did you leave in the first place?"

"I just needed to get away. I had a lot on my mind. My brother died, my dad had been gone for a while, my mom was drinking, and...well, I couldn't handle it all, really."

"Christ. I can see why you left. Better that than staying and getting yourself in trouble."

"Exactly."

They smoked and sat quietly as the crack of bats hitting baseballs penetrated the air. "Do you know it's my birthday today?" asked Sophia.

"No, I didn't. And you have no plans?"

"At my age you realize there's no celebrating birthdays—just means a year closer to death. And I have no family that gives a damn, anyway. But, you are here and that's all that matters."

"Well, I wished I'd known—would have got you something."

"Stay for dinner. I'll order Chinese, and we can open some wine."

"Deal."

***

BACK IN THE APARTMENT, it was still too early for dinner, so Declan opened a bottle of wine. They sat on the patio and watched the throngs of people come and go from The Met, as the sun lowered over the Manhattan sky. Within an hour, they had finished off the bottle, and Lady Sophia phoned a local Chinese restaurant to order dinner.

They ate at a small dining table, and Declan wondered how many people had ever eaten dinner with Sophia in her apartment—he doubted many had. Sophia asked him to put "any" album on the record player. Declan looked along the dozens of records on her shelf and found they were mostly ballet or opera. He picked out Puccini's Tosca and, on sliding the record out of its sleeve, noticed the vinyl was covered in scratches.

The wine made him comfortable, and he realized that on all the occasions he had been with Sophia, he had been nervous. Her stature, background, and apparent wealth intimidated him. The wine made him calmly think through things and understand that this woman was smart enough to know he was nowhere near her class. Knew he was most likely from a council estate; knew he had no security, no safety net, no network of friends or family to support him. Knew, in fact, that he was running from something more than he had told her. But, after all this, he knew for some reason she liked him and wanted him around. He decided they were friends.

"Why did *you* come here in the first place, Sophia?"

"I'll tell you, darling. But first, go and open up another bottle. Get that 1975 *Romanée-Conti*. It's on the top shelf. Been sitting there for bloody years—it reaches its peak right about now."

Declan retrieved the bottle. The label read: *Appellation Ro-manée-Conti Controlée, Année 1975*. Declan was unsure what this meant in English and felt too embarrassed to ask Lady Sophia. He knew enough French to recognize that it was a wine controlled by Romanée-Conti, so it came from that specific region, and, of course, was from 1975. More than that, he did not know.

"What region is Romanée-Conti?" asked Declan.

"Burgundy, darling."

"Oh."

They drank, and Lady Sophia told Declan some of the details of her past life: her days at Roedean Girls' School, her time at La Sorbonne, and her attempt to become a professional ballet dancer. "But I was not small enough, you see. I am too big-boned. You have to be a nymph to excel as a professional. It's all I ever wanted, but no number of years of training would ever be enough to overcome this big arse of mine. Believe me, I tried. I practiced night and day and literally starved myself. But it was no good."

"So, you came here after not making it in the ballet?"

"No. No. I became a choreographer at The Royal Ballet and was eventually promoted to Artistic Director. I was doing quite well until I fell in love."

"What, your late husband?"

"No. NO."

"Sorry."

"It's OK. I get a little irritated sometimes. Anyway, I had been married, had children—you know one of them—but then Phyllis came along."

"Phyllis?"

"Phyllis Bernice Spira. You must have heard of her?"

"A ballerina, I think."

"Not just a ballerina: *Prima Ballerina Assoluta*. An angel. An angel sent from heaven to earth. The most beautiful, elegant, exquisite creature that has ever been on this earth. To watch her dance is to watch God himself. I fell in love with her the day I first laid eyes on her."

"You were married at the time, then?"

"Yes, that was part of the scandal. We started spending time together in a cottage I had in Seaford, Sussex. But once the papers got wind of it, it was all over. They got a picture of us walking the beach hand in hand and put it on the front page of the *News of the World*. Well, that was it. Marriage over, sacked from my job, and Phyllis even left me. My whole life was over, so I came here. Here to the bloody colonies!"

Declan was unsure how to reply. But now it all made sense to him: Sophia's isolation, the absence of her children, the sense of betrayal from her home country. "Things are a little different now, but back then, that sort of thing was very hush-hush. Caused quite a stir in the establishment, I can tell you."

"What happened to Phyllis?"

"Oh, everyone forgave her and forgot about her little 'transgression.' Once she started dancing again for the Royal Ballet, it was like our whole time together never happened. But, for me, my life was over. I couldn't get a job in the industry I loved," she said with a cracked voice.

Sophia wiped her eyes, and Declan looked down.

"The sad thing is I loved her."

"I'm sorry, Sophia."

"Not to worry. At the end of the day, all you are left with in life are a few good memories. A kiss here and a kiss there—that's all you'll ever get to cherish."

A third bottle of wine was opened, and Declan wanted to cheer up Lady Sofia somehow, so he walked to the nearest grocery store to find a cake. He found no real birthday cakes but was able to buy a box of half a dozen pink cupcakes.

When he returned to the apartment, Lady Sophia smiled and ate half of one. "Thank you, Declan. It really is so nice to have you here."

"It's no problem. I like to visit you. I really do wish I'd known it was your birthday so I could have brought you something."

"There is something you could give me, if you don't mind."

"What's that?"

"I want you to kiss me on the lips. I want to feel such young, beautiful lips on mine—just one more time."

Declan sat rigid for a second, took a deep breath, wasn't sure what to say, and then found himself replying: "OK. But then I will leave."

"Yes, very well."

Lady Sophia slowly rose to her feet. Declan did the same. Sophia edged her way around the table, not looking at him. Then, as she stood in front of him, she lightly stroked each of his cheeks with her fingertips. She looked up into his eyes, paused, and said, "Darling, you'll have to bend down. I'm not that tall."

Declan slowly bent down and brought his lips to hers. He could smell her flowery perfume and closed his eyes as she gently put her lips on his. She opened her mouth slightly and pushed onto his lips firmly, and moved her lips around his. Declan was only able to hold onto the kiss for a few moments before pulling away. "I think I'd better go."

"That was a wonderful birthday present, Declan. Thank you."

"But Sophia, please tell me something. I don't understand this kiss with me, and yet you and Phyllis?"

"It's quite simple, my boy: I adore true beauty of any kind."

***

ON THE WAY HOME, Declan's mind swam. He was not sure how to comprehend the evening—such a strange evening. How was he to tell Marie about this? He decided not to tell her anything and realized it was the third time he had withheld something from his fiancée.

Still drunk and wanting to talk with someone familiar, Declan phoned Chris from a street phone. "'Allo mate. You all right?"

"It's fucking four o'clock in the morning! What's going on?"

"Not much. Just checking in. Have you seen my mum?"

"No mate. And look—I can't keep babysitting her. It's been months now, and you really should have fixed her up with a mobile. If I see her, I'll ask how she's doing. But it's not my problem. OK? I've got my own fucking business to run now."

"Your own business. What do you mean?"

Silence.

"Well?"

"The Russians. They're not bad blokes it turns out. Gave me a pretty good gig dropping off deliveries for them."

"Deliveries?"

"Yeah, you know what I mean. Merchandise delivery and collections. They like the fact I've got me dog, Death Row. And the money I'm earning is incredible. Plus I can still sign on the dole."

"So, you are working for the Russians? The bastards that killed my brother?"

"Dec, they didn't kill him. And I've been thinking I might be able to help cut some deal with them to help you out too."

"Deal?"

"Yeah, a way to pay back Sean's debt quicker with you doing a few jobs for them."

"Fuck that mate. I'm disgusted by this. This is bollocks. Bollocks."

Declan hung up the phone.

CHAPTER NINETEEN

THE FOLLOWING MONDAY AFTER work, Declan was to meet Marie at Bin 71. Earlier that day, he had found what he thought would be the perfect apartment for them to rent: an Upper West Side location, clean, affordable, and promised to him by a workmate who was returning permanently to Ireland. Declan was excited to share the good news with Marie.

The bar was almost full as he made his way through the crowd and sat opposite Marie at a small table. A less than half-full bottle of wine sat next to her empty glass. "Am I late?" asked Declan.

"No. We said seven p.m."

"Oh, just wondering since you'd already had a couple of glasses."

"Was here a bit early and got carried away."

Declan could sense something was not quite right. It was the way Marie's shoulders hunched, how she crossed her arms on the table, and how she seemed to lean over her wine. Her face, too, had deep frown lines. The woman he knew—strong, carefree, and lusty—was absent.

"What's the matter? You look a little...different."

"I don't know. I've just been thinking. That's all."

"Oh, right. You don't seem yourself."

"Have a drink, will you?"

They drank. Ordered another bottle. Marie talked about her trip to Washington D.C., and Declan told her about his visit to Lady Sophia's—except for the kiss. Through this, Declan could sense there was something on Marie's mind, but he tried to ignore it. He hoped she would tell him what was wrong when she was ready.

"I heard about another apartment coming up. The bloke works with us and is moving back to Ireland next month. I'm going to take a second look at it tomorrow after work—it's just around the corner from the Shakespeare Company Bookstore."

"Declan. I need to tell you something."

"I can sense that. Something's not right."

"I know that us being engaged and moving in together is a big deal. You know, once we do it, I'll have to get another job and, well, you know, it gets really serious for us."

"Yeah. What's wrong with that?"

"Well, I guess I'll just say it. Because I've got a feeling you won't feel the same when I tell you this."

"Tell me what?"

"I was raped two years ago. In college. By several guys. I don't want to lie to you anymore about my past."

"Jesus Christ. By *several* guys?"

"Yeah. They were in Delta Iota Delta Fraternity."

"A fraternity?"

"It's like a club. Anyway, I was a freshman."

Several tears slid off her cheek, and she covered her face with her hands. Declan moved to the chair beside her and put his arm around her shoulder. "I'm sorry. I'm sorry this happened. But it doesn't change anything with us. It's over now anyway. Been a couple of years, so we can move on. Together."

"But it's not over. It'll never be over. I can never get it out of my mind, and I'm sorry, but it keeps on and on in my mind."

"Christ. Well, you might as well tell me the whole story."

Declan gulped his wine and shakily placed the empty glass on the table.

"They always had these off-campus parties that were kind of in-famous. I had only been at school a couple of months and thought it would be cool to go. I went with just my roommate. That was the stupidest thing I did—going in the first place. We went and got drunk really quickly. They were feeding all the girls margaritas—they had huge bowls of the stuff everywhere in the house. Outside, they set up this big bubble machine, and girls and guys were making out to deafening music. I thought it was fun. There were football and basketball players—and all the prettiest girls from the best sororities."

Declan drank his wine as he watched her anguish grow.

"I got invited to play pool by one of the fraternity brothers. We went inside and downstairs to a basement game room. I felt a little funny down there since there were at least five guys and only me. Two were playing pool, and the other three were drinking shots. They gave me a drink, and it must have been spiked because I don't remember anything much more, apart from being carried to a taxi by those guys."

"How do you know you were raped then?"

"How do you think? My underwear was missing and I had. I had..." She cried again.

"It's OK, I can guess," replied Declan.

"There was blood and stuff in between my legs."

Declan put his arm around her shoulders again, and she leaned into him and cried into his chest. Declan felt like he might vomit, and had to steady himself on the chair as his head became cold and sweaty. He suddenly felt the whole world had again decided to try and destroy his happiness. A sickening, nauseating feeling gripped him deep in the pit of his stomach—it was the same feeling he'd experienced while watching the ambulance men lift his blood-soaked brother from the pavement onto a stretcher and pick up a piece of his skull and place it next to his body.

Neither said anything as they finished the bottle of wine. Declan walked Marie home towards Riverside Drive. As they crossed Amsterdam Avenue, they stopped at Verdi Square and sat on a bench directly in front of the gaze of the statue of Giuseppe Verdi. "There's something else," said Marie.

"More?"

"The two fraternity guys who put me in the taxi told my roommate that if I went to the police, they would post a copy of the movie they took of the whole thing onto the internet. They seemed to be the ringleaders."

"They recorded it? Jesus fucking Christ!"

"That's why I never went to the police. They seemed to know exactly what they were doing—like they had done it lots of times before. They made the videos for security and for their own amusement."

"I can't believe all this."

"I hope we're going to be okay. I'm sorry to spring all this on you."

"I'm glad you told me. I just don't know what to say. I'm sorry. Angry. I don't know. I'm just so sorry it happened to you. I can't understand it."

Declan felt numb. Then he asked, "But why would they release the tapes? Wouldn't it implicate them in the rape?"

"Yes. But I didn't care, I didn't want the whole world to see the videos. But I hate the fact too that those recordings are sitting down there in North Carolina."

"Sure, I can understand that."

"And one more thing came out of it too. I found out a year ago I am HIV positive, and I most certainly caught it during the rape."

Declan couldn't speak. It was as if he was unable to compute everything he had just heard. Each detail seemed to tear away at all that he had accomplished since he had arrived in New York City. But, more than that, seeing the pain in Marie as she tried her best to compose herself brought out an anger in him that he had never known before. Again, the world was a cruel, dark place regardless of how hard a person struggled.

Declan walked Marie home from Verdi Square. Their goodnight hug and kiss weren't as long as usual—just a short hug and peck on the cheek. Declan looked into Marie's eyes. Her face was a mess of mascara and dried tears. "I'll see you on Saturday," he said.

"OK."

"One more thing. What were their names—the two ringleaders?"

"Why? What does that matter?"

"I don't know why. I just somehow want to know everything so I know there's nothing else to tell."

"Ben DeLuca and Josh Belmont."

***

THAT NIGHT, THE NEXT day, and the following days, all Declan could think about was Marie's rape. He kept going over what had happened and hardly slept. He went to the library and researched on the internet all he could on fraternities in American colleges. He learned about the organizations, who ran them, and how a person could join. He also read as much as he could about Marie's school, North Carolina State University. He looked at maps, class schedules, history—anything he could find out about the University. He stopped pursuing the new apartment. But, most of all, he became obsessed with Ben DeLuca and Josh Belmont.

Finally, over the weekend, he saw Marie. They were supposed to go to Lady Sophia's together, but on meeting at Central Park, Declan told her, "I'm sorry, I can't go today. I have to do some overtime for Ray. Plus, I promised some of the lads I'd see them down at The Fiddler's tonight."

Marie looked at him and appeared to understand the change—almost as if she expected it. "It's OK. I'll see you during the week then?"

"Yes. How about lunchtime on Monday in Riverside Park?"

"Sure."

***

DECLAN HAD NO OVERTIME to do for Ray. His mind was still full of emotion and confusion over Marie's disclosure. He walked to The Fiddler's and watched a game of soccer broadcast from England via satellite. He was amongst his own kind: working-class English and Irishmen. He felt at home and ordered pint after pint. He missed England, Brighton, and even the familiarity of the council estate. But, more than anything, he felt angry.

The days of thinking, days of swirling everything around in his mind, had brought him to the conclusion: *Ben DeLuca and Josh Belmont have ruined my life.* He believed they had made irrelevant every hardship he had gone through since arriving at Port Authority back on that cold early-spring evening. They had done a great injustice to Marie...and him. The world seemed more unfair than ever to Declan. His brother had been taken from him, and now his future happiness had been ripped from him. But one thing became clear even through the haze of half a dozen pints of beer: Marie should not have to suffer anymore from this. Someone had to recover and destroy any electronic copies of the incident. But he had no idea what he could do. He didn't trust the Police, and he knew everything would become public if he went to them.

He staggered back to the youth hostel and collapsed onto his bed—one of the rare times he had returned later than Zane. The alcohol only helped him sleep until three a.m. He woke, and his body was in a state of hangover and rage. He pictured Marie being raped by laughing, obnoxious fraternity boys. He hoped it was all a bad dream, but sat up in bed and realized it was not: this was another horror he would have to live with. The rage welled in his stomach—a gushing torrent of hot anger that spread to his mind and made his head pound. "Aaarrgggghhhh!" he shouted and punched the wall: once, twice, three times. Plunging his fist into the brittle plasterboard and cutting his knuckles. "What the fuck is that?" Zane asked sleepily.

"Nothing. Nothing!" replied Declan, breathing heavily.

***

THE NEXT MORNING, HE decided to go to the library and read for inspiration. He knew this was not a situation Roger de Coverley would ever find himself in—but he knew he had to try to come to some sort of resolution in his mind on what, if anything, he should do to try and resolve this distress from which he could find no relief. Declan had risen before the two other men in the room and made his way to a coffee shop close to the main library. He entered the library within minutes of it opening. Already in his mind, he had books he thought might give him some answers: *The Confessions of Augustine*, *The Trial*, *The Essential Confucius*, and even *The Bible*. He spent the entire day—a beautiful, end-of-summer day—reading everything he could.

Finally, by the end of the day, Declan had completed a plan. Such was his anger that his plan contradicted most of what he had read earlier in the library. With a pencil, he wrote the action items of this plan:

> One: Find out where Ben DeLuca and Josh Belmont live.
> Two: Buy a pistol and learn how to shoot it.
> Three: Travel to the rapist's home by Greyhound Bus and retrieve, by force if necessary, all copies of the recordings.
> Four: Destroy the video copies and the gun.
> Five: Greyhound Bus to Washington, D.C., and then

fly home to England.

Six: Help his mother move home to Ireland.

Seven: Once everything is settled, return to Marie in America.

Chapter Twenty

After completing his list, Declan made his way to the New York Public Library's large public computer room. In there, he spent the rest of the day trying to find out the addresses of the rapists. It took a good deal of searching, but by sheer number of online search attempts and cross-referencing multiple different websites, he was able to find their address. They lived together at 212 Pogue Street, Raleigh, North Carolina.

He was then able to plot directions from the Greyhound Bus station to their house, located close to North Carolina State University. He calculated it was less than a two-mile distance—he could walk it in thirty minutes. He printed the map and route. Step one was now complete.

***

That night, Declan invited Zane to The Fiddler's. They sat at the bar drinking Guinness and stepped outside for the occasional cigarette. "So, what's on your mind, Dec? You have a huge frown on your face—what's going on?"

"I have to go home for a bit. I have to take my mum back to Ireland. Plus, I've decided to let things cool down between Marie and me."

"Not breaking up, are ya? You're totally head over heels with her—doesn't make sense you'd break up."

"No, nothing like that. I have to sort my mum out, so thought it would be a good time to just take a break. I don't know, it's hard to explain but I suppose it's like I need to go home and tie up a lot of loose ends so I can come back and really settle down here."

"Yeah, I think I know what you mean, mate. Good on yer. I'm gonna miss yer, though, so you better come back. I need yer now."

"I will. I promise Zane...I will."

Declan felt sad that he could not tell his friend what he was about to do, as if he were deceiving him. Zane had been his best friend during this most crucial time in his life. But he couldn't face telling him what had happened to Marie. He felt the unspeakable should remain unspoken. It made him all the more determined to get this task over so he could move on and get back to where he was with Marie, Zane, and his life in New York. As he thought about this, Declan came to realize that what he was doing wasn't at all logical. He knew it didn't make complete sense. Moreover, regardless of what he did to Belmont and Deluca, Declan knew it wouldn't change the fact that Marie was HIV positive, and that would affect their future forever. But there was a powerful element of anger driving him to do it.

The two friends drank until the bar closed at two a.m., then staggered north on Broadway to the youth hostel.

***

THE NEXT MORNING, DECLAN packed his small number of possessions into his backpack, threw his asbestos-riddled gear into a garbage can, telling himself he could get a clean set on his return, and then walked with Zane to 5 Riverside Drive.

"Arghhh...shite. I always lose me best ones," said Ray.

"It's only temporary—I'll be back Ray. I promise."

"That's what they all say. Mind you, I can't complain. You've been a top-notch employee, so yer have. Phone me when you have your plans to come back, and I'll see what I can do about getting you set up with a supervisor job."

The two men looked into each other's eyes as they shook hands. Declan felt a tinge of sadness on leaving Ray. The man had taken to him and given him stability in an otherwise unstable environment. Declan wanted to say something to Ray, but the words just didn't materialize.

Outside, Zane was smoking a cigarette, waiting to say goodbye. "Now, you will come back won't you? You've been a bloody decent mate, and it's just not going to be the same for me without you around."

"Yes, mate, I will. I want to come back and help sort out your problems back in Oz."

"Yeah. That would be bloody great if we could go over there together. In fact, I'd bloody love it."

The two men looked at each other. Instinctively, there was no handshake—just a hug. Declan could smell the mix of asbestos and Stetson in Zane's hair. They stood back, and as Declan lifted his backpack to his shoulder, he noticed Zane's eyes were watery. "Goodbye, mate, I'll see you soon."

Declan walked the thirteen blocks to Marie's apartment building and dropped off an envelope at the front desk for her. The letter inside read:

Dearest Marie,

I'm so sorry not to have the courage to see you in person, but I have to return to England to sort a few things out. My mum's situation has worsened, and I need to get her moved back to Ireland as soon as I can. It's just a matter of time before the Russians do something stupid over there.

This really has nothing to do with what you told me the other day, although I must say it has upset me. It seems like a good time to return and fix some things I should have done sooner. I believe I'll be in England for four to six weeks. I do hope you will wait for me so that we can build our plans for the future. I will phone you once I know more.

Please say goodbye to Lady Sophia for me.

All my love,
Declan

Next, Declan phoned Dwayne Jefferson in Brooklyn. "Who dis?"

"It's me, Declan. The bloke from England. Remember—I stayed at your flat one time?"

"Shit man. Yeah. How ya doing? Was wondering what happened to you. Me and the boys thought you must have gone home."

"No. I've been busy with my new job."

"That's OK. So, waz up? Wanna drop over for some 40s?"

"No. I have to ask you a favor. I need a gun."

"A gun? What for?"

"It's a long story. I don't expect to shoot anyone. Just scare 'em. Can you get me one?"

"You talking 'bout a pistol, right?"

"Yeah."

"I can get you one. But, I'm not sure I like dis. I don't wan you in no trouble, you know."

"I know. But I have to have one. I can explain later."

"OK. But, you know it'll cost yer, probably three hundred."

"No problem."

"Well, come over to the Pink Houses after two p.m. I'll be on watch in my usual place."

Declan phoned Isabella. He didn't quite know why. But he felt an obligation to her and didn't want her to find out he had left the U.S. More than that, he wanted to do something for her—show her he did care. Show her she did mean something to him. He called her number, but no one answered. He left a message on the machine, "Hello, Isabella. Declan here. I have to leave America in the next few days. I'll be gone for about two months, and I wanted to say goodbye. I'll be at Columbus Circle at six p.m. if you happen to be able to see me. Thanks. Bye."

As he hung up the phone, he suddenly felt a sensation of fear that he might not be able to see Isabella. He realized not seeing Isabella again would upset him. He felt confused: how could he be in love with Marie but have such deep feelings for Isabella? It didn't seem right to him.

***

DECLAN CAUGHT THE "B" train to the southeast of Manhattan and withdrew $4,000 from the Lower East Side People's Federal Credit Union—leaving $1,000 in the account. He put the cash in his money belt, strapped the belt to his stomach, and pulled his shirt over it. From the bank, he caught another subway train to Brooklyn. As the subway crossed the East River, the travelers on board filtered down from white to Black at each stop. Declan exited the train at Euclid Avenue and made his way south—passing the same boarded-up, but open, corner grocery store, then down through the Catholic Church parking lot, across Linden Avenue, and then into the labyrinth of the twenty buildings of the Louis Pink Houses.

It was a warm afternoon. Children rushed along the paths of the housing project. Several followed Declan on their bikes—curious about the white man who was in their midst. It took only a few minutes to arrive at the courtyard he had visited months earlier. Dwayne had a serious look on his face until he was sure it was Declan coming towards him, and then his face gleamed with white teeth as a broad smile emerged. "Waz up, my man?"

"All right, Dwayne?"

Dwayne gave Declan an exaggerated handshake with thumbs locked. On seeing this, the kids following Declan split off in several directions. Dwayne seemed relaxed—early afternoons were not busy times for the drug trade at the Pink Houses. "So, why you need this gun, my man?"

"It's a long story," replied Declan, who then gave an abbreviated account of the situation he was in with Marie. It was the first time he had shared this with anyone, and it felt good to release some of the stress that had been plaguing him. He did not mention any names or places.

"So, you gonna kill those motherfuckers?"

"No. That's not my plan. I plan to use the gun to get any copies of the video they have. You know, hard drives, backup drives, et cetera. Then I'll tell them if they report it, I'll turn the copies over to the cops with names and addresses."

"Yeah. Thing is bro. You got a gun, you gonna have to be willing ta use it, if necessary."

"Yeah, I see what you mean."

Dwayne looked around the courtyard, saw just two children playing by a corner tree, so pulled from his pocket a small silver revolver. "Smith and Wesson six-forty with enclosed hammer. Can shoot .38 and .357 Magnums."

"Nice. Very nice. So I don't need to pull the hammer back?"

"Nope. I got you something simple. You just have to remember to pull the trigger—that's it."

"Can I go practice with it around here?"

"Shit no! Cops be here. You need to take it out to the country. But, anyway, this thing gonna fire. It's as simple as it gets. I didn't want you to have no automatic—you need this as a first gun."

"OK," replied Declan warily.

"Listen, all you do is just point the motherfucker at the motherfucker and pull the trigger. Then he be a dead motherfucker."

"Sounds good to me."

"Gonna cost yer four hundred. Cash. I got yer a box of twenty hollow point Magnums, too."

Declan turned to shroud the money belt from Dwayne and pulled out four one-hundred-dollar bills.

They made the exchange—Declan put the gun and cartridges into his backpack. "You be safe now. You hear?" said Dwayne.

"I will mate. I will."

"I don't want to hear 'bout no English boy been shot."

"I'll be back mate, and drop by and see you."

With that, they shook hands. Declan turned and lit a cigarette as he walked out of the Pink Houses and north towards Euclid Avenue. With the revolver in his backpack, Declan felt he had crossed a line. He decided he could not waver and must focus on his plan at all costs.

***

DECLAN HAD THREE HOURS to spare before he hoped to meet with Isabella, so he exited the subway at Times Square and walked 42nd Street and then south on Eighth Avenue to remind himself of his first night in New York City. He came up on the cavernous entrance to the Waverly Theater, and for some reason wanted to go inside—see for himself if it really was the place where he slept on his first night.

He paid seven dollars to the sickly-looking old man in the box office to see a "Waverly Cine Classic": *Breakfast at Tiffany's*. Inside, Declan was surprised by how much cleaner the place felt compared to his first night. He took a seat close to where he had sat before. The cinema had only a few patrons, all of whom appeared to be interested in the movie.

He then thought of Marie—her rape, her HIV. He felt sick. He felt the need to vomit, but nothing came from his stomach. He got up and left, lighting a cigarette as he exited the building.

He walked north on Broadway and into an internet café. He then bought and downloaded Nick Drake's *Pink Moon* album. This was the album his brother played night after night before he killed himself. Declan listened to the songs on his MP3 player while walking north towards Columbus Circle. The sparse, dolorous, graceful songs put Declan into a sort of trance as he recalled his brother's death.

***

Declan sat down on one of the large semi-circle benches within Columbus Circle. The statue of Columbus cast a long easterly shadow across the plaza. Declan smoked a Camel as he waited until he saw what he thought was Isabella, walking across the crosswalk at Central Park South, but she looked different. This time she wore tight jeans, heeled shoes, and a snug sweater. As Isabella walked closer, Declan could see that her hair made her seem taller, her face bore makeup, and her ears displayed pearl stud earrings.

Declan rose to meet her and could sense her awkwardness. Declan had a vision of her trying on all her new clothes, makeup, and earrings in her room, trying to find the right combination. She certainly was attractive to him, but she lacked the confidence to convince Declan that this was who she really was. Instinctively, he hugged her, wanting to let her know her work had not gone unnoticed. More than that, he genuinely was glad to see her and worried, too, that he might not see her again. He understood his journey was coming full circle. It was Isabella who had been there from the beginning, and it seemed fitting that it was she who would be one of the last people to see him in New York.

"Shall we take a walk?" asked Declan.

"Sure."

They walked from Columbus Circle and into the Park's sanctuary of trees.

"So, tell me why you are leaving?"

Declan realized he couldn't really tell Isabella the truth about why he was leaving. He had wanted to see Isabella one last time, but now, suddenly, he was caught having to lie to her. He couldn't deny an attraction to her—a slow-burning, fermenting attraction. But he threw it out of his mind. Marie was the woman he wanted, the woman he loved. He was seeing Isabella today as a good friend.

"I have to go home to sort out some problems with my mum. She's been having some issues. And there's no one over there to help her out. I'll be helping her move back home to Ireland."

"I'm sorry. You seemed to be getting established here."

"Well, I'll be back."

"I hope so. You can always call me, you know."

Declan stopped and turned to Isabella. She had a look of antici-pation. Her eyes widened slightly, and she took a deep breath. Declan said, "Do you fancy taking a horse and cart ride? I see them every day around here and haven't done it yet."

"I'd love to."

They hurried to the horse stand on 59th Street, where the man at the front of the queue was brushing down his horse's mane. The man turned and said, "Horse ride, sir?"

"How much?"

"Fifty dollars for twenty minutes, Sir."

"I'll take forty minutes, please."

"Are you sure, Declan?" asked Isabella.

"Absolutely. I really want to do this. Plus, the Mayor is trying to ban the horses, so it may be our last chance to do this."

Declan helped Isabella into the cab and then climbed up after her. They sat next to each other on the rear seat. The heavy clop of hooves on the road sent the buggy on its way through the south end of Central Park. Declan was pleased to see Isabella with a childish smile. Her hands gripped the edge of the seat front. As they made their way north, Declan leaned over towards Isabella and pointed out the carousel to their right. As he brought his hand back down, it brushed Isabella's. Declan put his hand on top of Isabella's. She looked at him. He tried to brush the gesture off as nothing, took his hand away, and said, "We should be passing the area where I slept my first night here."

The horse ride continued to the Tavern on the Green and then onto the *Imagine* area, where Declan pointed out his sleeping spot. "I still can't believe you did that," said Isabella.

As the horse and cart turned south on their return trek, Declan sat back in his seat. It was as if he didn't want the trip to end—he sensed Isabella didn't either. He was confused. Confused since he now felt that if he could, if it were possible, he would rather stay in New York. What he had been planning to do to solve his situation with Marie suddenly seemed irrational.

The horse ride was over too quickly for Declan, and, it seemed, Isabella.

"Would you like to go for a glass of wine or a beer somewhere?" asked Declan.

"I'm not twenty-one. And I always get carded."

"Don't you have a fake ID? You can get one easily at a couple of places off of 42nd Street."

"My parents would kill me if they found out."

"Yes, I see. Well, we could always buy some beer and drink it in the park."

"That would be good."

Declan bought a bottle of Old English 800 from the nearest grocery store, and they walked to the Great Lawn in the park, where they sat as hidden as they could under a perimeter tree. "That stuff is what street people drink!" said Isabella as Declan removed the brown paper bag covering the bottle.

He felt stupid. Forgetting what company he was in. Forgetting where Isabella was from. "I'm sorry. I wasn't thinking. It's normally what I buy since it's cheap. Plus it says 'Old English' on the front so it sort of reminds me of medieval England."

Isabella laughed, "Oh, so you think maybe Shakespeare drank that stuff!"

"Yes, I think he references it in *Romeo and Juliet* during Act 2!" replied Declan, grinning.

Isabella fell back on the grass and laughed. Declan put down the bottle and rolled over to her side. He could smell the faint, orange-blossom fragrance on her neck. He realized she had put it on for him as he kissed her lightly on the lips. She wrapped her arms around him, and they kissed passionately. He kissed her neck, kissed her ears and the pearl earrings, kissed her chest. He wanted more. She breathed hard and could feel his stiffness against her thigh. But Declan pulled back and said, "Sorry, I got carried away."

"It's fine with me. Really," replied Isabella.

"I have to go soon. I'm sorry. Let's just have a drink."

"You care about someone else, don't you?"

Declan paused for a few moments, then replied, "Yes. How did you know?"

"I didn't, but it's kind of obvious."

"I feel awful, Isabella, but there is something about you I can't stay away from."

"Are you serious with her?"

Declan looked down at the grass and replied, "We are planning to get married."

"Oh."

"I'm sorry."

"That happened pretty fast."

"Yes, it did."

"Will you keep in touch with me?" asked Isabella.

"Yes, we can even try the new video chat over the internet when I'm in England?"

"Sure."

They shared the malt liquor but didn't finish even half the bottle. Soon, Declan got up and helped Isabella to her feet. They walked hand in hand to Central Park South and over to a cab parked at Columbus Circle. They hugged and kissed—tightly. Declan saw tears flow down Isabella's cheeks, and then she quickly pulled back and scurried into the cab, which then drove away. Declan was left standing on Columbus Circle with his money belt hiding over three thousand five hundred dollars and his small backpack containing all his worldly goods, including a Smith & Wesson 640 revolver and a box of twenty .357 Magnum hollow point bullets.

Chapter Twenty-One

It felt strange to Declan, knowing that as he walked his familiar territory of Broadway to 42nd Street and on through the hectic Port Authority bus station, he had a revolver in his backpack. It gave him a sense of power and safety. He wondered how many other people in America were walking around with guns on their persons at that particular moment.

His mind was on a sort of high alert. He had set into motion his plan—a quickly conceived plan, but one he felt would succeed. So far, Step One (find out where the ringleaders who raped Marie lived) had been accomplished. Step Two (buy a pistol and learn how to shoot it) had only been partially achieved in that Declan was unable to practice shooting the revolver. However, he trusted Dwayne's advice, "Just point the motherfucker at the motherfucker and pull the trigger. Then he be a dead motherfucker."

He kept saying to himself that, at all costs, he must make sure no traces were left of his journey or plan. So far, only Marie could connect him to Ben DeLuca and Josh Belmont—Dwayne did not know Marie or know of any connection Declan had with North Carolina. In fact, Dwayne did not even know Declan's surname. He had told no one else about Marie's rape or his real reason for leaving New York. He kept telling himself that if he could retrieve the electronic copies and leave Raleigh without being caught, there would be no way for him to be connected with any crime that might result.

He bought a one-way ticket to Raleigh. The Greyhound Bus trip would take over twelve hours. By paying cash, he could do the trip anonymously—flying would require identification, and, in any case, he would not be able to take the handgun due to the security checks. The bus left at eight-forty-five p.m. and he only had to wait five minutes before boarding. Sitting on the hard plastic bolted-down chair in the waiting area, Declan felt an odd sensation as he realized that in less than two days, he could be walking the beach in Brighton after having held up two Americans with a gun.

"Bus Three-Sixteen to Raleigh, North Carolina, now boarding," came the announcement over the intercom. Declan was a little concerned that out of the thirty-or-so people in the waiting area, only eight other people got out of their seats to board the bus, and only one other person was white—he was hoping to somehow blend in with the passengers. He rose slowly and decided to take a seat behind the other white person. His idea was that by sitting close to the only other white person, the bus driver (if questioned) would have a better chance of getting them confused and perhaps even giving cause to believe the operation was performed by a "team." The other thought running through his mind as he took his seat was that he must refrain from speaking to anyone in order to make sure no one knew he was English. Therefore, he would act sleepy or pretend to sleep for the whole journey. At stops, he would avoid people and answer questions with only "yep," "naw," or even a grunt. He had already practiced saying, "Raleigh, North Carolina—One-Way," in an American accent, on his walk down Broadway.

The seat on the bus was thin and coarse, the windows grimy, and a fecal-disinfectant smell filled the air. As the driver started the engine, the smell of diesel added to the mixture. Doubts again began to enter Declan's mind: *Is this the right thing? Should I wait a day or two and think about this?* He swept those doubts away and focused on his plan:

he must perform the plan at all costs. In less than two days, he would be home in England and could move on.

It was impossible to sleep—the details of his plan swam through his head. Several men in the back of the bus were laughing loudly, and someone else was playing a radio at a volume just loud enough for everyone to hear above the din of the engine. Yet none of this bothered Declan, who kept remembering a phrase he had heard a man say once, on a BBC Documentary: "Get the job done, get the job done." The Englishman had set a world record for running the entire length of Death Valley. Declan decided to borrow the phrase and make it his mantra: "Get the job done."

Within four hours, the bus entered Baltimore, Maryland. Everyone had to leave the bus for one hour while it was "serviced." Declan followed the white man fairly closely and sat just three seats from him. He avoided eye contact with everyone to prevent the possibility of a conversation. Thankfully, only ticket holders were allowed in the waiting room of the terminal. A security guard checked each person for a ticket as they entered the thinly partitioned waiting area. Three cigarettes later, Declan was back on the bus, where he took up the same seat behind the solitary white man. There were fewer people on the bus now—about six—since the laughing group had left.

The bus route was simple: south on I-95 and then west on NC-64. The view changed from densely populated areas to lonely, vacant wooded vistas as the bus entered Virginia. Declan recalled his flight to Raleigh and the vast panorama of trees. He wondered what downtown Raleigh would look like—he envisioned a farm community, but knew this was unlikely, given that there was a major university in the city center, North Carolina State University.

Declan felt a prodding sensation on his upper arm. For a moment, he thought he was in the Waverly Theater, but quickly realized the bus driver was telling him to leave the bus while it was again "serviced." Declan looked at his watch: six-thirty a.m. He was in Richmond,

Virginia, and as he sat in the waiting area, he was annoyed at himself for sleeping—now the bus driver had cause to look at his face. One slight transgression in his plan. However, he was grateful for over two hours of sleep.

***

As HE RE-BOARDED THE now-serviced bus, Declan knew the next stop would be Raleigh. His stomach churned, and he felt sick; he hadn't eaten in over twenty-four hours. *Get the job done, get the job done.* He went to the bathroom at the rear of the bus. Inside, he took the revolver from his backpack and pushed on the cylinder release latch, as Dwayne had shown him. He then slid a .357 magnum bullet into each of the five chambers before snapping the cylinder back into the body of the revolver. He pushed the pistol into the waist of his jeans, emptied the remaining fifteen bullets from the box of ammo, and put them into his jeans pocket, then threw the box out of the tiny upper window of the bathroom. Again, he did not want to leave a trace of himself on the bus—especially an empty ammo box. He sat back in his seat and felt strange as the revolver dug into his stomach.

***

At NINE-FIFTY-ONE A.M., THE bus pulled into the small Raleigh Greyhound bus station. Raleigh had no tall skyscrapers that Declan could see; instead, it seemed to be a sprawling town filled with trees and wide boulevards. Declan exited the bus quickly, but first went to the ticket counter and bought a one-way ticket to Washington, D.C. He figured it was better to buy the ticket before any possible incident occurred, since he was sure he would be nervous and possibly draw attention to himself after the crime. Also, he felt that news of a holdup might spread quickly in such a small town—fast enough to make it back to the bus station before he bought his ticket.

With his return ticket in hand, Declan rushed from the bus station, stopping briefly to look at the bus schedule posted on the wall close to the door. He now knew the last detail that eluded him at the New York Public Library: if he could complete the operation and be back at the bus station for the noon or two p.m. bus, he would have enough time to ride to Washington, D.C. and then make the last flight for the day back to England—a British Airways flight departing at ten p.m.

The directions were easy. Declan had a printout of the route but was in no need of it: west on Jones Street for two blocks, South on Glenwood Avenue for three blocks, west on Hillsborough Street for one-and-a-half miles, then north on Pogue Street for three blocks. His head was cloudy from lack of sleep, but each time he realized what he was doing, a shot of adrenaline brought him back to life. *Get the job done.* He passed a bar that purported itself to be an Irish pub: Napper Tandy's. He felt like going inside and drinking a few pints of Guinness to quell his nerves, but knew it was out of the question: more connections he wanted to avoid.

At one minute past ten, he had turned onto Hillsborough Street and was passing within the shadow of NC State University's Clock Tower. Students were coming and going, most with backpacks. Declan felt a little lucky since something he hadn't considered was in his favor: he was about the same age as most of the students and also carried a backpack. He blended in. He passed a frozen yogurt store and turned north on Pogue Street. Three blocks later, Declan O'Neill was outside 212 Pogue Street—a pleasant-looking single-storied house wrapped in trees with extensive open grounds to the rear. This was the residence of Ben DeLuca and Josh Belmont.

Declan stopped and coughed, felt like puking. *Get the job done.* He pushed on and walked the long length of the brick path and up the steps to a large, shiny green door. As he did, he looked around to check that no one was close by. His stomach, always a barometer of his state of mind, suddenly went numb. His whole body became numb. He had been thinking of how this would happen for days now, and it was as if he was now watching a playback of it on television. He no longer needed to think—all anxiety seemed to flow from his body. He knocked on the door four times and listened: nothing. He knocked again: nothing. He stood for a few moments and heard people walking along Pogue Street. He quickly walked away from the building and south towards the University.

***

BEFORE HE COULD GATHER himself, he found himself walking north on Glenwood Avenue and came upon another bar, The Hibernian, another supposed Irish Pub. He went inside. "Guinness," he ordered.

"ID please," replied the tall, balding American barman. Declan grew flustered. Knowing he had no choice—except leave and draw more notice to himself—he pulled out his fake New York I.D. The barman looked at it suspiciously but nonetheless poured Declan a pint. He drank two pints, said nothing, left a ten-dollar bill on the bar, and exited the pub. He decided to try the house one more time. If they were not home, he would forget about this plan and return to England. He also realized at this point that he knew he could not control his anger. He had a feeling that his entire trip to America had been building up to this point. As if the universe had set him up to do this. All the difficulties and hardships he had suffered seemed to act as a primer for what was about to happen. And he knew that something very, very bad was going to happen if Ben DeLuca and Josh Belmont were home right now.

***

He looked at his watch: five minutes past eleven. This time, as he approached the house, he felt almost in a trance. It was as if he had done this a million times. *Get the job done.* Fewer students seemed to be around at midday—perhaps the hot sun drove them inside, maybe morning classes were just more popular. Declan found himself again knocking on the door of 212 Pogue Street.

A shirtless man about his own age abruptly opened the door. He was slightly shorter than Declan, but had a broad upper torso, together with a fat gut that hung over a pair of red swim shorts. "Yeah?" asked the man.

Declan was on automatic pilot and moved through the scenario he had already made up in his mind: "Hello there, I'm looking for Ben DeLuca and Josh Belmont."

"Why?"

"I'm compiling a report for the British *Sunday Times* on life in American Colleges. I was given a list of possible students by the University. It will be a big feature for December."

The man smiled and shouted back, "Hey Ben, come here."

Knowing now that both men were home, Declan pulled out the revolver and pointed it at the man's head. "Get inside."

The man's jaw dropped, and he stepped back into the apartment. Declan kicked the door shut. Inside the small, messy, main room, another man lay on the sofa reading a magazine. Declan looked around and noticed several lacrosse trophies on a corner bookcase.

"Both of you sit down on the sofa."

"What the fuck is this?" asked Belmont, the man in the red swim shorts.

The two men sat together on the sofa, and Declan breathed a sigh of relief. "Is there anyone else in here?"

"No," said Belmont.

"You two bastards raped a friend of mine and apparently made a recording. I need any records you have of it right now—hard drives, backup drives, pen drives—or I will shoot you both."

"What the fuck are you talking about? We don't know anything about that," said Belmont.

"Josh. Just give it to him. Can't you see he's got a gun?" said DeLuca.

"So you just want the drive? Then you'll leave?"

"Yeah."

"OK. Well, can I get up and get it for you?"

"Yeah."

Belmont got to his feet, and Declan moved back two steps to keep both men in his view. Declan had his back to the hallway and watched as Belmont went to a small cupboard by the sliding glass door that led out into the large rear grassy area. Belmont then bent down and took a key from under the cupboard and unlocked the cupboard drawer. Inside was a stack of six portable hard drives—all with handwritten codes on them.

"Whose recording are you looking for?"

"Marie Cooper."

"Hmm...Cooper," said Belmont as he picked up what appeared to be a small pad that served as some type of index. Within a few seconds, he pulled out one of the hard drives from the middle of the stack and attempted to hand it to Declan.

"No. Hook it up to your computer and play it. Then sit back down."

Belmont plugged the hard drive into the laptop on the corner desk and then, with the mouse, clicked on a file. There was no introduction on the recording—just a sudden grainy picture of a dimly lit basement game room and loud thumping rap music in the background. In the foreground was a pool table with one youth playing alone. On the other side of the table was a couch and Declan was shocked to see

Marie—his Marie—lying on the sofa with one arm and leg flopped towards the floor. Declan cleared his throat as he recognized DeLuca walking into the frame and pulling Marie's skirt up over her chest, then saying into the camera, "Let's check out this pussy." He then tore off Marie's white underwear while the camera zoomed in on Marie's vagina. "Very nice," said the cameraman, whose voice Declan recognized as Belmont's. DeLuca then pulled down his jeans and boxer shorts, exposing his already erect penis. He knelt down on the couch and entered Marie forcefully; she groaned.

Declan turned to the two men and noticed DeLuca had pissed in his jeans and had a petrified look on his face. "Please, don't hurt us. It was all a big mistake. We didn't mean to harm those girls," said DeLuca.

Belmont shifted his weight. He looked at his friend and seemed to wake to the reality of the threat in front of him. "Man, it was just a fraternity thing. You know? They were just parties that got out of control."

"Do you have any other copies of this?" asked Declan.

"No, we just back them up on these hard drives and erase the copies in the camera," replied Belmont.

"Shit man, don't hurt us. Please," said DeLuca.

Everything to Declan slowed down. The anger entered his mind again. The rage—like an old friend—had returned. He thought of his brother, and he thought of Marie. His head was then pierced by a sharp, high-frequency sound. He pointed the Smith & Wesson 640 Revolver at Belmont's head and squeezed the trigger. It was the loudest noise Declan had ever heard. Belmont's chin blew off his face, and the man fell back on the couch—his face was astonishingly grotesque, with just his upper teeth exposed and no lower jaw, and a gargling scream coming from his exposed throat. Declan shot him again. The bullet pierced his forehead, and part of the back of his head blew out onto the rear wall: blood, brains, and bits of white skull.

DeLuca had risen, opened the sliding glass door and ran out the back of the apartment. Declan fired two shots in quick succession, and DeLuca fell to the grass, but then got up and stumbled to the side of the house.

Declan put the revolver in the waistband of his jeans, ripped the hard drive from the laptop and put it in his backpack, then threw the remaining five hard drives from the cupboard over the body of Belmont.

***

THROWING BACK THE SLIDING door, Declan raced out of the apartment and followed droplets of blood around the side of the house, across Pogue Street, and into a wooded area that suddenly turned into row upon row of rose bushes. Continuing to follow the trail of blood droplets, Declan walked through an open iron gate that led into the backstage area of an outdoor amphitheater. Standing on the stage, Declan looked out over dozens of rows of benches forming a large semi-circle. It was as if all the events were unfolding in a play and were not real. It was as if his life had turned into a Shakespearean drama being played out at The Globe Theater.

Then he noticed DeLuca trying to hide under one of the benches. Declan removed the pistol from his jeans, jumped off the stage, and walked up to the man curled up under the bench. DeLuca was clutching his bloodied and limp left arm. Declan raised the pistol at him and pulled the trigger. The round entered DeLuca in the stomach. He screamed. The noise of the blast intensified in the amphitheater and seemed to permeate the entire town of Raleigh. Declan then said, "This one is for the HIV."

He pulled the trigger. Click. Again, and click. He then remembered this small revolver only had five shots, and he didn't want to try reloading the gun in the open.

"Shit," said Declan, and he turned and ran from the amphitheater and south on Pogue Street.

Several students were standing and talking outside a house just a block south of the amphitheater—apparently alarmed by the noises. Declan kept walking as if he was late for class and turned left past the yogurt store and west on Hillsborough Street.

***

BEFORE HE HAD A chance to properly assess the situation, Declan was heading north on Glenwood Avenue. He checked his watch: 11:35. He had forty minutes before the next bus to Washington, D.C. He quickly decided it was better to wait at Napper Tandy's Pub rather than at the bus station. As he entered the pub, which had gone out of its way to try and be an authentic Irish spot, police sirens outside wailed from all directions. The bartender, another American, distracted by the sirens, didn't ask for Declan's ID and instead handed him a Guinness.

Declan was no longer nervous. *Get the job done. Get the job done.* He had now completed step three of his six-part plan. The other steps were relatively easy. And he knew everything else was out of his control. As long as the bus left on time for Washington, D.C. he would be safe. At exactly eleven-forty-five, and after two pints of Guinness, Declan left a ten-dollar bill on the bar, said nothing to the barman, and walked the short block to the Greyhound Bus station.

***

THE BUS WAS ALMOST ready to go and half-full of passengers. The driver was loading luggage into the lower baggage storage under the bus as Declan stood by the bus steps. The busman walked up to him, took his ticket, and with an experienced action, clipped the ticket with a clipper stored in a holster, of sorts, attached to his belt. Declan was fixated on the holster and thought of the revolver he had in his waistband. *Get the job done.* Declan then realized he had to get rid of the gun and hard drive before he arrived in Washington, D.C. He sat in the bus and put on his MP3 player to listen to his Nick Drake songs. As soon as the engine of the bus roared into action, he fell asleep.

***

WITHIN THREE HOURS, THE bus pulled into the Richmond, Virginia, bus terminal, where there was a two-hour layover. Declan looked at a map on display in the information area and realized he had just enough time to walk two miles to a place called Maymont Park.

Once there, he tossed the gun and bullets into a lake within a beautiful Japanese garden. He then threw the portable hard drive onto the path and stamped on it several times—breaking the case open and then snapping the spindle in several pieces. He picked up the parts and threw them into the lake. He stood for a few seconds and suddenly became aware of how striking the Japanese Gardens were: filled with colorful Maple Trees, Cherry Blossom Trees, Black Pine Trees, and Azaleas. He left the park and, within forty-five minutes, was back on board the bus for Washington, D.C. Step four was complete.

***

TWO HOURS LATER, DECLAN took a taxi from the Washington, D.C. Greyhound Station to Dulles Airport. He paid cash for the 10 p.m. overnight British Airways flight to London.

As the flight left the airport, the adrenaline and alcohol started to fade. Declan felt nauseous, nerves twisting in his stomach. He puked three times in the bathroom during the flight. The whole experience felt like a dream. He was now a killer, a murderer. It suddenly didn't seem right to him that he could get away with it. Although he had planned everything carefully, he wondered how he could escape justice. Logically, he knew it wasn't the police's fault they couldn't catch him—how could they ever connect Ben DeLuca and Josh Belmont to him? It seemed impossible. More than that, the hard drives were likely to trigger a massive investigation into the fraternity's activities and expose dozens of potential vigilantes—all of whom would make it even harder for Declan to be found.

***

AT TEN-FIFTEEN A.M., THE British Airways flight arrived at London's Gatwick Airport. Step five had been completed. Declan caught the train south to Brighton and, after a short walk, arrived at his mother's flat just before noon.

As he approached the block of flats, he recognized one of the Russians sitting on the car park wall smoking and talking with another Russian he didn't recognize. They both noticed Declan and watched him intensely as he entered the block of flats.

He caught the elevator and made his way directly to his mother's flat. "Oh, so you're back then? Nice of you to let me know you were coming."

"Sorry mum, got caught up in a few things."

"What happened over there?"

"It's a long story. But don't worry. I've got enough money to get you out of here and into a new place back home in Ireland."

His mother burst into tears and hugged him.

Chapter Twenty-Two

THERE WAS NO RISING sun to see the next morning as the patter of rain fell on the semi-rotted wooden window frame. A cool sea breeze sneaked through the gap between the frame and wall. The air felt fresh and the outside of the bedspread cold to the touch. Declan sat up and reached for his pack of Camels. He wondered if Camels were sold in England, and then wondered if Marie was smoking one at that moment. He sat and listened to a distant train scuttle from the station. Declan took a long drag on his cigarette. His mother tapped on his bedroom door.

"Fancy a voddy?"

"No. For Christ's sake, are you trying to kill yourself?"

"What I do is my own business," replied his mother.

"Fine. Anyway, can you start packing? I'll go down and buy some boxes today. I'm going to start sorting out your move back to Ireland."

"Thanks, son."

***

LATER, AFTER A CUP of tea and some toast, Declan checked out the window to make sure the Russians were not posted at the front of the building before he left the flat. He caught the elevator down and was saddened to see the same bold graffiti on the wall above the button pad: *Fuck Off You Loser*. He walked the familiar streets: passing the butcher's shop, the corner newsagent's, the pub, the second-hand car dealer, the chip shop, and then up the steps to Chris's flat door. He rang the bell once, and then twice. "All right, all right. I'm coming!"

Chris opened the door, and Declan stared at his rakish figure dressed in only a pair of skinny jeans. "Fuck me. What you doing 'ere?"

"I'm back, mate."

"I can see that. What happened? No phone calls or nothing and then you just appear at me door. Come in."

Inside, Chris's room appeared much smaller than Declan remembered—the low ceiling, small gas stove in the corner, unmade pull-out sofa, threadbare carpet, and lingering smell of fish and vinegar all depressed him.

"Your amplifiers—you got them back," said Declan as he stared at the stack of audio equipment piled up in the corner.

"Yeah, me and Tony went down there and apologized. In the end, it turned out fine. The Sergeant Major geezer turned out to be all right. Bought us a drink and we wound up staying all night. They all thought it was funny, more than anything."

"Wow. Well, that's good. Glad that's all over. Practicing at all, are you?"

"No. Not really. Sort of lost our drive since you left. Are you staying then?"

"For a bit. Maybe more. I'm not really sure yet."

"Right."

"What about the Russians? You still working for them?"

Chris turned and walked to the window, picked up a pack of cigarettes and lit one.

"Yeah. Look, mate, they're not too bad once you get to know them. They're just like us—trying to make a living. They're bloody industrious too—running all the doors of the clubs, they deal all the big estates. They're also running most of the betting shops, and now they've even started running a few pubs. The pay is great, and there are chances of promotion too since they are expanding."

"Expanding?"

"Yeah. Prostitutes. They can't bring enough in from Moscow. And they need managers here."

"It just don't sit right with me mate. Not after what happened to my brother."

"Well, like I told you on the phone before, I talked to the gaffer about that and he said they'll be happy to wipe the slate clean for one or two easy jobs you could do for them. It's not dangerous stuff—more like their way of saving face. They're funny like that—it's all about how they're perceived. If you know what I mean."

"No mate. Good luck to you. But I'm not in on that."

"Understood."

"So, that's it for you then? Career with the Russian mob pushing drugs and prostitutes."

"Oh leave it out. What else can I do?"

"There's every opportunity in the world, Chris. I've seen it. I know England has them too."

"But the Russians are here right at my doorstep with cash in hand right now."

"Yeah. And there lies your answer."

Declan shook his head, rose from his seat and left.

***

AFTER ONE WEEK BACK home, Declan was still no closer to moving his mum back to Ireland. Rose O'Neill was dragging her feet with packing, and Declan was finding it hard to get any help from his family in Ireland. Avoiding the Russians was becoming increasingly difficult, and he knew it was only a matter of time before they caught up with him and confronted him.

But, more than anything, he was most concerned as to why Marie had not contacted him. He had left his mum's address and his UK mobile phone number (which was now switched back on) and a working AT&T calling card number in his last letter to her. He had begun to worry she knew about the killing and was in some kind of trouble. More than that, he began to realize he should not have left her the way he had. Realized, too, he wanted more than anything to be with Marie. And realized that his flirtations with Isabella were just that: flirtations.

He decided he would have to phone Marie's employers, the Mortons. He went to the pub, bought a pint of Guinness and sat in a quiet corner seat where he dialed their number. "We are sorry to have missed you. Please leave a message." He left a short message apologizing for calling and asking them to ask Marie to please contact him. He then called directory enquiries and tried to find Lady Sophia's number. The American telephone operator said, "That number is not listed, Sir. Is there anything else I can help you with?"

***

ANOTHER WEEK WENT BY, and there was still no word from Marie. Declan became desperate for answers and thought of contacting Zane and asking him to try to find out what had happened to Marie. But, he didn't want to involve Zane—didn't want his friend to get messed up in all this business. To keep himself occupied, he walked a lot during this time. Often visiting sites from the *Quadrophenia* movie that Marie had watched and known: the alley on East Street, The Sealife Centre, The Brighton Palace Pier.

He wandered through the labyrinth of Brighton's Lanes aimlessly. Avoiding the hordes of French tourists. Eventually, he happened on the central Brighton Square, where he sat on a bench. As he fumbled for his cigarettes, he looked up and noticed a sign, Seaside Tarot, nestled between a coffee shop and an antiques store. Instinctively, he disregarded the cigarettes and rose and walked over to the tarot shop. He pushed aside a heavy, beaded curtain strung across the open door and stepped into the dusty, dimly lit, cramped interior. A middle-aged, plump, purple-haired lady wearing a burgundy shawl wrapped loosely around her upper body sat directly opposite the door behind a small table.

"Can I help you, please?" she asked tersely.

"Yeah, just wondering how much a tarot reading is?"

"Twenty pounds for thirty minutes, thirty pounds for an hour."

"Anything shorter? I don't think I need so much time," responded Declan, nervously scratching the back of his head.

"I can do a one-question reading for a tener."

"OK."

"Take a seat."

The lady closed her eyes, took a deep breath, and slowly exhaled. As she did, Declan looked over to her right side and noticed a hand-written notice taped to the wall that read, "Internet Readings: £15. PayPal accepted." The table had a red wool tablecloth covering the top, a small lamp with a green lampshade, and a deck of well-worn tarot cards stacked neatly next to the lamp base. Declan could smell gin on the lady's breath as she exhaled. The lady then opened her eyes and asked, "What is your question, young man?"

Declan wriggled in his chair and replied, "Well, I want to know what will happen with me and my fiancée, Marie."

The lady took another deep breath, asked Declan to shuffle the deck of cards in order to, "assimilate your persona into the cards," and then she expertly spread them, face down, across the table in a quick, efficient manner. She moved her right hand to the left side of the line of cards, drew one out, laid it face up on the table, then selected and placed two more beside it. The cards revealed were:

THE FOOL.
KNIGHT of SWORDS.
WHEEL of FORTUNE.

The lady drew some breath and slowly shook her head.

"What does it mean?" Declan asked nervously.

"This is a rare combination. The fool card. This was the first card picked and reflects a situation you got into without knowing how it would all work out. A big change where you went into without knowledge. The knight of swords card. This indicates you are, or have, taken dramatic action in some form or other. You have battled a situation that was a hard fight. The wheel of fortune card talks about what is next for you. It suggests that life is now beyond your control. The past is gone, and things are set in motion that are outside of your influence."

"Oh."

"Young man, you should be very, very careful in the next few weeks."

Declan quickly rose, paid the ten pounds, and left.

***

FROM THE LANES, DECLAN walked back to the Brighton Pier area and caught a coastal bus to Seaford. He wanted to see if he could find the bungalow Lady Sophia described to him where she had stayed with Phyllis Spira. He walked east along the beach towards the Seven Sisters chalk cliffs. The series of peaks and dips of the bright-white cliffs were enthralling as he imagined Lady Sophia and Spira treading the same path along the coast.

He thought about Sir Roger de Coverley and imagined what he would have thought about Declan's trip. He knew too well Sir Roger would not have been impressed. Knew he most likely would have been appalled by how Declan had conducted himself in many of the situations he found himself in.

Declan began to worry about his own fate. He went back to see his friend, Chris and finally told him the whole story. "But, why did you shoot those blokes?" asked Chris.

"I don't know, I got so angry. I shouldn't have gone down there in the first place. Or, once I did, I should have just called the cops."

"You always did have a temper. Problem is, over in the States you can vent it with a gun. It's a bit different here, where you can only punch or stab someone."

"I messed it all up. I couldn't control myself. I let go of all my anger on those two guys. Yeah, they were a couple of scumbags, but exposing their game would have been a much better way to go."

"Right mate. Right."

"I've really gone and fucked it up, ain't I?"

"Yeah. You did a fantastic job all the way. You did so well. But now you've got a couple of murders on your hands."

***

THE NEXT MORNING, DECLAN's mobile rang on his bedside cabinet. As he fumbled for the phone and checked the number, he became excited on realizing it was a New York City number. "Allo," said Declan.

"Hi, is this Declan O'Neill?"

"Yeah."

"I'm calling from the *New York Times*. Are you aware of Marie Cooper's suicide?"

Silence.

"Hello, are you still there?"

"What do you mean? I don't know what you mean."

"Sir, I'm sorry if the police haven't contacted you. This happens a lot. We are trying to find out why Miss Cooper killed herself. The family she works, worked, for is distraught—especially the children she cared for. The father of the children, a Mr. Morton, was recently nominated UK ambassador to the UN. So, this is causing a stir here in New York."

Declan turned to his mother, who had opened his bedroom door and was leaning against the door frame, sipping her orange vodka. "You OK, son? You've gone all white," asked his mother.

Declan looked around the bedroom at his boxed-up belongings.

"Mr. O'Neill. Is it correct you were engaged to Miss Cooper?" asked the reporter.

"Yes, sort of. I don't know. I hadn't heard from her for weeks since I got back. I couldn't get hold of her. She stopped contacting me."

"Were you planning on getting married?"

"I don't know. It was all up in the air."

Declan could hear the reporter typing. "Mr. O'Neill, do you know of any reason why she would do this?"

"Of course not. I can't believe it," mumbled Declan.

He realized the receiver was shaking in his hand. "Just one more question, if I could. When and where did you first meet Miss Cooper?"

"About six months ago at Riverside Park."

"Thanks for your time, Sir."

"Hold on. How did she die?"

"She hung herself in her bedroom. I'm sorry, Sir."

***

Declan sought refuge in his bedroom. He became sick. Could not talk. Would not see anyone. He listened to his Nick Drake MP3s. Over and over the bleak, short, poetic melodies caressed and enhanced his deep depression. After three days, even his mother was worried: "Won't you come out and have somat to eat?"

On the fourth morning, he woke to find his head swimming with a strange dream: he was walking through Central Park with his brother, Sean. They were laughing as the hazy sunshine broke through the bright green leaves of a canopy of trees overhead. Then they began running—running along the path, passing the carousel, passing The Boathouse Café, passing the lake. All the while laughing, all the while enjoying each other's company.

Up ahead, they saw Marie sitting on a bench. They slowed to a walk and waved to her, and as they approached her, she stood up. Her glossy dark hair glistened in the bright rays of sunshine streaming through the trees. She wore a red silk scarf around her neck. She smiled and murmured, "I'll always be yours Declan. Always."

About the Author

KEVIN POLIN was born in England and grew up between County Armagh, Northern Ireland, and Brighton. He has spent most of his adult life in the United States and now lives in North Carolina. He holds a master's degree in creative writing. When he isn't writing thrillers, he's hiking, running—he's completed more than thirty-five marathons—and traveling.

https://www.kevinpolin.com

www.ingramcontent.com/pod-product-compliance
Lightning Source LLC
Chambersburg PA
CBHW020352110726
47899CB00006B/1695